I

His thirtieth birthday tomorrow. He would, of course, go home to his mother who, rosy and refulgent with leaning over a hot stove, would have made him all the things he liked best to eat – or, more precisely, some of the things he no longer cared to eat. She had had little opportunity to observe the changes in his taste. But tonight, dinner at Baumann's.

He was curious as to what he should see. He had been out with Clive often in the last five years to pubs and to restaurants; but never to his house. It had been a good five years, marked by spells in Frankfurt and in Paris, and it seemed to Toby that he had done rather well. Certainly he earned a good deal of money, and he was prepared to say that few things were as sound as merchant banking. He had a good ear for languages; French he already spoke well, German he had acquired.

He bent down, frowning, to tie his tie in the mirror that was a little too low. Were his freckles spreading? It cheered him to think that they had never put off a girl he fancied. Was there anyone he was likely to meet this evening? Claire might be there, since her father and his patron, Lord Llangain, was a director of the bank. She had married soon after her affair with Toby had come to an end, and he knew that she had a son and was expecting another child.

The time seven forty-five, which, if he took a taxi from his small flat in Chesham Street to Hyde Park Place, would get him there only a little after eight. Well, that would be all right, since he did not care to be first comer in an unfam-iliar place. His assessment was correct, and he arrived at eight five. He entered a spacious hall, was shown into a rather dark drawing-room, the walls brown, the lighting, so far as he could see, confined to the picture-lights and to two small standing lamps. The effect was that of an Aladdin's cave, from which one might hope to scoop up a handful of rubies and emeralds.

He adjusted his eyes from the glare outdoors and saw that his host was advancing with a pretty but rather stout woman. 'Clarissa, you haven't met Toby Roberts, though you've heard a lot about him. Toby, my wife.' Toby could not have riposted that he had heard a lot about her, because he hadn't.

Claire bore down upon him, in full sail, her flaxen hair arranged on top of her head. 'My sweet, how nice to see you! Alec's not here tonight; he'll be disappointed to miss you.' (Why should he be?) 'Mummy and Daddy are here.'

So they were, Idris and Moira Llangain, stepping out of shadow.

'Well, my lad,' said Toby's patron, 'it's been quite a time since we last saw you.'

'He's deserted us,' said his wife, 'and I dare say we deserve it.'

'No, why should you?' Toby said. 'But they keep me pretty busy. I haven't much of a social life.'

'Oh, nor have we.' Moira took a sip from her glass of vodka – her usual tipple, as he remembered it. 'But I don't like what I see of it. A lot of noisy pop.'

'Make a distinction, Mummy. Most pop is trash, but some is special. What do you think, Ann?'

Claire brought forward a tall, smiling woman in white, wearing no jewellery but a string of jet beads around her neck.

The Good Husband

Pamela Hansford Johnson

ISBN: 0 333 25501 1

First published 1978 by
MACMILLAN LONDON LIMITED
4 Little Essex Street WC2R 3LF
and Basingstoke
Associated companies in Delhi, Dublin,
Hong Kong, Johannesburg, Lagos, Melbourne,
New York, Singapore and Tokyo

Photoset, printed and bound in Great Britain by
REDWOOD BURN LIMITED
Trowbridge & Esher

*

TO ALAN AND ROBIN MACLEAN,
FONDLY

'Oh, as you do. Some are nice and fresh and clean, and they make a kind of fresh noise.'

'Ann, this is Toby Roberts. Toby, this is Mrs Thorold.'

Toby looked at her with interest, and put her down as in her middle thirties. She and Claire went on discussing pop music. Another couple was brought up by Clive and introduced. 'Mr and Mrs Packer . . . Mr and Mrs Steinlen. What are you drinking, Elissa, Jane? Toby, let me freshen up that glass.'

What with the introductions, the filling and freshening of glasses, the pools of light in semi-darkness, Toby felt a little bewildered. He began to look at the paintings, so elaborately lit, and thought they could only have come from the gallery of an expensive department store. (He was not his mother's son for nothing.)

'Now, you're not looking at the right one,' a voice said. 'Come out with me for a moment.' Ann Thorold was at his elbow, trying to propel him forward. After a second's hesitation he went with her out into the hall, where she showed him a small, familiar painting of Mrs Robert's, one of her schoolchildren pictures, the children trooping in crocodile, their blazers bright under a sodden sky. 'So you see, I know who you are.'

Toby murmured something appreciative.

'Clive bought this about six months ago. It's a beauty, isn't it?' she went on.

'I think so.'

'Does your mother really work at home, without a studio, just with an easel in one of the bedrooms?'

'It's not even an easel. It's a chair with a good hard back. The house reeks of turps.'

'Well, I think she's a very special person.'

At that moment, the bell sounded for dinner and other guests came out to join them.

'Wait a moment. I must consult the table-plan and see where I'm sitting.' When she leaned over, her white dress fell away slightly, to reveal the curve of small breasts. 'Oh, good, I'm on your left and Claire's on your right. You mustn't let me bore you, though. I'm given to talking.'

'I'm given to listening,' said Toby (which was true), 'so we shall get on well together.'

The dining-room dazzled with glass and silver. Beside every plate was a full-blown rose in a brandy-glass. This room was more brightly lit than the other, chandeliers augmenting the candles on the table.

'I do', said Mrs Thorold, 'love to see what I'm eating. It's always splendid here, but in some places, if the lights were too low, you might be confronted with a squid in its ink, sitting up with arms akimbo. I experienced that in Malta once, believe it or not.'

As the meal began, he was able to look at her more carefully. Her arms were long and slender, without being thin. She wore her black hair cut short, in flat curls framing her forehead and cheeks. She had a high-bridged nose, clear hazel eyes. She reminded him suddenly of the portrait of Princess Lieven.

He turned to murmur congratulations to Claire, whose condition was obvious.

'Yes,' she replied, 'and it's bliss. I only feel one-hundred-per-cent well when I'm with child.'

He thought of them both, nearly ten years ago, sitting up in bed and sharing a bottle of wine after love-making. How easily he had lost her! And yet he now knew that he had never really wanted her.

Moira Llangain spoke to him across the table. She was on Baumann's right. 'Tell me how your mother is. I always think of her at that first show Maisie arranged for her. Such a wonderful woman! Wonderful, wonderful.' Her words were already a little slurred, but he knew by experience that they would get no worse.

For a moment Mrs Roberts, retiring, proud, keeping herself to herself, was the talk of the entire table.

'So how will you ever know', Mrs Thorold murmured in his ear, 'whether anyone loves you for yourself alone?'

The talk ceased and Toby was glad. He had, not for the first time, felt overwhelmed by his mother.

'Now you will never know,' Mrs Thorold murmured on, 'but you are liked, just for yourself. Clive goes on and on about you.'

'That I find it hard to believe.'

'Well, perhaps not on and on, but just on.'

He was silent for a while, eating caviare with some suspicion and not too much liking.

As the meal continued, she interrogated him, finding out where he lived and if alone. 'Well,' she said, 'it's only round the corner from me, in Ebury Street. I expect you've got a car?'

He told her that tonight he had come by taxi.

'Then let me drive you back. Do, please. I may sound forward,' she added, 'but if one can't be forward at forty when can one be?'

Ten years older than he. He would never have guessed as much.

She went on talking. She had been widowed, she told him, for five years and had been left with two sons, one at Charterhouse and the other at a preparatory school. 'But I'm being boring about myself. It's your fault; you're such a good listener.' This was an ancient charge to be laid at Toby's door. He made no comment. 'You are,' she insisted.

'When there's something as fascinating as this to listen to, I suppose I can be.'

She had a low, rather harsh voice, as from a long-term

9

smoker. However, when the party began to smoke, he noticed that she did not.

When the women had left them, Baumann drew Toby nearer to his side, determined not to let him seem too much a junior member of the firm.

'And how is our wandering boy tonight?' said Llangain, facetious. 'Going off on your travels again? Is he, Clive?'

'Well, nothing's quite fixed, but he might make a trip to the New York office, just to see what goes on there.'

Toby, whose skin flushed easily, flushed with pleasure now.

'Would you like that?' Llangain enquired.

'Very much.'

'Well, we'll see what can be done.'

After fifteen minutes with the port and a pair of not very dubious stories, Clive rose to announce exodus. Turning his patent-leather head from side to side, he surveyed the drawing-room. His wife and Claire were in a corner, talking embroidery patterns. Mrs Packer and Ann Thorold were in another corner, on the sofa. Everyone seemed satisfied, and Clive, who liked to see his guests quite comfortable, never left the women after dinner for more than twenty minutes and saw to it that they, too, could have port if they wanted it. Toby noticed that Mrs Thorold had some. The party once more became amorphous.

Claire went to Toby and smiled upon him. 'We've lots to gossip about, haven't we? At dinner you were too immersed with Ann to pay much attention to me.'

He asked her boldly, 'How is Maisie?'

'You mean you don't know, then?'

'No. Why, what is it?'

'You know she has provided Edward with a daughter? He was as pleased as two dogs wagging two tails.'

'I never knew.' He had felt his stomach turn over, as he

had done when Edward told him that he was to marry her, so amazingly much her senior.

'Good for her,' he said, and it seemed to him feebly. 'Is he still working? I haven't seen a play of his for ages.'

'He thinks he's washed up,' Claire said openly, 'that the theatre hasn't any use for him anymore. He writes well-made plays, you know, and people seem only to admire badly made ones. At least the critics do, though the box-office receipts for the bad ones aren't encouraging. Edward's receipts are more so, though he can't take comfort from it. He's always got a play on in rep, though.' She stared at him. 'You and Maisie, that was a shame. Or ought I not to mention it?'

'Perhaps you oughtn't,' Toby said, but he smiled. 'It was all ages ago.'

'So were other things,' Claire said, with energy.

Clarissa Baumann came to join them. She was indeed a pretty woman, much bejewelled. 'Do you mind if I butt in? Mr Roberts, I've hardly had a word with you. How is life?' she asked vaguely.

'Very pleasant, thank you. Especially here.'

'Now, isn't that gracious, Claire?' To Toby, 'Thank you. I do enjoy a party, especially a small one like this.' She spoke with enthusiasm, as if parties were rarities for her, but Toby guessed that she gave one about once a week. 'You must come to us again before long, really you must.' She spoke a thought reproachfully, as if it were entirely his fault that he was not a regular guest.

The clock struck eleven. Ann Thorold came to them. 'Clarissa, I have got to go. I must be up early tomorrow.' Toby wondered why. 'Mr Roberts, my offer still stands if you can tear yourself away.'

The Steinlens rose to go, and soon the whole party was on the verge of breaking up.

Claire gave Toby a moist and exuberant kiss on his cheek. 'Don't disappear again. Anyway, you just must come and meet Alec.'

'Oh, Idris,' said Moira, 'don't let's go now, not until I've finished my drink.' They sat on.

Toby, having made his round of good-byes, waited at the hall door for Ann Thorold. It was a steaming-hot night, though this had not been apparent indoors, because the Baumanns had air-conditioning. Mrs Thorold had brought no wrap with her. Stepping out into the air was like stepping into a steam bath.

'My car's the yellow one over there.'

At her side, waiting for her to tighten her seat belt, he was suddenly overwhelmed by her scent, fresh, woody, and what the makers described, he believed, as 'green'. As they drove off, he remarked on it.

'I like it, too,' she said. 'It's the one I always wear.'

They moved along Bayswater Road to Marble Arch and Park Lane.

'I shall call you Toby,' she said abruptly. 'I'm old enough to do that.'

'I shall like it if you do, but not because you think you're old. That's lunacy.'

'Brusque graciousness, I call that.'

They stopped at the red lights.

'Do you know why I've got to get to bed fairly early? It's because I've got a job. I'm a producer for the BBC World Service, at Bush House. It seems to me that whatever you don't know you don't want to ask. Or perhaps you're not interested.'

'Of course I'm interested.'

'I send out talks on novels and novelists to Australia, God help the Outback.'

She was talking easily, with relaxation, but hardly

seemed to need much in the way of comment from Toby. At last she brought him to his door.

'I suppose I can't ask you in for a last drink?' he said.

'No, I don't think so. I really meant it about an early night.'

She did not unstrap the seat belt, but waited for Toby to get out. Before he did so, he kissed her lightly in the manner now fashionable, high on her cheek-bone.

'Good-night, Toby,' she said, 'and you must come and have a drink with me some time. Are you in the book?'

He said he was. Through the open door of the car, her scent pursued him. 'Good-night, and thank you, Ann.'

She drove off.

2

Toby went down the short path bordered by yellow privets to his mother's house. This was the terraced house in SE1 which she had steadfastly refused to leave despite her comparative fame. Nevertheless, she had made it different from all the other houses in the row by relining the curtains so that, when drawn, they should present a homogeneous face to the passer-by, and by repainting the door to match them. All this work she had done herself.

As he put his key in the latch, the familiar smells of cooking and of turpentine came out to greet him. So did Mrs Roberts, in a rush, as rosy as he had imagined her from the stove.

'Happy birthday, son,' she said. 'And don't linger there in the hall. I've got a present for you, but not if you don't like it.' He knew she was about to give him a picture, and decided to like it very much.

'Come upstairs, and I'll show you what I've been doing.'

'Cooking,' said Toby. 'It smells wonderful.'

'This is something else.' He noted in her voice a touch of pride, which was rare with her. 'Come along.' She led him upstairs to the bedroom which had been his, and where his bed still was. In the middle of the floor were two chairs: her painting-chair and the one used as an easel. On the second stood her latest work. It showed a sunny room with a window, containing only a bed covered with a glaring patchwork quilt, in the middle of which slept a large black cat. Toby exclaimed with real pleasure.

14

'It's for you, if you like it, though it seems a mean thing to be giving you.'

'Mean, nonsense. As you well know, Mummy, this picture's commercial value is something more than I can afford. I love it.'

'I hoped you would.' Mrs Roberts spoke in the small voice she was accustomed to use when she was forced to discuss her works. 'Your dad wanted to give you an electric shaver, but I told him that was just what you already had.'

'I haven't, but I don't want one. No, really, Mummy, this is terrific.'

'You haven't met that cat yet; we took him in as a stray.'

'I must certainly meet the cat. And, Mummy, thank you very very much.'

'You'd better come down now, and have a drink before supper. I know that's what you usually do.'

They went down the narrow stairs into the kitchen, where supper was laid. It was only with a touch of defiance, these days, that Mrs Roberts used the front room. Toby remembered Maisie there, before a tiered cake-tray. He said he would have a small whisky, and she supplied him literally.

'Well,' she said, 'and how did you get on with your grand party? Was it grand?'

'Grandish,' he replied, 'but not quite what you'd expect.'

'See anyone you knew?'

'The Llangains, of course. And Claire.'

'That Claire,' said Mrs Roberts.

'Now, Mummy, don't say things darkly.' But he grinned. 'You know I nearly married her.'

'Flibbertigibbet.'

'Not at all, now she's married her baronet. She's expecting another baby.'

'One born every minute,' said Mrs Roberts, continuing

to be dark. She had changed very little in the past five years, her little bun of hair still reddish. Her comparative fame had on the surface not altered her by one jot or tittle, and she did not intend that it should do. The little house was often a place of pilgrimage by dealers, who were invariably surprised by the two chairs.

Toby drank his whisky and asked for more.

'If you don't think it'll hurt you.'

He said he was quite sure it wouldn't hurt him, and that, anyway, this was a birthday. At that moment Mr Roberts came in with his greetings and a box of cigars.

'Well, boy, how does it feel to be thirty?'

Toby said that he felt rather old, and was at least grateful that his job was secure.

'That old bank,' said Mrs Roberts scornfully. She had never lost the illusion that her son worked behind a grille. She had been so intent, in his Cambridge days, on wanting him to be a don.

She laid the table for supper – a bright checked cloth and blue china, nasturtiums in a blue bowl.

The cat came in.

'Welcome, old man,' said Toby. The cat was handsome except for his ears, which were a trifle chewed. He had a fine bold face. Toby put out a hand and the cat sniffed at it, finally deciding that it was good enough to do the stroking. 'What's his name?'

'Blackie,' said Mr Roberts, who was somewhat lacking in imagination. 'Suits him, doesn't it?'

'I've been given a picture of you,' Toby said to the cat. 'It's splendid. But, then, you're splendid, aren't you?' The cat thrust his chin up so that his admirer might scratch it. He gave a faint mew, surprising in a cat of his bulk.

'There,' said Mrs Roberts, 'he likes you.'

'He has good taste, don't you think?'

'Oh, get along with you. I shall be dishing up soon.'

The same feasts to which he was accustomed, the centre-piece being a large chicken-pie. 'And there are brandy-snaps to follow.'

'An innovation, Mummy. I bet they're good.'

She asked what they had given him to eat at the Bau-manns', and he told her. 'That caviare,' she said, in much the tone of voice with which she had commented on Claire. 'I had some at that picnic of Mrs Ferrars. I took it and had to finish it, but I had to swill it down with water as if it were pills. By the way, I see pictures of Maisie with her husband from time to time.' Her voice had an undertone of disappointment. She had wanted Maisie so much for her son, had loved her for her own sake.

'She's often with Edward at first nights.'

'Now *there's* a girl—'

'Don't rub it in, Mummy.'

'I'm not rubbing anything in. Eat your supper.'

For 'starters', as Mrs Roberts called it, there were shrimps. The cat immediately leaped upon the table and with poised and delicate paw began to pick some for himself from their plates, as though at a wine-tasting. 'Now, you get down,' said Mr Roberts, but feebly. 'You know you're not allowed on the table.' But the animal obviously was. Grave as a reverend signor, he condescended to leave them to their meal.

Toby thought that his mother had not been completely unchanged by her success, though she would not have liked to think so. She was a touch more sharp, a shade more wary. A year ago she would not have made the remark about Maisie.

'Any news of your other friends?' she said.

He told her that Bob Cuthbertson, as expected, had been made a Fellow of the Royal Society.

17

'Even I know what that is,' Mrs Roberts said, and Mr Roberts added, 'He's a one.'

Bob had not remarried, but, able to afford it now, had a woman in to look after Estella during the day. He was still besotted with the child, having quite forgotten her mother.

They were disappointed that he had to leave them early. He was sorry, too, but they were people meant to be left, self-sufficient, nothing grudging. As a matter of fact, he had nothing else to do, but was finding his parents increasingly stifling. He did not want to discuss his friends with them, not Bob, Maisie, Edward nor his new-found acquaintances. He had liked being with them, but now he was looking forward to solitude for a couple of hours, with no questions to answer.

So he went away, taking with him, with great praise, the picture of Blackie on the patchwork quilt. 'By the way,' he said to his mother, as he kissed her at the door, 'where did that wonderful quilt come from?'

She tapped her forehead. 'From up here. I've often thought I should like one like it.'

Toby determined that she should have such a quilt, though he had not the faintest idea where to look for it. 'You shall have one, if I have anything to do with it.'

'Stuff and nonsense,' said Mrs Roberts. 'They come at huge prices these days.'

'Stuff, certainly,' said Toby with an air of wit, 'but nonsense, no. Mind you, you may have a time to wait.'

When he had left the house and gone to his car, which was parked two streets away, he wondered why she had this attachment to this neighbourhood. She was like a limpet on a rock, unable to shift. He knew he had one of her very best pictures, and was grateful to her. But how might she receive Ann Thorold?

3

She did not telephone him. He had thought about her a good deal, but without sexual excitement. His main feeling was admiration, for her long neck, her sloping shoulders, the way the hair clung to her nape, cheeks and forehead. At last he telephoned her. It was not yet late enough for the school holidays to have started, and he thought he might find her free. She answered at once – with a note, he thought, of pleasure in her voice. Would she come and see the new painting his mother had given him? Come for drinks, any time in the next few days?

The only time she could give him was that night. 'I'd love to see the painting. By the sound of it, it seems rather outside her usual line.'

'Well, this time she has a model. The cat.'

When they had made their arrangements and she had rung off he went around tidying the already tidy flat, and out to buy cocktail bits and pieces. Everything must be nice for her.

She was there on the stroke of six, wearing a grey suit, a pink roll-topped sweater. 'I like this place,' she said at once. 'I can see you have a collection of Robertses. And, yes, this is the new one. Do you mind if I look at it more closely?' She did so. Then she said, 'Your mother has been gaining in technique, recently. She was shy about flower-vases, but this bed is sitting quite firmly on the floor, and the cat firmly on the bed. I like it very very much indeed. But let's talk about you.'

She accepted a gin with bitter lemon, refused a cigarette. He then remembered that she had not smoked at Baumann's. 'No, thank you, I've managed to cut it out. I'm a slave to propaganda.'

He did not believe that. He asked her if she minded his smoking. 'Not in the least,' she replied, it gave her vicarious pleasure. 'Are you off anywhere?' No, he said, not at the moment, but he had New York to hope for.

'You've never been?'

No, he said.

'It's a bit large for the human scale. It makes me feel intimidated. I lived there for a few years, when my husband was working at NBC and the boys were very young.'

Toby said, in his speculative way, that he supposed they must be about eight and fifteen.

'Well, Sam is nearly nine. You're right about Tim.'

She told Toby that Tim was old enough still to miss his father. It had been a good marriage, she told him, and she fancied that Tim, though only ten, had been conscious of it. It had been a pile-up in fog on the M1. 'At first I could hardly believe it. For months I listened for Mike's key in the lock.'

'But you needn't always be lonely,' said Toby.

'You mean marry again?' she said directly. 'I could have done, but I haven't. I have certain consolations.'

Toby wondered what she meant by that, but made no comment.

'But we're still not talking about you. A little bird told me that you were once keen on Claire.' Two little birds, in fact: Llangain and Baumann. He smiled and said nothing. 'Oh,' she continued, 'not my business? But people interest me so much, and I'd like to think you had your consolations, too. Thirty is rather too old to be a bachelor still.'

The talk verged on the intimate. Toby poured her

another drink, and said, after due reflection, that nothing had tempted him since Claire. 'And that wasn't serious.' He thought of the engagement-ring he had brought her, and had taken away again, mildly forlorn. 'I've never met her husband,' he said.

'Alec Wallace? He's nice enough but he seems rather tame for her. She's a wild girl. However, two babies ought to settle her down.' Ann crossed her elegant legs and took a long drink. 'I'm afraid I love gossip. It's truly creative, not to say inventive.'

Toby took his courage in both hands. 'Would you care to come and see my mother some day? You'll find hers a strange little house.'

'I gather that's part of her *mana*,' Ann said. 'Yes, I'd like to very much. Will she show me any pictures?'

He said he was sure Mrs Roberts would be delighted, and suggested a date. 'Could you eat a huge, old-fashioned "high tea"? My mother's set in her ways, and she's a fine cook.'

'I shall do without lunch that day.'

'That's arranged, then,' he said, and shortly afterwards she left.

He thought about her when she had gone. She was an attractive woman. What had she meant about consolations? Her children, or a lover? He was pretty sure she would tell him sooner or later. The cat slept on above his head.

At lunch-time next day he had a telephone call from Claire. 'That you, old boy? Am I interrupting anything? I'm sorry we had so little time to talk the other night, but then I saw you were taken by Ann Thorold. I could tell you a lot about her. Will you come and have drinks with Alec and me tomorrow evening? Do, do, do.'

Toby said Ann had told him a good deal about herself and that, yes, he would like to see her and her husband.

21

'And you can see my son. He's two. He's called Luke.'

He felt easy with Claire, quite as though there had been nothing between them. She lived in a large, rather ornate flat near the Park. Her husband was not yet in when Toby arrived. He was, she told him, a stockbroker and his hours were all over the place. She showed him the fat child, and he duly admired. He seemed bright, strong on his legs and with a surprising flow of conversation.

'He gets it all from Alec. Alec is very clever, though you would never think it.'

When Alec himself came in, Toby, indeed, would never have thought it. Beneath rather a fine brow were colourless eyes, a large nose and a small chin dimpled in the middle.

'Good to meet you after all this time,' he said. 'Claire tells me you're a high proud banker.'

'Not a high one, just one of the shoal.' In Toby's mind banks and fish had been connected, but Alec merely looked puzzled.

They talked of generalities. Toby supposed they had a place in the country, too.

Claire said, no, they didn't; they could always go to the parents for week-ends. 'This flat is pretty plushy for our liking, but we took it furnished. It will do for another year or two, won't it, poppet?'

Alec said it would have to, until the present heir was stronger on his feet.

'Oh, and talking of heirs,' Claire said, 'Hairy has been over from Germany with his wife. You did know he married?'

She was referring to her brother Ivor, called Hairy in the family not because he was hirsute, but because he was Llangain's heir. 'She's German, you know, Anneliese. I like her myself, but the parents took it rather hard.'

Toby suggested that they must have been married for

22

some time.

'Oh, yes, for nearly three years, but there's no sign of a baby yet, which irks Father even more. Maisie and me, we breed well enough, but Anneliese doesn't oblige. I don't know whether she can't, or whether they don't want to do so while Hairy's still in the Army. He's getting out of it in another year, or so he says. He's a lieutenant-colonel now, by the way.'

'Plushy we may be,' said Alec, 'but we don't live in comfortable sloth. We go riding in the Park before breakfast, two days a week – or, rather, we did.'

Toby remembered Claire as he had first seen her at Amanda Ferrars's picnic, in white shirt and jodhpurs. She was still as pretty. He saw her likeness in the little boy who, while they had been talking, had been pottering silently about the room, only pausing now and then to give one or other of them a beam of pure gladness. Now Claire seemed to be aware of him.

'Come on, young man, bedtime,' she said and picked him up. 'Say good-night to Daddy and to Uncle Toby.'

'Uncle Toby?' the child repeated. 'Oh, that's Uncle Toby. That's Daddy.'

'I should hope you knew that,' Alec said. He stood up and took the boy from Claire. He was a shortish man. 'I'll put him in his cot. You give Toby another drink.'

He went out. 'He's so good with Luke,' said Claire. 'Like a mother to him, I always say. Do you like Alec? I hope you do. I've been wanting you two to meet.'

Toby said he liked her husband very much, which was an exaggeration, but, yes, he liked him all right.

'And you liked Ann Thorold very much. We haven't talked about her yet.'

He supposed she was a connection of the Baumanns.

'No, just a friend. But he often asks her because he thinks

23

she may be lonely. Life is very rough on widows,' Claire added thoughtfully. 'At first they don't get asked out, as everyone assumes they'll be too grieved to go, or else spend the evening bursting into tears. After a time, though, people forget they'd ever asked the poor woman at all, and her social life collapses. Mind you, I don't see Ann as particularly lonely. She's got her BBC work, and it keeps her busy. Besides, she's naturally high-spirited.'

'So are you,' said Toby. 'I've never met anyone like you.'

'There isn't anyone like me,' Claire said teasingly, but he believed she had meant it in part. He wondered how much she had known about Maisie.

'But about Ann,' she persisted, 'you were very taken, weren't you? Of course I know she's older than you are, but with her that never seems to matter. She's damned well-preserved.'

Toby protested. 'You make her seem like an octogenarian.'

'Well, good hunting, if she's what you want.'

Toby was protesting this time that she jumped to conclusions, when her husband came back, and the topic of Ann was dropped.

'All right?' she asked him.

'Snug as a bug in a rug. He didn't even ask for a story.'

'Luke's an awfully good child,' said Claire. 'Everything interests him so much that he doesn't want to cry. I hope our next is going to be the same.'

Yes, Toby thought as he walked home, she had obviously been lucky, with the little boy and with that quiet husband. He started to feel his life was being wasted.

4

Ann asked him to tea on Saturday. When he got there he was disappointed to find another man with her, whom she introduced as Colonel Clover. 'He commanded Mike's regiment during the war, didn't you, Percy?'

'Good chap, Mike.'

He was like a caricature of a certain type of senior soldier, sharp as a fox-terrier, with small feet and hands, small head, and small moustache. 'What do you do, Mr Roberts?'

'He's a banker,' said Ann. 'Have a cake.'

'Cakes I never can resist.'

'But you can resist a drink, so that's why I ask you to tea.'

'Don't drink or smoke much. Small virtue to me; I don't like either.'

'Toby likes both, so he's going to suffer till about half-past five, when it's not indecent to open the drinks cupboard.'

The Colonel went on interrogating Toby, in his rasping way. Toby felt like an inept subaltern.

'Now, stop it, Percy,' said Ann, 'or I shall send you home in disgrace.'

'Hear how she bullies me? Knows I can't get back at her.'

'I should think very few people could get back at Ann,' Toby said. His eyes admired her.

They talked in a desultory way through the meal, until Toby, still disappointed, said he must go.

'Have you got your car?' she asked him, getting up with

what he felt to be alacrity.

He told her he had walked. It had been a fine day.

'Which way are you going?' Clover asked.

Toby told him. 'Then I'll walk part of the way with you. Must keep up my exercise.'

'Grand girl, Ann,' said Percy Clover, as they stepped out into the warm September evening.

Toby wondered aloud about loneliness.

'Lonely? Ann? Flies round a honeypot.'

Toby felt the sudden jerk of jealousy.

'She doesn't have time to be lonely,' Clover went on. His eyes snapped, as if with malice. 'I'm just an old friend, though. I imagine you're a new one.'

They passed a front garden adorned with an espalier pear. 'Yes, quite a new one.'

'Well, watch out.'

Toby asked why he should watch out.

'No particular reason. Just do.'

The little terrier of a man quickened his pace. 'Well, I must be getting on. I'll leave you here. Enjoyed meeting you. Remember, grand girl, Ann.'

Toby continued his walk. He was not at all sure that he liked Colonel Clover; despite his barking and appearance of directness, he was an allusive sort of conversationalist. He wondered whether Clover had any hope of marrying Ann, decided that he was too old for her — whereas he, Toby, was too young. Not that he had any idea of that. But his jealousy had been awakened by Clover, and he disliked him accordingly.

On his doorstep he found Adrian Stedman, hopelessly ringing the bell. Adrian was a friend from Cambridge days, now a priest in a featureless and rambling parish in Lincolnshire, where he had first been a curate, then been given the living when the old priest died. Adrian was

26

spectacularly handsome in an Italianate fashion, which had been a disadvantage to him because, during his celibate years, he had been a focus of feminine attention in the parish. Now he had married the daughter of a local doctor, renouncing his private vow of celibacy, and Toby guessed he had done so because the burden of the parish was too much for him to take alone. Not flattering to Ruth, but she, small and plain, was only too delighted with her situation.

'Glad I caught you,' Toby said. 'Come on in. What are you doing up here?'

Adrian told him. He was to see the publisher who had, surprisingly, taken a short book called *Windows on the Parish*.

'I never knew you were a writer,' Toby said, pouring Adrian a large whisky, of which the latter was fond but could not afford very often for himself.

'Nor did I,' said Adrian. 'It was Ruth's idea.' He looked around him at the small but handsome flat where Toby lived.

'Good for her. By the way, how are things going? Any more women wanting themselves exorcised, or wanting to ditch their husbands for you?' There had been examples of both in Adrian's past.

'Not so many women doing either,' Adrian replied, with the ghost of a smile. 'But, by the way, I'm still hearing from Rita.'

Rita was the ex-wife of Bob Cuthbertson; at one time, she had pursued Adrian with singular tenacity, driving him farther into retreat. Toby asked how she was doing: he had not the slightest idea of what had happened to her since she had let her husband divorce her. 'Has she married again?'

'No, and never will, I think.'

'Is she still besotted with you?'

'I'm afraid so. I thought that when I retired from

London I'd be lost to her, but she had the genius to look me up in *Crockford's*. I don't answer her letters, but Ruth sees them coming and they make her furious. Or, rather, not furious – she's not like that – but touchy. Even now, she finds it hard to believe that I never did the slightest thing to encourage the woman.'

Toby knew a spring of sympathy with poor Ruth, so plain, so hard-working, being eaten up by a jealousy which had not the least foundation. He believed that Adrian had had a bad time renouncing his vow in order to marry her and that, even if it were a marriage of convenience on his side, he could never conceivably be unfaithful to her.

'What Rita wants', said Toby, 'is the black eye Bob gave her.'

Adrian was shocked. He mustn't say that. He remembered how Bob's assault, though under severe provocation, had landed him in a magistrate's court.

'I ought not to say it, but I do say it.'

'I show her letters to Ruth, and then tear them up. Honestly, I do feel beset.'

'Well, I don't see what else you can do.'

Adrian said he had come to dread the sight of her handwriting. Toby suggested that he could always tear the letters up unread or send them back. Not that, said Adrian. It would be putting myself in touch with her in a queer way.

'Then destroy them.'

'I think I must.'

They went on to talk about the affairs of his parish. Adrian said that, but for the money his mother had left him, they would be as poor as – 'Appropriate, this' – church mice. In any case, they had to be careful. He had acquired a very young curate who didn't seem much good but who took much of the visiting off his shoulders.

At that moment, the telephone rang. It was Ann.

'You were cross today because I had Percy with me. Do you think you know me well enough to be so?'

Toby replied, 'I wasn't and I don't.' He kept a weather eye on Adrian, who was prowling around his books.

'Good. There will be another time soon.'

'At my mother's.'

'Yes. I'll ring you. By the way, you have someone with you now, haven't you?'

'Yes.'

'So I won't say any more. Bless you.' She rang off.

Adrian had seated himself again, as one preparing for a good long stay. He had been known at Cambridge as one who never knew how to go home. So he talked on and on, face eager above the clerical collar; and Toby pretended to listen, while thoughts of Ann threaded themselves through his mind. At last Adrian looked at his watch, and exclaimed, 'But I must be going or I'll lose my train and Ruth will be worried stiff.'

When he had actually gone, after a delay of another ten minutes, Toby sat in the light of the green converted oil-lamp that Maisie had once given him, and pondered the mystery. Was Ann always so direct, or was she forcing an intimacy? Was she like this with all her friends? She was a very odd woman, he thought. But it seemed unlikely that she was forcing her way with him, so much younger. Indeed, when he was with her, he felt rather like a pet animal she had picked up somewhere, and for a moment he was violently irritated. He must soon put a stop to that. He turned on the radio. There was an interview going on with a skiffle group who played on washboards outside pubs. Then the news. Cuba recognises Communist China. Sylvia Pankhurst, the suffragette, dead. Nothing much for Toby here. He went out for beer and a sandwich, and remembered how, long ago, he had walked the streets in the wet, like a lunatic, after hearing that Maisie, his first love, was to marry someone else. There were times when he still hankered after her. He had seen her once since her marriage, but that was at a cocktail party and, amid all the din, he could think of nothing to say to her. She had been as pretty as ever, with the curls of damp-looking fair hair clinging close to her face, but she might then have been a million light-years away. On his way back from the pub he wondered why thoughts of Ann should bring back so acutely thoughts of Maisie.

5

After Adrian's talk about Rita, Toby fell to thinking of her ex-husband, his old friend Bob Cuthbertson. Toby felt like spending an evening with him in Cambridge. His letter was warmly acknowledged. 'But when you get here I may still be in the lab. So go into my set and wait for me and pour yourself a drink.'

Toby arrived by the afternoon train and went straight to the college. Bob had a handsome set of rooms with linen-fold panelling, three of them, including a dining-room across the staircase and three steps below. A gown lay tossed over the arm of a chair and there was an ashtray full of cigarette butts. On a small Regency sideboard was an array of bottles and a thermos container of ice. There were some good prints on the walls. Books had overflown their shelves and were stacked on the floor. He wondered how Bob managed to keep up the small house in Chaucer Road, but realised at once that this would not be a strain on him these days. He poured himself a whisky and tried to find something to read, but all he could find were scientific works and a few ancient detective stories.

After a while Bob came in, bullet-headed, fairly tall and with a pugilist's shoulders. He was the son of a steel-worker in Sheffield, and had never lost his accent nor tried to. Toby mused how his own mother, who had no discernible accent at all, had brought him up to have none and how he had laid over this an accent of his own.

'Hullo, Tobe. Good to see you. You don't mind dining in

Hall tonight? Mrs Flax is on duty with Estella in Chaucer Road.'

He fetched a can of beer from a cupboard and opened it for himself. 'Well, how's life? How's the big banker getting along? I bet you're glad you never became a don.'

'When I was looking round your place, I was rather sorry I hadn't.'

'Oh, it wouldn't have suited you. You like to get around. Seen anyone we know lately?'

'Adrian,' said Toby, and wondered how much to reveal.

'Poor bloody parson — I must say I don't envy him. Funny, him marrying at last, isn't it?'

'I think he actually needed a "helpmeet", if ever anyone did. He seems happy with Ruth, though.' He decided on the giving of information. 'He's still being bothered with letters from Rita.'

Bob banged the dripping can down on a pile of papers. 'Bugger Reet! Why the devil couldn't she get married? She was going to, but then she didn't. What sort of letters?'

'Love-letters. I don't think she's quite sane where Adrian's concerned. He shows them to Ruth and then tears them up, but they make her mad all the same.'

'If I could stop her I damn well would, but I never see her these days. She's long given up coming to take Estella out.'

Toby remembered the shotgun marriage, taking place decorously in the registry office. Rita had been a pretty girl.

'I'd like to see Estella.'

'You really would?' Bob was released from his angry thoughts. 'Well, there's plenty of time to stroll round there before dinner, and she won't have gone to bed.'

Bob's house was exceptionally clean and tidy, probably owing to the efforts of Mrs Flax, a bonny woman in her fifties who had come to let them in.

'It's you, Doctor Cuthbertson! We didn't expect you so

early.'

'You don't know Mr Roberts, do you?'

'I haven't had the pleasure. Estella!' she called, and down the stairs came a very pretty little girl of about five, who threw herself instantly into her father's arms. 'Daddy! Daddy! You've come back.'

'Just for a little while. You don't remember your Uncle Tobe, but he remembers you when you were about as small as your teddy bear.'

'How do you do?' she said politely, putting out a little plump hand to be shaken. She bounced up and down in Bob's arms. 'Piggy-back.' He hoisted her up, and ran up and down the room.

'Now, don't excite her too much, Doctor,' said Mrs Flax, 'or we shall have tears before bedtime.'

'I'll just take her up the stairs to bed,' said Bob. 'Come along, Tobe.'

Upstairs it was not quite so tidy, toys lying about on the landing, with picture-books and games. One of these was a Meccano set.

'She's good with her hands,' said Bob, 'and I'm not going to have her grow up without knowing a thing about science. Mind you, when she's older she can choose for herself, but I want her to have the same chance as a boy.'

He carried Estella into the bedroom and tossed her on to the eiderdown, to the accompaniment of a squeal of bliss.

'Where are you going, Daddy?'

'To eat in Hall.'

'I wish I could eat in the hall.'

'When you're a big girl, maybe.' He featly undressed her and put her into a pink dressing-gown. 'Now, off to Mrs Flax with you.'

'Come and see me in the bath.'

'Well, only for a moment.'

33

She splashed about happily, looking at him with the odd flirtatious air of the young female child. Then she seized a rubber duck and threw it at him, spattering his shirt.

'Hi, that's enough of that!'

'Daddy's all wet. Poor Daddy.'

Mrs Flax tried to mop him up. 'She's a bad girl,' she said, 'aren't you, lovey? Now I'm going to scrub your back.'

'And Uncle Tobe and I have got to run. I'll be back by eleven, Mrs Flax. Get yourself something to eat.'

Toby enjoyed dining at High Table, where he had been once before at Bob's invitation, and afterwards drinking claret in the Combination Room. Yes, this was a good kind of life, a timeless life, but not for him. At ten o'clock they retired to Bob's set and drank some whisky.

Bob said suddenly, 'I'd better take a hand with Reet, though I've no standing there.'

'I wouldn't. Do you even know her address?'

'No, but Adrian would. Do you think he'd like a spot of help?'

Toby wondered. Adrian was not proud, and was tired of being harried. Toby said, 'He might do, but then he'd have to know I'd told you. No, on the whole I wouldn't interfere.'

'I should have thought I was the one you'd naturally tell. What's Adrian's address?'

Toby told him. The same. All that had changed was that since his marriage he had got the living.

'I shall think about it. But something ought to be done.' Bob sighed and rose from his chair. 'I must be going, to release Mrs Flax. You can have my bed here. I'll be round about nine tomorrow.'

When he had gone, and Toby had begun his preparations for bed, the latter began to think afresh about Rita, and what might come of a new encounter with her divorced husband. Then he turned his thoughts to Ann Thorold. This

34

would have been a good background for her; he could imagine her as a Master's wife. He was not obtuse, and he knew very well that she was attracted by him, freckles and all, but was not at all sure just how deep this went. Did she want an affair, or did she still regard him, as she was prone to pretend, as a boy? However, events there could take care of themselves. He rolled on to his left side, and comfortably into sleep.

Next morning Bob had breakfast brought up, and did not speak again of Adrian or Rita. Perhaps he had thought the better of his impulse. Toby said he had been glad to see Estella.

'She's a good-tempered kid. Do you think she's pretty?'

'Very. Your eyes, Rita's profile, but more robust. Mrs Flax looks a good sort.'

'She is. Sometimes she spends the night at Chaucer Road when I have to be out. She'd be a treasure if only she didn't nick things, but I always pretend not to notice.'

'Good God, what things?'

'Knick-knacks from around the house. Serviettes. Spoons. She thinks I'm blind, poor sod. But I keep an eye on the household, though you wouldn't believe it, and I don't miss much.'

'Just so long as she doesn't start Estella on a Fagin-like career.'

Toby thought how many people must condone offences in such circumstances with such servants as they could get. He said good-bye to Bob, but instead of going straight to the station walked through the college and on to the Backs. It was a misty autumn morning, the sun just struggling through like a great chrysanthemum. There was a slight shine upon the waters where two Indians were blissfully punting, seemingly unaware of the chill. He remembered how he had taken his mother here, and what a charming

35

picture she had made of men and girls lying in the sun. That had now been sold to an admirer in Cleveland, Ohio. How he had walked here with Maisie, half in love with her but always chary of saying so. He had never wanted to commit himself – he had once done so to Claire and had been turned down – and he still didn't want to. But no one is asking you to commit yourself, an inward voice said.

The ground was damp, and bright blades of grass clung to his shoes. He stooped to wipe them with his handkerchief, then thrust it back deep into his pocket. Almost time to go and catch his train. He bought a *Daily Express* to read on the journey.

No news that much concerned him. A long puff for a pop concert. A story about a much-married film star who was about to repeat the mistake again. And a notice about the forthcoming play of Maisie's husband, Edward Crane. Edward was still good box-office, but his vogue, if he had had any, was gone. That would sadden him, though he had anticipated the new trends. Maisie would be saddened, too, though her mother would be keeping Edward among her lions. He wondered if, that rather chilly summer, she had still given her lavish picnics. He had not been asked since that day, years ago, that she had told him she knew about him and Maisie. Though Amanda had been so liberal in her attitude that Toby had expected life to go on as before. Now he only got Christmas cards. The 'permissive age' was upon them all, and Amanda, who liked to be in the swim, had seemed to accept it. She had been glad, though, when Maisie married Edward, so much her senior. It must all have seemed very safe.

Bishop's Stortford. A bore Toby had known at Cambridge got into his carriage, and he had to listen the entire way to Liverpool Street.

Next morning, Ann rang him up at the office.

'I want you to take me out to dinner tonight,' she said. 'Nothing grand. A hamburger joint will do. I shan't dress.'

He was taken much aback. 'That would be fine. But I'll have to put off—'

'Of course you must put off. Well, will you call for me? About seven thirty?'

When Toby said he would, she immediately hung up the receiver.

Now what was she up to? He would certainly like to take her to dinner – he marvelled at her self-confidence – but it would not be to a hamburger joint. He thought for a long time where he should take her, decided on Le Jardin des Gourmets, where, all those years ago, Amanda had told him what she knew. Well, surprisingly, that was not a memory that held much pain for him. Indeed, it seemed to him sometimes that, with the exception of Edward's announcement of his marriage, life had held very little pain for him at all. He tried to understand Ann, but could not. It seemed to him that she was making all the running, but only as an older woman would make it for a man much younger. She must have felt it was up to her to set the pace. What would his mother have said? he wondered. 'Isn't she a bit forward?' Oddly enough, she did not seem so, but rather as though, when she wanted anything, she had to have it as a prize for her seniority.

He was attracted by the idea of her, but not precisely to her as yet. Yet he was flattered that a woman so beautiful (he had decided that she was) should so seek him out. He rather liked it that she had not given him a chance to ask her first.

6

He took his car, hoping to find parking-space somewhere.
He was let in, not by her, but by an elderly maid who said
that Madam would be down in a minute.

And so she was, wearing a yellow dress and a white wool
coat. She put up her cheek casually to be kissed.

'This is very nice of you, Toby, to accede to my last-
minute demands.'

In the minute of his waiting he had been looking round
her room. Pretty panelling, well-stocked book-cases, and
the things Bob had described as 'knick-knacks', strewn
around the room, but not so much as to make it look
cluttered.

'We'd better take taxis, I think,' she said.

'No, I've brought the car, hoping we can park it in Soho
Square.'

'Not a hamburger joint, I imagine? And I love them, but
hardly ever get taken there.'

'Come on,' he said. 'Hamburgers another time.'

'Masterful,' said Ann.

As they walked into the restaurant he saw eyes rest upon
her in admiration. He felt as though he had feathers which
had puffed up with pride.

'I've never been here before. Is it good?' she asked.

'You shall see for yourself and give me a report.'

'More and more masterful. Don't change too much,
Toby.'

The restaurant, with its faded garden murals and its

trellises, made her seem very fresh. Somewhat to Toby's surprise, when she consulted the menu she did not spare his pocket. 'I'm very hungry,' she said. 'I've put out two interviews today, wondering just who the hell will hear them. I'll start with whitebait and then have lobster. A fishy meal.'

'When you come to see my mother, you'll have a classic high tea. I warned you. Can you cope with that?'

'Certainly I can. What will she think of me, or won't she think of me at all?'

'Of course she'll think of you. She'll take you in from head to tail and be sorry she can't do portraits. She is still astonished by what she can do.'

'Does she look like you?'

'A little, I'm told, but she has reddish hair and I haven't.'

'You nearly have, when a light shines on to it.'

She then addressed herself to her dinner and didn't talk much while she was eating. At last she said, 'And what do we do after this? Don't tell me you've got tickets for the opera, because I loathe opera unless it's on the radio where I can't see all those stout people.'

'I haven't got tickets for the opera. I thought we'd go back to my flat for a drink. Then I can show you the richest Roberts collection in London.'

'And then?'

'Another drink.'

'Toby, you are definitely growing up. But, if I come to see your mother, you must promise me to see my boys. They've very considerately got long leave in three weeks from now.'

Toby said he would much like to see them, and went on with his meal.

'Well,' said Ann, when she had come to the end of hers – she ate slowly and daintily – 'they're good boys. Tim is the spitting image of me, and Sam of his father. Tim is

39

remarkably clever, and Lord knows where he gets it from.'

Toby felt he was being sucked into intimacy, and hadn't yet decided whether he wanted it. But to see her in the fairly dim lights – watch her, in fact, stuffing herself – had been a revelation. He had no idea whether she was the most spontaneous woman in London, or the least. His thoughts were mostly on Mrs Roberts: this was a riddle she would be able to answer at once. He decided that there should be no fuss about cake-trays in the parlour this time.

'Now tell me all about yourself,' Ann said suddenly. 'That is what I've come to hear. You're such a clam, you know.'

He demurred at this.

'No fencing, Toby. You've already extorted quite a lot of information from me, but I want the same from you.'

He said, surprising even himself, 'Why should you want it?'

She did not answer, but said instead, 'Why are you still a bachelor?'

'You don't expect me to confess that I'm a homosexual, which I am not.'

She said scornfully, 'I never make that sort of crude mistake. What held you back from matrimony?'

'A girl I liked but didn't tell her so, and another who sent me packing.' It seemed to him that this was the only personal confession of his whole life, and he marvelled at her.

'The one who sent you packing was Claire, I take it. Well, that was all to the good. And the other?'

'You want to know too much,' said Toby, boldly for him, but he had to hold his own.

'All right, I won't pry. Shall we go back to your flat now? I've eaten like a pig and it has been so nice.'

Toby called for the bill, and congratulated the waiter.

40

'The Calon Ségur was very good.' And to Ann, 'We could perhaps have done with another bottle.' But she said, 'No, I don't want to get drunk. It isn't my thing. And I have the drinks to come to consider.'

He was amused to see, later, that she entered his flat watchfully, as though it were some sort of den. He took her coat, waved her to the sitting-room. But once she was seated she sprang up again. 'I'm going to inspect the Robertses again.' She prowled around the walls. 'I love this!' It was the patchwork quilt with the cat recumbent. 'Have you got a quilt like this?'

'Has she, you mean. No, but I'm going to see if I can buy her one.'

'Let me help. I'm quite good at serendipity, and we don't want a new one. Second-hand would be far better.'

Toby said he would be glad for her to help. It was no part of his life to search antique-shops. He gave her a drink without asking what she usually had, and sat down on the sofa. He watched her as she moved from picture to picture. Then he said, 'I've a beauty in the bedroom. Would you like to see that?'

'I'd love to. Your intentions are honourable, I trust?'

'Perfectly,' said Toby, and indeed he felt that they were. In the bedroom were a couple of Mrs Roberts's late flower paintings, with the vases scarcely sketched in.

'Pretty,' said Ann. Then, 'Has your mother got a cat? What's he called?'

'With a total lack of imagination, Blackie.'

'But it has an honest ring. Blackie is what he is.'

She walked back to the sitting-room, waiting for him to follow her. I could have her if I wanted to, he said inwardly, but do I? It struck him that, where she was concerned, he simply didn't know what he wanted.

So they sat side by side talking, mostly about the theatre.

Ann showed, he thought, a pretty critical wit. After a while he slipped his arm round her shoulders, turned her to him and kissed her on the lips. She responded in a comradely manner, then moved away from him and said, 'No more of that, old boy.'

'Why not? Wasn't it nice?'

'Of course, but you are so young.'

'I'm thirty.'

'Not a great age, or not to me. Toby, I must go.'

She rose and so did he. 'I'll run you back.'

'No, but you can get me a taxi. I'm a little doubtful how you would react to a breathalyser.'

'I'm not drunk.'

'No, but we've both had a good deal this evening. It's been a lovely evening, so thank you. I'm looking forward to meeting your mother. Now go out in the cold, cold street and find me a cab.'

He did as she had told him, and when he had seen her off he returned to ponder more. Her response to his kiss — which had cost him much daring — had been rather like a sister's. He thought he could change all that, given time. And, since he did not wish to realise the loss of her presence too easily, he sat down to write about her to his mother.

'You've heard me speak of a Mrs Thorold, whom I met at the Baumanns'. She's a widow, a good deal older than I am, and she's very keen about your paintings. May I bring her to tea next Saturday, about four o'clock? And will you show her more of your work? She tremendously admired the portrait of Blackie. She is very handsome, I think, and good fun. You'll like her.'

Though he was not sure of this. Mrs Roberts had a mind of her own, and her 'that Claire' had had all the force of a commination. Still, he knew she would, at least superficially, make Ann welcome. She was far more used to visitors

42

than she had been, though these were usually dealers, for whom she did not provide high tea. She would be suspicious of her, of course, but what did that matter? She had been suspicious of every young woman he had brought to her, had judged them and had found some of them wanting. He closed the letter and took it out so that it might catch the morning post.

His father would like Ann, of course. He had always had an eye for a pretty woman – a fact not at all resented by Mrs Roberts who, though not pretty, knew herself to be the right wife for him. Toby remembered how cordial he had been to both Maisie and Claire. He was without a vestige of class-consciousness, though the same could not be said of his wife. Dora Roberts had always been uneasy with Toby's smart friends, wondering what they would think of her. It was only her pride in her own work that had allowed her to fraternise with persons of a different class, and this pride was self-evident. Nevertheless, she worried about what people would think of herself and her home. Yet she had been sufficiently shrewd to know that to move elsewhere would have destroyed her charisma, and she was proud also that she had decorated her little house with some skill.

Toby had added a postscript to his letter: 'High tea will be fine.' Ann would have seen through that cake-tray at once.

He called for Ann next Saturday. 'I've remembered your warning,' she said, 'so I haven't had any lunch. I shall be ravenous for tea, however high.'

The moment Mrs Roberts set eyes on Ann, Toby knew that she had bristled. Here was not just one of Toby's girls, but a woman of practised poise and charm. 'It's very kind of you to come all this way,' she said.

'It's even more kind of you to let me,' Ann replied. 'Toby will have told you that I'm an admirer of yours. Will you

43

show me some paintings?'

'After tea,' said Mrs Roberts stiffly, 'if you don't mind.'

She had put herself out. Cornish pasties, sausage-rolls, fruit-tart, two kinds of cake. Certainly Ann's claims to be ravenous were justified, since she ate in a fashion which mollified even Mrs Roberts. In the middle of the meal his father came in.

Mr Roberts was tall where his wife was dumpy, and Toby's features could be seen in him, though Toby's had fined down.

'How do you do, Mrs Thorold?' he asked. 'Nice of you to come and see us.'

'I've told her that,' said Mrs Roberts.

'I've shut up the shop for about three-quarters of an hour, so I can get a quick cuppa and indulge myself.' He took two Cornish pasties on to his plate. 'How long have you known our Toby?' he asked Ann.

'On and off, about six weeks. I've been hearing all about your wife.'

'She's made quite a name for herself,' he answered proudly. 'We get people from all over the place, especially Americans.'

'They seem to think I'm rather like that Grandma Moses,' said Mrs Roberts, 'but actually I can't hold a candle to her.'

'Let others say what candles you can hold, Mrs Roberts,' Ann said. 'I think they'll say a great many.'

Mrs Roberts said nothing, but pressed a sausage-roll upon her. 'Do have one,' said her husband, 'you've nothing in the weight way to worry you.'

'That's good to hear,' said Ann.

Then Mrs Roberts took Ann to the bedroom, Toby following. She had a good many paintings to show, stacked along the walls. Toby noticed how, over the years, she had

44

become far less shy about exhibiting her work. Ann examined them all closely and, when she began to praise, did it knowledgeably.

'But I haven't seen Blackie today,' she said, 'and Toby tells me he's your model.'

'Oh, he's a roamer.' Mrs Roberts's face softened; she loved the cat. 'He'll be in for his supper.'

'If I want to buy one of the pictures, must I go to your dealer?'

'I'm much obliged to you, but I'm afraid it's yes. He gets cross with me if I sell on my own.'

Toby liked the idea that anyone could get cross with his formidable mother, and he saw Ann smile.

'I'll get his name from Toby,' she said.

'Come down and have a smoke and a drink,' Mr Roberts called up the staircase. 'I'll take quarter of an hour more off.'

So they went down, Ann nearly into Mr Roberts's arms. This time they went into the parlour, where she praised the colour-scheme. 'No, I don't smoke,' she said in answer to his father's enquiry, 'but a drink I should like.'

Toby thought she was obviously in for a long stay, and knew this would please his mother who, whether she liked the guest or not, would regard a short stay as a slight.

'Nights drawing out now,' Mr Roberts said. He looked frankly at Ann, at her delicate head, her Roman hair-style. 'And I've got to draw out with them. We don't really shut till seven. Pleased to have met you. Come again.'

'I certainly will, if I'm asked,' Ann said, 'and I hope I shall be.'

'Oh, you won't have the time to come traipsing out to us,' said Mrs Roberts. 'Toby told me you were with the BBC, and I expect you've a lot to do.'

'Not so much that I can't get free sometimes. I appreciate

the privilege of meeting you.'

It was kindly meant, but Mrs Roberts was flustered. 'Oh, I'm no treat.'

'I think you are. Thank you very much.' Ann stood up; she was only an inch or two shorter than Toby. 'I had a lovely tea, much the best I've had for ages' (if ever, Toby thought) 'and I'll be in touch with your dealer over that painting. I'd be so proud of it.'

So the afternoon came to an end.

When Toby was at last informed of Ann's dealings, he almost blushed, which was something he did sometimes, not always significantly. The dealer wanted five hundred pounds for the painting which had taken Ann's fancy.

'I don't think your mother did like me,' she said thoughtfully, 'or I suspect she'd have let me buy direct.'

'She's terribly tied up.' Toby was defensive. 'I don't suppose she ever makes a private sale these days.'

'You may tell that to the marines,' Ann said. 'All the same, I'm very satisfied to pay five hundred for anything as lovely as that.'

Meanwhile, in a bemused way, he continued to see her. He found that she loved walking, as he did, and they met for long tours of the metropolis which ended usually in his flat or her house. Sometimes he felt like a boy out courting; if he were that, then he wasn't getting very far. He had not kissed her again except for the obligatory peck on the cheek for hail and farewell. She told him, as they rounded St Paul's churchyard, that she was planning a small cocktail party. 'I don't suppose your mother would come?'

'I'm afraid I don't suppose so, either,' said Toby. 'It's a pity, but she gets more and more of a recluse.'

This was not entirely true. Mrs Roberts had ventured out for luncheon with dealers or with art editors whose interest she had caught, but had seemed to scuttle home, as to a burrow. Otherwise she was content to do the shopping round, sagely buying enough for one week, and that was all. Mr Roberts, to Toby's surprise and hers, had taken up ten-pin bowling, which he practised every few days. He had certainly asked his wife on one occasion whether she would accompany him, but had been scornfully brushed off. She was too busy.

His thoughts returned to Ann's cocktail party. How many would she ask?

'Oh, only about twenty. My house isn't geared to more than that in a room.'

He wondered whether she would invite the Cranes. He knew that she knew Maisie slightly, but not of his own past involvement with her. He wasn't sure whether he would dread a meeting, or welcome it. The last cocktail party where he had glimpsed her must have been a hundred strong. They came to the Monument, where she said she was a little tired. 'Taxi, then,' said Toby. But she would not hear of it. They were right by an Underground station which would take them to Victoria, and they could walk on to Ebury Street.

The train was very crowded and they had to strap-hang. This was no hardship for a woman of her height, and they talked all the way back.

'I enjoyed that,' Ann said, as she took out her key. 'It was good. Tell me, would you like an early drink, or would you like tea?'

He said he would like tea, if it wasn't too much of a bother. But they had just sat down to it when Colonel Clover called.

'Ha, Ann. Ha, young Roberts. What have you been doing with yourselves, eh?'

Ann told him that they had been walking in the City.

'Good for you, too. I bet you weren't dull.' She went out

47

to ask the maid to get a tray ready.

'No being bored when Ann's around,' Clover continued. 'I wish you'd met Mike. He was a live wire, always on the go. Tragic thing, that. What he wanted out of life, he got.'

Toby murmured something suitable. He did not wish he had met Mike.

'Went right through the Normandy beaches, too, never got a bruise. Then, to die in that damned smash – it's too bad.'

Ann came back. 'Tea won't be a minute. Are you coming to my party, Percy? I'm planning it for the first of November.'

'Just try to keep me away. Am I to know the other guests?'

'I don't know myself, up to now. You and Toby will form a nucleus.'

He seized her hand and kissed it.

'Thank you,' said Ann.

'I try to be gallant, but an old soldier would need some practice.'

The tea came. 'I don't think you do so badly, Percy, but you are a bit archaic.'

'Hear the names she calls me, Roberts? Now I'm in the doghouse.'

'No, never,' she countered – with a trace, Toby thought, of tenderness. Could she really be planning to marry this silly man, or did she see him purely because of his contact with Mike? Clover left soon after tea, with some hand-kissing, but Toby stayed on.

'You've never seen a picture of Mike,' said Ann when he had gone, 'because I don't believe in putting up pictures in a room. I keep them in a drawer.'

Toby, who would have liked Mike to be uncomely, was taken aback by the sight of a fair young face, the features sharply cut, the eyes bright. 'He was very good-looking,' he said.

'I certainly think so.' She put it away again. 'Will you have a drink? I think you deserve one after all that walking. We must have done at least six miles.'

Toby accepted and sat beside her on the sofa, but made no attempt to kiss her. He said, 'I should like to be special to you, like Colonel Clover.'

She gave a shout of laughter. 'Oh, but you are! Poor Percy, he's not at all bright but he's a link.'

'Is that really all?' It was rare for him to ask a question.

She answered him rather soberly. 'That's all. What on earth were you thinking? And, if you were thinking anything, it would be ridiculous and impertinent.'

'I wasn't, really. And I didn't mean to be impertinent.'

This time she kissed him, but on the cheek. 'Oh, Toby, don't be so hangdog. I was joking.'

He took her hand and held it. 'I think I'm half in love with you.'

'Only half in love? Not the whole. That is so like you.'

'Don't laugh at me.'

'Of course I shall laugh at you if I like. You don't seem much older than Tim to me. Which reminds me,' she said, withdrawing her hand, 'they're coming home for the day on Sunday next. I want you to meet them.'

It seemed impossible to turn the subject back to himself again and soon he got up to go. 'But remember', he said to her boldly, 'what I said.'

'I shall remember you as a flatterer of elderly ladies. Run along now, and don't forget about Sunday. You may come to lunch.'

He went, a little encouraged, on his way. To be asked to meet her sons was somehow significant. He had begun to hope that he might become her lover.

49

7

It was the day after he had met Ann's sons, and had been impressed by them. Tim looked very like her and, for a schoolboy, had a ready wit. Sam was rosy but silent. Toby fancied he had passed muster with them both.

Now he was tired. He had returned to his flat after an unusually long and hard day, had cooked himself scrambled eggs and was now lying on the sofa trying to relax. Baumann had praised him and had hinted that his American trip might not be so far off. Outside was a misty October evening pressing itself against the window panes. As he often did, when alone, he admired Mrs Roberts's decorations, her pictures bright on the walls, Maisie's lamp. He was satisfied with his lot and disinclined even to read.

And then the bell rang. Who the devil at this time of night? He got up reluctantly and answered it.

On the step was Rita, wearing a mini-skirt and an anorak. Time had made her more ravaged.

'Can I come in, Tobe?'

'Do.' He led her into his sitting-room, poured her a sherry. 'Now what's up?'

He had not asked her to take off her coat, but she now did so. 'You remember me?' she said.

'Of course I do.'

'I have something special to ask you. And think twice before you answer. You're thick with Adrian?'

'Yes.' Toby was bold. 'And if you don't stop writing him letters he'll go mad.'

'*He'll* go mad! What about me?' She drained her glass of sherry at a gulp.

'There's nothing for you. You know he's married?'

She said triumphantly, 'Of course I know. I've seen them together. I went down to Lincolnshire and crept into a service. She's what the Yanks call a dog. I took care that they didn't see me.'

'Look, Rita,' said Toby, 'this is all wrong. He told me you were persecuting him with letters and, believe me, there's nothing in him for you.'

'Persecuting him! Doesn't he persecute me – never an answer in an ordinarily friendly way?'

'Your letters aren't ordinarily friendly.'

'How do you know?'

'Because he told me.'

'Thick as thieves,' said Rita. She leaned back on the cushions, her sharp face profiled by them. 'That's what I always said. Whose side are you on? His or mine?'

Toby was thrown out of course by this mad conversation.

'Look, Rita, I can't seriously discuss this. Adrian is married, and he's happy, and your letters disturb him.'

'He's happy with a church helper, that's all.'

'It's more than that. So shut up, Rita, and let's talk about something else.'

For a while she was silent, and he was able to study her. Under the anorak she was wearing a very short skirt, up to her thighs, and a white sweater, nibbed all over by what could have been a cat. Her hair was pulled back into a rubber band.

Then she said, 'Do you know what this is?' Out of her handbag she produced a flick-knife. Toby was chilled with horror.

'Put that away, Rita; it's a beastly thing.'

51

'You tell your holy pal that, if he doesn't answer my letters, I'll give him this. I can find an opportunity.'

'Do you know you can be jailed for uttering menaces?' That sounded pompous even in his own ears.

Scornfully she said, 'I know all about that. My old dad was a policeman. He's dead now and so's my mum. So just tell your friend what I said.' Her voice had roughened with the years, and her daintiness had gone.

'Of course I shall tell him, and warn him. But I don't think you really mean it.'

She snapped open the blade. 'You'll see if I mean it. Why can't he answer my letters?'

'Put that knife away, I said. And we can't go over all this time and time again.'

'Aren't you going to offer me another drink?'

'No, I'm not. I want you to go away. And you'd better give me that knife to keep.'

'Some chance,' she said. But she had begun to cry. 'It was never anybody but him, from the first time I set eyes on the bastard.'

The tears streamed down her cheeks. Toby felt a sudden pity for her. What would have happened if she had not slept with Bob and made him marry her? If she had never left the child she had abandoned? It was a wretched life for her.

'Come, wipe your face.' He did cross the room and pour her another sherry. 'Here you are. This is all moonshine and nothing to cry about.'

As she reached in her bag for a handkerchief she let the knife fall to the carpet. Toby pounced, and put it in his pocket. At once she threw the glass at him, contents and all.

'Give that back, you bloody swine!'

Toby, glumly trying to wipe sherry from his best suit, did not answer.

'Give it back!'

52

'No,' he said. 'You're safer without it. And now get out.'

She said, 'Can't you see that I love him? People who love as much as I do have to get something in return.'

'No, not necessarily. He has nothing whatsoever for you, and you'd better make up your mind to it. Come on, get your coat on.'

She got up as if to let him help her into the anorak but, as he held it out, made a dive for his pocket.

'Oh, no, you don't,' said Toby, morosely reflecting that she could easily get another like it.

'You're stealing. It's my knife.'

'All right, I'm stealing. But I shan't give it you.'

Her tears had dried. She shrugged, and said, 'All right, but remember what I've told you.'

He showed her to the door and watched as she went down the stairs.

The moment she was out of the way he telephoned Ann, looking for a sage head upon those Princess Lieven shoulders. She was in.

'And what can I do for you at this late hour of the night?' she asked.

He told her, as quickly as he could, the whole story.

'So now you're in possession of a flick-knife,' she said. 'Offensive weapon.'

'What would you do if you were me?'

'Write and warn your friend Adrian at once. The bad thing is that she's already been down in Lincolnshire looking him over. You must treat this thing seriously, whether it is serious or not. She's mad, I take it?'

Oddly enough this had not occurred to Toby. Now it did.

'I suppose she might be,' he said. 'Anyway, she's changed enormously since I first knew her. She's scruffy, which she used never to be.'

'You must take this as if it were meant. Warn Adrian,

and let him take what steps he pleases. Legal ones are due, but she seems too cut off from anybody; there doesn't seem to be anyone at all responsible for her.'

'You know', said Toby, 'what makes me think you may be right, she's mad? Not the flick-knife – that could have been show – but when she threw the sherry at me.'

'She threw the sherry?' Ann was laughing too much to go on, and to Toby her laughter had a sane, releasing sound. At last she said, 'And have you tried to get it off?'

'I don't know how to do it.'

'Try cold water only. If that doesn't work, you'll have to send it to the cleaner's. Now, go to bed and try to forget all about it.'

'I doubt whether I can. Adrenalin is pumping through me.'

'Well, if you can't, I can. I've had a very hard day.' She added, 'Good-night, pet,' which was what he had always said to Maisie, knowing she wanted him to say something different.

'Good-night, darling,' said Toby, greatly daring.

He took the flick-knife downstairs to the street, and dropped it down a drain. But what good could that do, since no one was likely to charge him with possessing an offensive weapon, except when Ann laughed at him?

Next morning, on waking still troubled, he sat down before work to write both to Adrian and to Bob. What Bob could do, having no *locus standi*, Toby couldn't imagine. But he knew Rita better than they did, and Toby thought he might attend to matters. The interview with the girl had shocked him more than he knew, since when he went into the sitting-room he fancied he could still see her there, in her red skirt, showing him the flick-knife. But, he said to himself, it is no good worrying, because it is no affair of yours.

54

By return of post he had a telephone call from Adrian, who was much calmer than he was. 'I shall write to her, of course, which is what she wants, but she won't like the contents of my letter. I'm going to tell her to stop sending me letters, or I shall have to take steps. Of course I'm sorry for her since she's evidently round the bend. You couldn't come down, I suppose, and talk it over?'

Toby said he was afraid he couldn't. The pips went. 'Good-bye,' said Adrian.

He was sorry in a way that he was too busy to go, for he had never visited Adrian in his parish, not seen him in the pulpit where, he imagined, he looked like an Italian portrait above the white collar.

Bob did not telephone: he wrote.

'Dear Tobe, Thank you for your letter. It is all rather like a madhouse, isn't it? Of course you can't just let it go. I shall write to Reet myself, if you can get her address from old Adrian, and tell her, if she doesn't give over, that I'm going to tell the police about her. What I've never told you is that, while we were married, I often thought she was off her rocker. Thanks for writing. I shall take steps.'

Well, at least she had got attention from Adrian, and from her former husband. From time to time he felt free, as if they were all exaggerating something petty. Then anxiety fell upon him again, as the phantom Rita smirked from the corner of his sofa.

A further surprise came from Ann. 'Look,' she said on the telephone, 'I have induced your mother to come to my party. She says she'll come for an hour, if you ferry her here and take her back. Of course there isn't going to be any nonsense about an hour. When the party's over, I shall take you both out for dinner, or give you a cold meal here.'

'How on earth did you do that?'

'I wrote and told her how much I wanted her, and that I

55

must return her hospitality. I talked about her paintings and about you, and this morning came a brisk note of acceptance. Though, she said, she wasn't used to parties.'

'Wonders will never cease,' said Toby, who often responded by a cliché when he was taken aback. 'What time do you want her there?'

'Early, I think. I don't want to plunge her at once into a roomful of people. She'll only close up, if I may put it that way.'

'I'll get her to you at six precisely. Will there be anyone else I know?'

'Not Claire or Alec – they're in Greece. Maisie and Edward Crane – you knew them, didn't you?'

He felt a deep inner plunge, as if he had gone down in a fast lift. 'Yes,' he said.

'And poor Percy, of course. The rest are more or less supers. Oh, and there'll be an art critic to talk painting to your mother, though I don't know who yet.'

'My mother doesn't know anything about any painting but her own.'

'Good. The critic shall be instructed accordingly.'

After this call, Toby was flooded with unease. Yet why should he be? He had got over Maisie, surely, and over Edward? He had never spoken about them to Ann, so her invitation had been innocent. The complication of having his mother there, with her cult of Maisie, was hard to imagine. Suddenly he knew why Mrs Roberts had accepted Ann's plea that she should come; it was because Ann had bought one of the more expensive of her paintings. She, too, must have felt she should make some acknowledgement. Well, he must look after her, spare her reclusiveness all he could.

He was not looking forward to Ann's party.

8

When he called for his mother, he saw that she was wearing the same blue dress that she had worn to her private show in Cambridge. It looked as though it had not been worn for nearly ten years, but the style was dateless.

'The things you land me into,' said Mrs Roberts ungraciously. 'You can't think how I dread it. But your Mrs Thorold was so pressing that I couldn't say no.'

'Lucky she didn't ask me,' said his father jovially. 'I'm not a society person, like your mum.'

'Oh, be quiet, Stan.'

Toby hurried her into his car before she could change her mind. She was wearing a string of good cultured pearls (so he supposed them to be) which she had bought with the proceeds of one of her sales. She looked neat, nondescript, and slightly fierce.

'Do you like Ann?' he couldn't resist saying.

'She's all right. Bit old in the tooth for you, though. I suppose there's nothing of that?'

'Not really,' said Toby.

'It won't be a big party, will it?'

'No, quite small. Edward and Maisie Crane are coming.'

She looked at him, and her mouth opened. 'What do they want to do that for?'

'They're old friends of Ann's, that's all.'

'Has she got a very grand house?' She could have asked Toby these questions the last time she saw him, but then had not been sufficiently interested.

'No, quite small. But everything's very nice, or so I imagine. I don't know anything about china.'

They sat in silence for the rest of the way. When they came to Ann's she began to tremble slightly. Toby laid a hand on her arm. 'Come, you're not going to the scaffold.'

Ann greeted them; they were the earliest visitors, she said, which was the nicest thing she could imagine. The maid came to take off Mrs Roberts's coat and they went into the drawing-room. The drinks were laid out there, ice-buckets, siphons, water. A man was there to serve them, and asked at once what they would have. 'Nothing for me,' said Mrs Roberts.

'Oh, don't say that! Would you like some tomato juice or tonic water?' Ann pressed her.

'Tonic water, thanks.' But Mrs Roberts was looking at her own painting, which hung above the mantelpiece.

'It looks good in this room, don't you think?' said Ann. 'I think it makes it.'

Mrs Roberts nodded stiffly over her glass. Soon other guests arrived, including Colonel Clover and the critic who had encouraged Mrs Roberts at her first show, all those years ago. Toby marvelled how Ann had come upon him.

'Sit down,' Ann said to her, motioning her to a wing-backed chair, 'and I'll bring people to talk to you. I know how tiring these affairs can be.'

'I can just as well stand.'

'Well, I won't let you. Toby, make your mother comfortable and give her that small table to put her drink on.'

And Mrs Roberts succumbed. Seated, she seemed more at ease and pleased when the critic came to squat on his haunches beside her. More people arrived, including the Baumanns, whom Ann introduced to Mrs Roberts. 'Mr Baumann is Toby's boss,' she said.

'Very nice,' said Mrs Roberts. 'I hope he works hard.'

'Like a beaver,' said Clive. 'We're all pleased with him. We may be sending him to New York for a trip soon.'

'I'm sure he'll like that,' she replied.

Toby lost sight of her then, to become involved in tedious conversation with the Colonel, and did not see Edward and Maisie come in. When he did spot them, they were crouched by Mrs Roberts, of whom they were making a fuss. Maisie looked much as she always had, in ruffled white blouse and black skirt; Edward, if anything, younger. Excusing himself to Clover, Toby came quietly to join them.

'This is a real surprise,' Maisie was saying. 'We thought we'd never see you again.'

'Oh, I sometimes come to a party,' Mrs Roberts replied mendaciously.

'Mother, it's only once in a blue moon, and you know it.'

Edward and Maisie got up, Maisie rather flustered, and greeted him.

'It's a long time since we saw you last,' she said.

'Five years, in fact,' said Edward.

'I hear you've got a daughter. Congratulations.' They were talking stiffly, or at least Maisie was. 'What's her name?' asked Mrs Roberts.

'Clemency,' said Edward, 'a good old Puritan name. She's very like Maisie.'

'She's beautiful,' Maisie said rather defensively, 'or I think so.'

Mrs Roberts reached out her arm and touched Maisie's hand. 'You deserve the best,' she said.

Then Ann came up with two women to introduce to Mrs Roberts, and they were on their own.

'I hear you've got a new play on the stocks,' Toby said to Edward.

'Yes, I have, and I rather dread it. It is not too pleasant to feel unfashionable, though I never was in the latest mode.

59

The audiences should keep up, though, if the past's anything to go from.'

Toby recalled the first night to which Edward had taken him and Adrian. It gave him pleasure to clip the years with reminiscence.

'I remember. It was awful.'

Ann came up. 'Toby, have you told your mother she's having a quiet supper with us? And will you telephone your father's shop — I gather he doesn't close till half-past seven — and warn him that she'll be late? The telephone's over there.'

'But I've got to tell her she's staying!'

'You don't fancy a *fait accompli*?'

'No, I don't.'

'Then I'll break the news.' She came up to Mrs Roberts. 'Toby thinks you will like to have supper here, with just the three of us. He's going to telephone your husband.'

'Mrs Thorold, I hope you don't mind me saying so, but I don't like being railroaded like that.' Heaven knows where she had got the word, Ann thought.

'But you must stay! Toby will drive you home soon afterwards. My cooking isn't as wonderful as yours, but I've made a lovely aspic jelly with patterns in it. I love to do that when it turns out firmly, but if it doesn't I simply have an urge to sling it at my guests.'

'I hope you don't do that to me,' said Mrs Roberts, capitulating without realising it.

'And we'll have a little champagne with it.'

'I don't drink—' she began, but Ann, not waiting for last-minute doubts, went off to Toby, who was standing by the telephone as though he had never seen such an instrument before.

'You can ring your father now,' she said. 'Your mother has succumbed.'

He just caught his father in the act of shutting up shop. When he explained why he had telephoned, his father gasped. 'Your mother? Staying out to supper? Strike me pink! But it's good for her to be out and about. Don't bring her back too late; and tell her she's an old gadabout.'

He returned to the party, which was just reaching the maximum height of noise and smoke. He thought of the nicotine deposit on Ann's window panes.

Maisie came up to him. If she were embarrassed, she did not show it. 'Tell me all about yourself, Toby.'

'There's nothing to tell, really. Same old job.'

'How long have you known Ann?'

'Only two months or so.'

'She's great fun, isn't she? Tell me about Adrian and Bob. What are they doing?'

'I'll tell you and Edward what's happened. I want you both to hear it.'

Edward was within touching distance, and Maisie pulled at his sleeve. 'Come here a minute. Toby's got something to tell us.'

Toby gave a brief account of what had been happening. 'I thought', he said to Edward, 'that you might be able to give us advice.'

Maisie was shocked and she showed it. 'I don't see how you can just let it go.'

'Give me a chance to think,' Edward said, 'and I'll write to you.'

It was curious, but while he had been talking to them Toby found himself almost unaware of Maisie, but conscious of Ann chatting to a couple just behind them. One of the pair was a man of almost Adrian-like good looks, who had put his arm around her waist. His thoughts were so much with her that he had to pull himself together and to thank Edward for the attention he had given to the story of

Rita.

'Mind you, I may not come up with anything brilliant, but I'd like to help. My first instinct is to get Adrian to inform the police.'

'I'm afraid there's only a local bobby on a bicycle to inform,' Toby replied.

'Give him something to do. Maisie, we must go. Another first night,' he told Toby, 'and we must get dressed.'

In a moment they had melted away to say their farewells to Mrs Roberts. The party was breaking up. Well, I have seen Maisie again and no harm done, Toby thought, and reflected on the tepidity of their conversation and of his. When the other guests had left, the man was dismantling the makeshift bar and Ann had gone to see to dinner, Toby sat down on the arm of Mrs Roberts's chair.

'Well, Mummy, you can't say that wasn't painless.'

She answered rather fretfully, 'It's all very well for you. I can never think of anything to say to these people.'

'Oh, come, they're doing all the talking themselves, and you have only to smile and say thank you.'

'I wish we weren't staying. Your dad won't know how to get on without me.'

'Don't you believe it. He was as pleased as Punch that you were stopping on.'

'I didn't see that Claire.'

'No wonder you didn't. She and her husband couldn't come.'

'I saw Maisie, though.'

'I know you did. She was talking to you a lot.'

'There was never anyone quite like Maisie.'

'So you always say.'

'I repeat myself, do I?'

'Why, Mummy, you sounded quite quarrelsome then. It must be the result of success.'

Ann came in to announce that supper was ready, and took them into a small dining-room with places laid for three. 'Now, sit down without fear,' she told them. 'My aspic has jelled.'

The aspic was indeed a remarkable sight. Ham, chicken, eggs, pâté had gone to its making, with cucumber as a decoration.

'Did you make that all by yourself?' asked Mrs Roberts, with a note of respect in her voice.

Ann said that she had. Toby said that it reminded him of St Mark's in Venice, and that it seemed a pity to break into it.

'Thank you, Toby. I am only a rather elaborate cook; it is when I make anything plain that I fall to the ground. Either my steaks burn, or they are totally raw.'

'I can't believe that,' said Mrs Roberts. 'I've never made anything like this.'

Ann said that a nice Liebfraumilch would go nicely with it and, when she demurred, reminded her that she had enjoyed half a glass of champagne after her first show.

Mrs Roberts said that she didn't abstain because of principle, but because wine and such things did not suit her.

'Nevertheless,' Ann said, 'I hope you are going to have half a glass now, just to celebrate.'

'Celebrate what?' asked Mrs Roberts, puzzled.

'Why, you being here at all. Toby told me you'd never come, but you did, and you made my party.'

Ann let Toby pass the wine, and attended to the aspic jelly.

He thought how graceful she looked in her black dress with the jet beads. Edith Swan-Neck, he thought. Mrs Roberts did accept her half-glass of wine, and before the end of the meal allowed it to be refilled. It relaxed her and made her more talkative, though Toby knew she would be worrying internally about whether it would make her drunk. She sipped at it again, though her glass was almost empty, and sat there, small in the blue dress, her reddish hair in a bun, which might have seemed arty to anyone who didn't know her.

'And now let's drink to Toby,' Ann said. 'He has troubles on his plate.'

'Why, what's on his plate?' Mrs Roberts cried, alarmed.

'Nothing that concerns me directly, Mummy, but I'll tell you all about it on the way home.'

So there was now a sizeable audience for Adrian's woes. Toby wondered if his mother would do the artistic thing and come up triumphantly as the sole sensible purveyor of advice.

'Just so long as it's nothing at the office,' Mrs Roberts said, and held up her empty glass.

'To Toby,' said Ann, and Mrs Roberts pretended to drink. 'Just fancy having a son who's a banker!'

'I wanted something else for him. College life, maybe.'

'Now, Mummy, this is far more paying, if you want me to be crude.'

'I suppose so. But I always saw you in one of those fine old buildings, teaching young men and doing your own work.'

The rest of the meal passed without incident, till Toby said that he must run his mother home. It was a quarter to ten. He had one problem on his mind, whether to give Ann the casual kiss fashion demanded, or whether his mother would make too much of it. He finally decided that he would do so, and was interested to see that Ann kissed Mrs Roberts without any gesture, or flinching, on the latter's part.

'I've had a day of it, haven't I?' his mother asked when they were back in the car. 'I wish I didn't feel so muzzy.'

'You don't feel anything of the sort; you couldn't do on one glass of wine.'

'That's for me to say. What about your trouble? What is it?'

Toby told her the entire story of Rita and Adrian. But, to his disappointment, she only said, 'Stupid girl. I'm glad you took that knife away. I shouldn't think you'll hear from her again.'

And she would not discuss the matter further. 'I quite like your Mrs Thorold,' she said, after she had said good-bye. She walked quite steadily up the small path, but Toby put this down to the power of the mind.

9

Next day, Toby received a note from Edward.

'I stand by my first impulse, which is the police. Adrian should consult the county constabulary. I can't say more than that. It was good to see you the other evening. We both enjoyed it. Perhaps you will come in for a drink one night.' (Night not specified.) 'Excuse brevity, but I wanted to get my idea to you as quickly as possible.'

The main point of this he conveyed by letter to Adrian, and received a letter in reply. 'We are urged not to retaliate when threatened, so I am going to leave Rita to dree her own weird. Don't bother any more about it. I dare say it was all showing off.'

But the day of this letter's arrival he had a telephone call from Bob Cuthbertson, who had already informed the Lincolnshire police. 'No one knows Reet as I do. When she wants trouble she gets it. I'll do the worrying from now on. But thanks a million for all you've been doing.'

After wondering just how much Adrian would like Bob interfering in his affairs, Toby decided that he might as well give up and leave it to other people.

He was beginning to have all his thoughts for Ann. Her air of fragility (misleading), her sense of fun had attracted him more than he knew. So he was greatly disturbed when a letter in capital letters reached him. 'She has dozens beside you.' Though he had seen no evidence of this, it maddened him to think that there were eyes peering at him. Who would think of writing such a thing? He would have suspected Rita had she known anything about Ann and himself at all. But she had not. He burned the note in an ashtray and made up his mind to forget about it. It was not so easy.

Next day, Baumann suggested that they should lunch together at a nearby pub. 'I want to talk to you, and it will be better there.'

Toby wondered, with a touch of unreasonable apprehension, what he could possibly have to talk about.

But it turned out to be his New York trip. He would go for six weeks, spending the mornings at the bank. Everything would be arranged for him. Would he like that?

Toby said it was great. He was, indeed, pleased, though there was a shadow in his mind about spending so long without Ann. He fancied that he could smell her green scent. What would she be doing? Whom would she be seeing? When they had exhausted the subject of America and had ordered more beer, he dared to ask Baumann how long he had known her.

'Ann Thorold? Oh, I met her shortly after her husband died. She was a friend of a friend.'

'Has she been very lonely?'

'I shouldn't say so. She has her BBC work and she's good at looking after herself.'

'Has there been anyone since?' Now Toby did blush, and was glad of the dimness of the bar with its great engraved mirrors and rows of fairy lights.

Baumann did not appear surprised by the question. 'Had lovers, you mean? Nobody knows. I shouldn't think she'd spent an entirely celibate existence for the last five years. But, then, she may be quite self-sufficient. You like her, Toby?'

'I admire her. And, yes, I like her very much. I think she's wonderful for her age, too.'

67

Baumann laughed. 'She'd hate to hear you say that, as though she was a sprightly ninety. But it is true that the years don't seem to touch her. Women like her, by the way, which is always a good sign. Clarissa is really fond of her.'

Toby wondered that, after those years, Baumann knew so little about her private life. But he said nothing more.

He took Ann out that night, to a small French restaurant equidistant from them both.

'So that's that. I shall be away for six weeks. You don't know how much I shall miss you.'

'Toby, you sounded so lachrymose that I thought you were going to say six years.'

'Don't laugh at me.'

'I shall laugh at you when I please and whenever I please. Fancy being so morose about a lovely jaunt, all expenses paid! You'll like New York, I expect. I don't, but thousands do.'

The lighting of the place became her. It emphasised her high cheek-bones, her broad white forehead, her brilliant hazel eyes. He could not believe that no one had slept with her during those long five years. 'Tell me about Percy Clover,' he said.

'Oh, poor Percy! Why do you want to know about him?'

'I just do.'

'He's just an old soldier. I put up with him for Mike's sake. Though Mike's sakes were incalculable.'

'He seems proprietary.'

'He wanted to be proprietary.'

'What do you mean?'

'He wanted to marry me. There was not a chance of that, but I could never completely disabuse him of the idea.'

An anonymous letter? Clover? 'And how did he take it?'

'Ill. But one can't marry everyone who asks.'

'You've been asked many times?'

'Not many times. A few.' She pursued a prawn around her plate, speared it and ate it.

Toby remarked that she could never have been tempted.

She ignored the implied question. Toby's questions were always implied, but she had the means of countering them.

'Oh, temptations,' she said, 'one has them, but they don't last five minutes.'

'Don't you ever feel lonely?'

'Toby, Toby, the moments fly. I've no time to be lonely.'

He saw that he would get nothing more from her. He said, 'I liked your children.'

'They're agreeable enough. Tim may be a nuisance as adolescence advances. I'm glad you found them amiable.'

'Ann, if you ever were to marry again, would they stand for it?'

'I don't know. I've never asked them.' She was looking with pleasure at a steak au poivre. 'Do you know I am always hungry and the canteen doesn't satisfy me? This is a good place. How clever of you to have found it.'

He told her he was glad she felt like that, but that he knew of several places equally good.

'Gourmet,' she said. 'How nice.'

'When I come home, we shall visit them all.'

'If you'll ask me, I'm sure we shall.'

Afterwards, when they went back to her house, Toby tried to make love to her.

'Oh, no, you don't, my dear,' she said, 'it's far too early for that yet.'

'But some day?'

'Write to me about your American adventures. Mind you, tell me everything.'

'And will you tell me everything?'

'Wait and see.'

She did allow him to kiss her, this time responding rather

69

more warmly. He felt he could never let her go. 'You won't let me make love to you,' he said. 'Why not?'

'Why should I? You're only half in love with me. You said it yourself. And I'm only half in love with you, my lad.'

'I'll ask you again when I come back.'

'Do. There's never any harm in asking. But you're rushing things, you know.'

He ran his finger down her nape and the back of her spine. 'Stop treating me as if I were a small boy.'

'Well, you are so young.'

'Nonsense,' he said and kissed her again. This time, however, she moved away.

'No more of that, now. You must be going, or you'll be all pasty in the morning.'

'And you'll see that I wear my socks and my under-vest and wash my neck.' He smiled, but his tone was a little bitter.

'All those useful things. But you won't be here in the morning.'

She got up with her usual lithe, uncoiling motion, and he rose with her. 'Toby, I'm very tired tonight. I had a rough day producing two other interviews for the Antipodes. You must see yourself out. Good-night, dear.'

And so he left her, but not altogether discouraged. He knew she was attracted by him, hoped that his six-week absence might make her grow more fond. Absence makes the heart grow fonder. Out of sight is out of mind. Which was it to be? He would have loved a light-hearted affair with her, but realised somehow that to her it would not prove so light. No Claire, she.

So he went to New York, was put up at the Stanhope Hotel, a comfortable place opposite the Metropolitan Museum, and was taken round the sights by a junior partner delegated to look after him. In the mornings he went to the bank, and saw how business was conducted there. His afternoons were his own, though he was usually taken out to dine in the evenings. He wrote a slow crescendo of love-letters to Ann. He would be in New York over Christmas, so he must buy her a present. He asked his bear-leader, who was called Dunstan, where he should look for one.

'Depends what you have in mind. There's a small antique jeweller's one block down, and I guess you might find something not too expensive there.'

Toby thanked him, and that afternoon investigated the shop. At once he saw an orange zircon set in a pendant, which seemed made for Ann. He enquired about it, found that he could just stretch his spare dollars to cover it. After all, he was having little to pay for himself. He wrote to Ann every two days, she sent him a letter a week.

'Dear Toby, of course I miss you. How shouldn't I? Your letters are most persuasive, but you really must wait till we meet again. I am suspicious of words on paper, since one can't see the writer's face.'

She added that the boys would soon be home from school, and would keep her busy. She was to have a month's leave from the BBC.

He wrote telling her that he had a Christmas present for her, but did not describe it.

He did and did not care for New York. It was very cold, and a stiff wind whipped along the canyons of the great tall streets. He was stifled by the heat indoors, and frozen outside of them. But, on the whole, the hospitality he received moved him, and he quite looked forward to spending Christmas at the Dunstans' home in Connecticut. The decorations were already up in all their lighted splendour along Fifth Avenue and they delighted him as much as if he were a boy again. He would bring Ann here one day and *make* her like it. He bought small – literally small – presents for his father and mother, knowing that he would have to pass them through the Customs.

When he drove out to Connecticut with Dunstan, he was delighted to see the snow. So much he had never seen in his life before. Their house shone redly through the trees, and Toby felt the excitement of childhood, though he did not relish putting his shoes and trouser-legs into snow nearly a foot deep. He found that they had their big meal on Christmas Eve, turkey with cranberry sauce, and pumpkin pie, which he did not care for. He did not really understand how anyone ever could. The young Dunstans romped about him, and were enthralled by his one parlour trick, which was to put his feet round his neck. Indeed, they requested this item so often that he feared he would have been stuck like it, as the Nanny he had never had might have warned him. Otherwise he felt wrapped in comfort, and, on saying he had never had a mint julep, on the following day one was produced. Biddy Dunstan was a comfortable young woman of thirty-five who, though less elegant, looked as old as Ann. She did everything she could to make Toby feel less far from home, though the truth was that he did not feel far from it. Toby was somewhat maddened by a record of 'White Christmas', with the verve and swoop of Crosby's voice, which the children seemed to play incessantly. He felt himself aloof from the more Christmasy sentiments of Christmas, and he wondered what sort of a holiday Ann was having.

His tour drew to an end, and, having addressed letters to all Americans who had entertained him, he flew to London on 29 December. Here he boldly walked through the 'Nothing to declare' part of the Customs, and at the barrier saw Ann.

He was breathless with surprise. It was nine o'clock in England, two o'clock Eastern Time. She was wearing a light fur coat, with an orange scarf round her neck.

'Ann! What on earth are you doing here?'

'Well, I couldn't let you arrive all dismal, with a jet lag, at this early hour. My car's outside, so come on.'

Exhausted, he had never been more sure that he loved her. He longed to show her his present. 'We shall go back to your flat,' she said, 'and install you decently.'

So they drove back, for Toby phantasmagorically, through the dark night. No snow for England. Along the route, past the deadly suburbs of the motor roads, he could find nothing to say to her. She drove beautifully as, it seemed to him, she did everything. It was still a miracle to him that she should have come so far to greet him.

At last he said, 'Did you have a good Christmas?'

'Certainly the boys did. They stuffed and stuffed, and afterwards got me to play that exhausting game, Monopoly. I won by cornering all the railway terminals. I left them at it tonight, and I think nothing more will be heard of them till I come in. Now let me unpack for you.'

He watched her as she did so, neat-handed as ever, and she paused only before a small suitcase with articles in tissue paper.

'I'll do that,' Toby said. 'They contain your present.'

He drew out the pendant, and let her study it before putting it around her neck.

'Toby, dear, it's lovely! But it must have cost a bomb.'

'It's only a zircon,' he said, 'but it seemed to me to look like you.'

She hugged him as heartily as if she had been a dairymaid. 'I really love it. I should have bought it myself. How nice to have a Christmas present a little late! But I must go now; you're tired.'

'Oh, don't! Or have a drink first! You forget that it may be late by your time, but it's half-past four to me.'

'That doesn't matter.' She accepted the drink. 'If you don't get some sleep now, you'll be worn out by tomorrow. You'll see.'

'What other Christmas presents did you have?'

'Oh, one of the boys gave me chocolates, and the other a box of Turkish cigarettes. They have never noticed that I don't smoke and don't eat sweets. You must come and eat them for me.'

'I don't like Turkish cigarettes, though.' He came to sit beside her, the strangeness of the muddled hours with him. 'And thank you for doing my unpacking, which is the part I dread.'

'Now I am really going, I shall have some important things to say to you, but not yet. Come to me on Wednesday night.'

'Or you come to me. If you can leave the boys, that is.' He never liked her better than in the green gleam of Maisie's lamp. But what could she have to say that was important? Was she going to tell him she was going to be married? The cold dread ran through him.

'All right, I'll come to you. Expect me about seven.'

When she had gone, he sat up drinking for a long time, having accustomed himself to it on the plane. Yes, what could she mean? He tried to remember the guests at her party. One of them? The good-looking man who had put his arm around her waist? Toby had been introduced to him, but could not remember his name. Who else? Surely not the ridiculous Clover. When it was one o'clock by English time, he went to bed and slept without a dream.

10

She came to him on the stroke of seven, wearing a fawn-coloured dress and the orange zircon. To his eyes she looked excited and half-amused; he had not seen her like this. However, she asked him for his American adventures first, with detailed interest. He tried to keep his mind on them. Then she stirred, kissed his hand and said to him, 'You want us to be lovers, don't you?'

'More than anything in the world,' he replied. He could feel a pulse beating in his neck.

She gave his hand back to him. Looked at him straightly and said, 'I don't want a lover. I've had lovers sometimes, during these years, and you must have guessed it. I'm tired of lovers, but I should quite like a husband. Does that appeal to you? Don't be afraid to say if it does, or I shall remind you again of my seniority.'

'You mean me?' Toby said, and felt foolish.

'I mean you.'

'Darling! But why?'

'Because I am half in love with you, as you put it, and I like your society, and I'm tired of being lonely.'

He turned her towards him. 'Dear Ann,' he said, 'will you marry me? That's something I thought I'd never say,' he went on, forgetting about Claire and her dismissal of him.

'Yes, I will marry you, if being half in love will do.'

'I am wholly in love,' he said, 'and couldn't be happier.' He felt as though he had been given a precious but frail gift.

Yet there was nothing frail about Ann but her appearance.

He could feel his courage rising. 'You must have a ring,' he said.

But she was determined. She unhooked the pendant and dropped it into his hand. 'I have quite made up my mind. You take this and have it made into a nice large ring. It will look wonderful.'

They had hardly embraced. Then she said, 'And you can move in with me. I've got a double bedroom and rooms for storing.'

This practicality made Toby cool again. 'I can manage for us both anywhere.'

'That's nice of you, but I have a decent private income. Better not to let it go to waste.'

He flung himself upon her.

'No,' she said, 'you must see first what you're getting.'

She went into his bedroom, and he waited. When she came out she was naked. He saw in a blur of emotion that there was nothing to say that she had had children, save a brownish stripe below her navel. She was thoroughly lean and beautiful.

'Like what you see, Toby?' she said. 'I don't think that anything's gone to rack and ruin.'

'I can be your lover now?'

'As a celebration,' she replied coolly, 'and I've no idea what place would be appropriate.' She turned back to the bedroom and Toby followed her. 'As a celebration,' she repeated.

He had her then, her lovely, agile self. He was happier than he had ever been in his life. She gave him far more pleasure than shy Maisie or athletic Claire. When it was over and she had retreated to shower and dress, he lay for a while and marvelled at this thing that had happened to him. It was all bewildering and, yes, just a little frightening.

What sort of a husband would he make her? A loving and a sensible one. He would match his good sense with hers.

She came out, sat down for a few minutes to comb her hair. 'Go on, lazy,' she said, 'and get dressed. We have to get a meal and talk about all the lovely boring details this sort of thing brings up. I love you very much, dear Toby, but I shall always be worried about the age-gap.'

'What, after tonight? I swear I'll beat you if you are.'

She gave an altogether uncharacteristic giggle. 'Where shall we go to eat? At La Relais?'

'I thought you'd like to go to the Ritz. It's quiet there at night, and seems to cost no more than anywhere else.'

So to the Ritz they went, ate at leisure, and talked over the details. 'We'd better be married at Caxton Hall,' she said. 'I don't imagine you want to go to church. Do you think your mother would come? And perhaps your father might take a day off for once from the shop. We don't want many people, do we? I thought perhaps Alec and Claire—'

'Not Claire.'

'Why are you always so mysterious about her? Were you her lover?'

'Yes. Years ago,' said Toby, looking around the beautiful room as if he expected to find Claire in a corner.

'You have some more champagne and try not to be stuffy. But we won't ask Claire if you don't want her. I'd better ask old Percy Clover.'

'He'll break his heart.'

'No, he won't. He has a perfect sense of occasion. Toby, do you suppose your mother is going to like this?'

'Her sentiments will be about middling, I think. She's always wanted me to marry. And she seemed to like you before.' He paused. 'The question is whether Tim and Sam are going to like me for a stepfather.'

'Sam will. Tim's coming up to a difficult age, but I think

77

he'll be all right. We won't have them at the wedding, though. That would be unseemly. But it won't be the break-up of a home for them, since you're coming to live with me.'

'You make me feel like a ponce. You must be careful not to.'

'Toby! From you, how coarse. I'll tell you what, we'll ask Clive and Clarissa. You haven't any objection to that?'

'No. That would be fine.'

'Then what have we got? Your parents, Clover, and Clive and Clarissa. And lunch here afterwards. Don't we make our plans quickly? No humming and ha'ing.'

'Honeymoon?' said Toby.

'Conventional. Venice.'

'There will be no need for you to go on with your job.'

'Oh, but there will! I'd go mad sitting around the house all day. So please don't try to stop me.'

'I shouldn't dream of doing anything you didn't want.' But his mind wandered to Bush House. Whom did she meet? With whom did she work?

'That's generous of you, Toby. I may try to cut down on the long hours, though. You'll always come home to find a meal waiting, whether it's my aspic jelly or not.'

'And all that's best of dark and bright, meets in her aspic and her eyes,' he parodied.

She laughed, and for a little while couldn't stop laughing. Finally she said, still gasping, 'That was very good. Give me some more champagne. Is there any left?'

'A little. Would you like another bottle?'

'No, I don't think so. Oh, my dear, we're going to get on tremendously well, aren't we?'

He thought how easily she had at last given herself. It would be good in bed, always. And he thought he could counter her lightheartedness with lightheartedness of his own.

They sat working out the details of their lives together until the waiters began to yawn. 'Oh, dear,' Ann said, 'get the bill. We're being pressured into withdrawal.'

'I want to make love to you again.'

'Oh, no! No, you don't. That was only for the once, till we've been, as it were, to the altar. Come, don't gloom.'

Then she said, 'When I come to think of it, it might be too early for Claire.'

'Why?'

'Don't you know? She's just had a second son. Llangain is furious. He wanted them to be Hairy's — no incest, you understand. But Anneliese or Hairy don't produce.'

He paid the bill, and they went out to wait for a taxi in the russet London night. He said, 'I'll take you back, but I won't come in. I want to do some thinking, and I don't want to face the boys tonight.'

'I don't expect they'd be up, not even Tim. Mary is pretty sharp on them.'

He made an enquiry.

'She calls herself my maid, but she's really a housekeeper who does a bit of cooking.'

'Well, I shan't come in, just the same.'

'To be quite sure of you, my boy, I shall put a little notice in *The Times*.'

'Do. But, darling, there's no danger.'

'The whole thing spells danger — but there, you don't like me to talk of that.'

He was indeed glad to get back home and think. The champagne had not touched him, so he poured himself some whisky. He was going to be a husband, to a most distinguished woman whom he happened to love. She still tended to call him 'My lad', or 'My boy'. He must put a stop to that. Partly because it irritated him, and partly because

79

it forced ridiculous doubts upon him. He had barely returned when the telephone rang. It was Ann.

'Sorry to disturb you, Toby and I hope you weren't in bed. But there was one thing I forgot to tell you. I found a patchwork quilt for your mother in an antique-shop. I bought it. Perhaps she will be pleased enough with me for that, and forget about other things.'

'I was to give it her. How much did it cost?'

'Twenty-five pounds, but I thought we were never going to be caught talking about squalid things like money.' And she rang off.

Yes, and he did think of money. He was earning a good salary, and so was she, only she had independent means. This meant that they would be quite well off, and not subject to anxieties of that order. It really seemed to him that everything was going their way.

When he was in his bedroom again he could still smell her scent, delicious, not at all cloying. As he lay down where they had made love, he wondered what magic had had charge of them that night. She had, nevertheless, seemed happy in a world of her own, half-comic, entirely delectable. Next day he would go home to break the news to his mother and father.

The following day was a Saturday, so he could get back to SE1 easily. Mrs Roberts, who had been warned of his coming in advance, greeted him with information about the food he was to eat. His father was in, and Toby suggested that they should have a drink. He had something to tell them.

'You're getting married,' Mrs Roberts said at once. 'Who to?'

'You might guess. But it's to Ann Thorold. I wonder how she's going to change a lovely name like that to Roberts.'

He had given his mother just enough time to draw

breath. She said, 'She's years older than you. She must be thirty-five.'

Toby did not correct her. 'That doesn't matter to either of us. And she's bought you a patchwork quilt as a peace-offering.'

'Why should she do any such thing? I'm not going to stand in your way and neither is your father.'

'Not me,' his father said. 'I liked the young woman. It won't do you any harm to settle down.'

'And you must both come to the wedding, shop or no shop.'

'I suppose we'll have to come, then. I hope it's not going to be anything too posh.'

'Nothing could be posh enough for famous Mummy. But, no, it's to be at a registrar's, and only a handful of people are coming.'

'You've got me confused,' his mother said. 'I don't know what to say.'

'I don't think it's at all peculiar, Toby getting married. It's about time for that,' said Mr Roberts.

'I'll need a new dress, won't I? Maisie always used to come with me and find things.'

Toby winced, but not because the mention of Maisie had hurt him. He winced because his mother had so baldly thrust the name at him. She was becoming a different woman from the one he knew.

'You can always wear your blue dress. It's fine.'

'Wonders will never cease,' said his father. 'Your mother even thinking of a new frock. Perhaps you could go with her.'

'Perhaps I could,' Toby said, thinking that if he did so he would take Ann, too. 'Mummy, I'm hungry and we have plans to make.'

'Where are you both going to live?'

81

'In Ann's house. It's a pretty large one.'

'I don't know that I like the sound of that,' said Mrs Roberts. 'When I was a girl, a man liked to make a home for the woman he wanted to marry.'

'It's the best thing for us,' said Toby. 'There will be room for storing some of my furniture, and there's plenty of room for my pictures. We shall be like a sort of Roberts museum.'

But his announcement that he was hungry had somewhat mollified his mother, who hastened both men immediately to table.

Toby thought again how much his mother had really changed. She had lost the inverted snobbery which had contributed to her dislike of Claire, since the modest fame she had made for herself caused her to look at all people from the same level. Occasionally she would go out – as she had to Ann's party. Before, her making her house her burrow had taken on a slightly pathological aspect. She was a little more tart than she had been, though her love for Toby had not diminished. And he himself? What had the years done to him? Well, at one time he had cared to listen rather than to talk, storing and using up the information silently collected. Decisions he had preferred to leave to others. Now he had made the greatest decision of all, and was glad of it. And, encouraged by Ann, he had begun to talk more. All of this was pleasant.

'Look here,' said his father as he sat down, 'we haven't drunk to you yet, given you our congratulations. Dora, have we got anything in the house? If not, I'll go out.'

'Not while the supper's on the table, you won't. You can have some of my cooking sherry.'

It was nasty, but it had to do. 'May you both be happy,' she said. 'And you'd better bring your Ann to see me again.'

The engagement notice was in Monday's *Times*. Letters of congratulation followed on its heels, from Claire and

Alec, the Baumanns, the Llangains, Adrian, Bob and others. Adrian said nothing of his troubles in his letter, Claire sent an exuberant telegram. Ann was duly taken to Mrs Roberts, who was a little stiff and stately, but she agreed that Ann should take her to choose a wedding outfit. She was much softened by the gift of the quilt, which had been mended and cleaned, and nothing would do for her but to place it on the bed and put Blackie on top. 'I may do more patchwork pictures,' she said. Mr Roberts, shutting the shop for the occasion, was cordial, though he was sorry Ann did not smoke with him.

The news had been broken to the boys without harm done, though whereas Sam was excited Tim was fairly non-committal.

'Well, that passed off nicely enough, I think,' Ann said. 'It's a bit difficult for them to accept you as a stepfather, but that will come with time.'

'I don't feel like anyone's stepfather.'

'And nor do you look it, pet.'

The wedding was fixed for the end of January. Meanwhile, Toby had given up his flat and Ann had helped him with the move. 'I don't think I like twin beds,' he said, surveying the bedroom that was to be theirs.

'Oh, I'm a restless sleeper. I get cramps and I toss and turn.'

'I should never have believed that of you.'

'You'll find out what to believe.' But until they were married she kept to the spare room. She would not let him make love to her again; it was as though she had never done so, and was determined to remain chaste for him. Meanwhile, he longed for her.

When she and Ann returned from shopping, to find Toby waiting for them, Mrs Roberts was slightly flushed as if with excitement. 'Ann's made me buy a pink coat and dress.

I tell her I'm not sure whether it's the thing for the winter—'

'Light colours are all the rage, Mrs R., and you'll find it very warm.'

'We've left it in the shop to be shortened for me. I've got a new hat, too.'

'She hasn't yet,' said Ann, 'but there's one to be made for her, to match the coat.'

Toby was amused that she had found a name for his mother, not too bold or too sentimental. Trust Ann for that.

The only person from whom they did not hear was Percy Clover. But he wrote Toby a letter. Was that the first or second Toby had received from him?

'Dear Roberts, I saw the news of you and Ann rather late. All my congratulations. Be good to her, because she's a grand girl, Ann is. I envy you. Yours, P.C.'

And Ann received a letter from him just as short and rather cantankerous. 'Really,' she said to Toby. 'If he doesn't behave himself better than this, he shan't come to the wedding.'

'You do know he's in love with you?'

'Of course I do. He's proposed to me three times. I tolerate him for Mike's sake, as I've already told you.'

The wedding day came, with a heavy mist all over the city, and it was bitingly cold. Ann wore a white woollen dress under her fur coat, and a hat. Toby had ordered her flowers, stephanotis and yellow roses, at which she exclaimed with delight. 'These are beautiful and so bridal! They take years off me.' This irritated him slightly, though he did not say so.

All the guests had assembled when they arrived. 'Hullo, Mrs R.,' Ann said, and kissed her. Mr Roberts expected a kiss, too, and got it.

The room was bright with daffodils and mimosa, but Toby could hardly take anything in. He was too excited. The last minutes of bachelorhood seemed to rush by him, and when the registrar appeared, smiling, the whole ceremony might have taken seconds.

Congratulations, kisses. Ann was his. He did notice one strange thing, though: Colonel Clover was crying. Ann saw him, too. 'Now, now, Percy, this isn't a wake, so dry your eyes, dear.'

'Can't help it. Weddings always take me that way.'

Toby had thought the wedding might have taken his mother that way, too, then shook so ridiculous an idea off. It was all over. Now the luncheon, and then back to the house for the night. They were travelling on the following day, but first he would take her to bed again. His loins stirred. He said, 'That's all, wife.' Everyone laughed and applauded, including the lachrymose Clover.

They went out into the street. The sun had broken through the mist, and Ann said, 'Pathetic fallacy.'

'Happy the bride the sun shines on,' said Mr Roberts, unexpectedly eloquent. There was a small knot of pressmen on the pavement. 'Like to take a few pictures, sir, madam.'

Toby and Ann obligingly stepped forward, but, after one brief snapshot, realised that this was not at all the pressmen's idea.

'Now can we have Mrs Roberts senior between you two,' said one of them.

'It's not my wedding,' she said, but was somehow manœuvred into the right position. Half a dozen more photographs were taken, and then one of Mrs Roberts alone.

'That's wrapped it up,' said a cameraman. 'Good luck to you,' and the knot broke up and dispersed.

'I'm glad I had my new clothes on,' Mrs Roberts said;

and Toby added, 'You look splendid in them.'

'Yes, but I wasn't expecting to butt in,' she replied.

'All over and finished, Mrs R.,' Ann said, 'and now for lunch.'

The Baumanns took Mr and Mrs Roberts in their car, and the others took taxis to the Ritz, where Toby had ordered a small wedding lunch in advance. Lobster bisque and grouse. Champagne, of course, though none of them was really fond of it.

'Let's leave our coats, Mrs R.,' Ann said, leading the way.

Clarissa Baumann came, too. 'I've had no chance to tell you how lovely you look, Ann. And what a lovely ring!' Ann had replaced it on her left hand, having taken it off for the ceremony.

'Thank you, Clarissa. So do you.'

'Too fat.'

'You're not. A little weight suits you.'

When they had rejoined the men at the table, they exclaimed at the flowers.

'This is a floral sort of morning,' said Clover, who seemed to have recovered himself. 'And our Ann's a flower herself.'

To this gallantry she seemed unable to reply, until Mr Roberts said heartily, 'To be sure she is. I can't get used to being a father-in-law.'

'You've only had an hour or less to get used to it,' said Toby.

'Well,' his father said, looking around, 'you can't say this isn't Ritzy!'

At this mild joke Mrs Roberts frowned. She wanted no one to think she wasn't used to such places.

'All right, Dora, joke over.'

She dipped her spoon in the soup, tasted it gingerly, then

86

smiled. 'Very nice.'

When the lunch was over, and they had lingered over coffee, Toby said it was time to go. He was suddenly tired, the excitement of the day and the champagne united to weary him. Ann, he saw, looked as fresh now as she had done that morning; even her flowers did not seem to be wilted.

When they were indoors in their own home, and when the housekeeper had offered her good wishes, he took the coat from Ann's shoulders, took off her hat, and hugged her to him. 'A most beautiful wife,' he said.

'And an admirable husband.' Her kiss seemed to him cool.

'What have I done that I shouldn't?'

She stared at him in surprise. 'Why, what should you have done?'

'You're so calm. I wish I were.'

'I thought it went off splendidly. I liked the registrar; Wordsworth would have called him a "grey haired man of glee".'

'I liked him, too.'

'And poor Percy, I was sorry for Percy.'

'I wasn't. That's one hanger-on I can do without.'

'Giving orders already? You're the calm one really, did you but know it. And asserting yourself at once.'

'Oh, all right, all right,' he said, holding her closely and feeling the desire for her, 'we'll have him every day if you like. Presuming he doesn't cry.'

'That was only a romantic thing for him. He really doesn't mind if I get married or not.'

'So you say. Ann, I want to go to bed.'

'What, now?'

'Right now,' he said.

'Toby, I said you were masterful! And I'll go to bed if you

87

want it. I must prevent Mary from bringing in tea, though.'

She disengaged herself and went to the kitchen.

They lay together that afternoon with joy. Sex for Ann, as he could see, was always to be a jocund business, no seriousness obtruding. Afterwards he said, 'You are going to be a most wonderful wife.'

'And you will be satisfactory, too,' she said, smiling. 'Now what do we do?'

'I'm ready myself for a sleep.'

'It always follows with you?'

'No. But today it does. I'm overwhelmed.'

'Sleep, then, and I'll inspect the wedding presents and tell Mary not to give us too heavy a dinner.'

'I feel as though I would never be hungry again,' Toby murmured, and then fell into sleep, as he had said he would.

I I

After the honeymoon, Toby returned to his desk with the feeling that, like a pigeon, he had fluffed all his feathers up. He was still unaccustomed to his new status, for, though thirty was no remarkably young age to get married, Ann still made him seem like a boy. She was not due back at her work till the following day, and was writing thanks letters at home.

Baumann came in to ask him what Venice in February had been like. 'Very cold but bright nearly all the time. I can't get over my first sight of St Mark's. Ann and I walked our feet off.'

Llangain also looked in. 'How's Benedick the married man, what? You know, I thought it might be Claire at one time.' He heaved a sigh, which might have been of relief.

'She wouldn't have me,' said Toby. He smiled. 'I'm glad she and Alec are so happy.'

'Two boys,' Llangain said, without much expression. 'It's about time for Ivor.' (This was Hairy.) 'They're coming over soon.'

Toby said that was fine, and that he was anxious to meet his wife.

'Oh, you will,' said Llangain, and withdrew.

For the rest of the day, Toby studied documents relating to a takeover bid and dictated a few letters to an elderly secretary who had been with the bank for nearly twenty years.

He really began to feel as if the holiday was over.

Ann was not there when he got in, and he felt an altogether irrational spurt of disappointment. Mary came to speak to him. Mrs Roberts had just gone to the shops, she said. She wouldn't be late. Without asking, Mary brought him a tray of drinks. He sat there over the whisky, listening for her key in the lock. At last she came in. 'I'm so sorry! But I've just remembered that it's Claire's birthday tomorrow, and I went to Harrods to look for something pretty. I got it, too — some place-mats, and had them sent.' She kissed him in a way that might have been a pat on the head, sat down and began to take off her boots, which she never wore in the house. 'I'll join you. Were you early home today? It's only a quarter to seven now.'

'Not especially. I was in by six. You look beautiful, by the way.'

'Don't ever stop telling me that. It's a sort of magic spell to keep me unwrinkled.'

'I wish you wouldn't say that. It grates on me.'

'Toby, I don't think you're being very nice. I expect it was because I was in late.' But she did not seem ruffled. Then she said, 'Oh, this came by the afternoon post.' She took a letter from her handbag. 'Edward and Maisie want us to dinner on the twenty-fourth. Of course we'll go. They say it will be just by themselves.'

He was a little jolted by the sight of Maisie's lovely handwriting, adorned by little tendrils. He supposed that Edward no longer considered him a menace, if, indeed, he ever had. But, had Ann not been late, he would not have replied so grudgingly that of course they would go. He was turning into a demanding husband, but could not tell how long she might meet his demands. He looked at her sidelong. She was sipping her drink thoughtfully, as if not sure that it was harmless.

She understood him. 'I'm sorry. I'm sorry I wasn't in to

welcome you. That's what you want, isn't it?'

'That's what I want.'

'We shall have to see whether I can always oblige you. I'll be home by about a quarter to six tomorrow, all being well. But it may not be well. I can only see. The day after tomorrow, by the way, I'm producing Edward in a chat programme.'

'I think you might consider giving up that damned job, some time,' Toby said. 'We don't need the money.'

'You mean, I don't. You don't get any of it. Ah, sweet, don't be so glum! I'm home now and everything is cosy and quiet. I had another letter today, from Tim.'

She showed it to him. 'Dear Mummy, I hope you both had a wonderful time in Venice. When can you and Toby' (he had been taught to use Toby's Christian name) 'come and take me out? Any Saturday will do. Work goes well here, and I don't fear dreadfully for my A Levels. Then I hope I shall get to Cambridge. Much love.'

'And I don't think he need fear for his A Levels. He's a bright boy,' Toby said.

The tension between them had passed away now, but Toby felt that they would have been on the edge of quarrelling – that is, that he had. Ann never quarrelled. Mary had laid dinner for them at opposite ends of the table. 'Oh, dear,' said Ann, 'this is all very stately and remote. I'd like to sit by you and not shout over space.'

'It would be nicer when we're alone,' said Toby, and moved his place to her right hand.

'It's OK, Mary,' she said when the maid came back, 'We just like to talk without shouting.'

'Sorry, I'm sure.' Mary was slightly huffy. 'I'll remember in future.'

'Funny things one doesn't know. Do you prefer to carve, or shall I?'

'Just as you like, though I haven't had much experience.'

'Then I will.' She went to the hot plate, and inspected the crown of lamb. 'Hungry?'

'Pretty. You can give me quite a lot.'

The meal seemed to confirm them in their domesticity. The slight cloud had passed over, and Toby felt comfortable and easy with her. He told her Llangain's remark. 'Would you think he knew any Shakespeare?'

'No, I wouldn't, but perhaps that's an old tag left over from school.'

Toby said, looking forward to bedtime, 'You carve as nicely as you do everything else.'

She thanked him gravely. 'Do you feel at home?' she asked him.

'Now, yes. I shall get a pair of bedroom slippers that you can warm for me.' He thought he had never loved anybody so much as this cool, delightful woman who was now his wife. They spent the rest of the evening in talk, being too newly married to have recourse to television or games of Scrabble. There was so much they wanted to know about each other, and Toby told her more than he had done before, though by no means everything. He had his secrets, and Maisie was one of them.

'We must have the best Dora Roberts collection in London,' she said, gazing about the room. 'She must come here as soon as you can coax her, and see it.'

'You'd be better at the coaxing,' he said. 'You've done marvels already.'

And indeed she had. Mrs Roberts, a woman not too affectionate outside her own little circle, had taken to Ann and was always pleased to see her. She did not love her, as she had Maisie, nor dislike her, as she had Claire. She was simply willing to be instructed, where Ann's knowledge was wider than her own. As for her husband, he was inclined to be gallant, though always regretting that she did not smoke. Toby thought Ann had done exceptionally well. She had accepted with delight a painting as a wedding present, despite the fact that Mrs Roberts's vogue showed signs of dropping off. And when she took her shopping for clothes always insisted on a lunch in the Dress Circle bar at Harrods. It was true of Ann that she could turn almost everything into a party. Toby hoped she would be a lively party influence when they went to dinner with Edward and Maisie.

The night was frosty but fine. Maisie came herself to open the door of their apartment in Hyde Park Gate, with Edward close behind. Edward, twenty-five years her senior, but as burly, as grey, as quartz-eyed as ever.

'Dears,' said Maisie, 'it's wonderful to see you.' She kissed them both, without embarrassment. 'Come on in and have a drink. It's frightfully cold outside.'

As she led them into a large drawing-room, Toby saw that she had lost none of the girlish prettiness he had himself so much admired. Her dark gold hair, looking always damp, was in close ringlets round her neck. It was natural. He remembered her telling him once that she never went to a hairdresser except for cutting. She was wearing a black velvet skirt, a white lace blouse and an onyx brooch which Toby knew well. He saw for the first time her engagement-ring, which was an emerald, with a mount of small diamonds. 'This is a lovely room,' Ann said.

'Well, we're not quite moved in, only a fortnight. We lived in a rather poky flat before.'

'We loved your wedding present,' said Ann. 'We were terribly in need of a coffee-table.'

'I'm glad,' said Edward. 'It was the subject of much debate. What else did you get given?'

'Well, two sets of herb-shelves, which was excessive,'

Ann replied, 'a splendid Spode dinner-service from the Baumanns, a salver from Claire and Alec, and of course a painting from my mother-in-law. One of her best. Oh, and there were lots of other things. We were so lucky.'

Toby noticed that over the mantelpiece there hung the picture he had called 'Smile in a Garden.' It seemed to draw Maisie light-years away from him.

'I've got another new play coming on,' said Edward, 'and it will be my first double on Shaftesbury Avenue.'

'That's very exciting!' said Ann.

Edward pondered for a moment. 'Yes and no. It will receive a vile reception from trendy critics, and run for about six months. Can you both bear to come to it? Only not for the first night. I am poor company then.'

'But we'd be good company for you,' said Toby. 'You know that.'

'Nevertheless. You are not invited.'

'Honestly,' Maisie said, 'he's *had* first nights. Of course you could go by yourselves, but Edward and I won't be there. We'll be funking it.'

How easily she had said it, 'Edward and I,' as though she had completely identified herself with him.

He said, 'How is Amanda?' This was her mother, who had been, and still was, hostess to the arts.

'Where you'd expect her to be,' Maisie replied, 'in Marrakesh, out of the cold and the rain. You must see her when she gets back, all full of party plans. They used to include a string quartet' — Toby remembered, he had seen them — 'but I don't think she always has them now. How I long for a warm spring and summer, so she can have picnics!'

Toby remembered those picnics, bossed over by Amanda Ferrars, and with the most delectable food. It was there that he had first tasted pâté de foie gras. He remembered Claire turning up at one picnic, wearing white shirt and jodhpurs. But he turned his mind resolutely from this. 'Bless Amanda,' he said.

Edward was engrossed in talk with Ann. Toby fancied that his attitude towards her was not that to a younger woman, but to a coeval.

'Let's go in to dinner,' said Maisie, rising.

The dinner was mediocre but the wine excellent, this always being a comfort to Toby. 'And after that I'd like to see your daughter,' he said to Edward, 'even though she will be asleep. Bob's daughter – you remember Bob Cuthbertson?' he said to Maisie, who had been present at Bob's wedding, 'doesn't seem to be put to bed till about seven thirty. But Bob's a good father.'

'Bob's a great man, I hear, these days,' Edward said. 'FRS, which means they'll soon find him a chair. I met him in Piccadilly the other day, and he had more horror stories to tell about that ex-wife of his.'

'Do you know what happened when Bob told the police?'

'Yes. They were pretty desultory and seemed to think that anyway it was not Bob's affair. They interviewed Adrian, and he told them about the letters – not the flick-knife, which he thinks was just a piece of melodrama – and then they told him to tear them up. And so we go on.'

'I like Adrian,' Maisie said. 'He doesn't deserve to be persecuted. Have you ever met him?' she asked Ann. 'He's a kind of male beauty. To give him such looks was hardly kind, as they only make trouble for him. He's not in the least vain, and it maddens him when parish wives try to get too intimate.'

'I suggest that he wears a yashmak,' said Ann.

When they rose from the table, Toby observed that Maisie was not so narrow-waisted as before, and no longer looked as though you could snap her in two. But her air of filigree frailness was undiminished. Edward followed her

95

eyerywhere with his eyes; the years had never diminished his passionate love for her.

'It's a pity', Maisie continued, still on the subject of Adrian, 'that he isn't brighter, because he would make an admirable bishop. Bishops are sometimes allowed to be handsome.'

'He got a two-two,' said Toby, 'but I agree that he's hardly bishopric material. He'll go on from parish to dim parish until his looks cease to trouble him.'

'Toby, my love,' said Ann, 'this is the first time I have ever known you to be catty. Shame on you!'

'If you knew Adrian, you'd cry less shame on me.'

'I can't wait,' she replied.

It was, in all, a pleasant evening: two pretty women and two men in love with their wives. Toby drank rather a lot and regretted it later. Edward drank moderately, and Maisie not at all. She seemed to have a fancy for tomato-juice. Ann also drank modestly.

'I'm sorry, dear,' Toby said, 'but you've got to be the driver. I can't risk it.'

'I was going to offer.'

'You must come to us again,' Maisie said, 'often. We'll have people to meet you next time.'

'But this is the nicest sort of party,' Ann said. 'We don't really want anyone but you two.'

'Nevertheless, we shall give you more people,' said Edward.

12

'Isn't Maisie sweet?' Ann said when they were home again. 'Maisie's a daisy.'

He laughed. 'And Edward is besotted. You'd never think there was all that difference between them, would you?' He was remembering, even while he laughed, that horrible evening long ago when Edward told him he was going to marry her. To drown the memory he drew a finger down Ann's spine, kissed her neck.

'I'm very tired tonight,' she said. As usual, when she said this, he felt a chill of disappointment. 'I'm going up pretty soon.'

'And nothing for Toby?'

'Don't be arch, pet; it doesn't become you.' And, indeed, she was looking rather tired as if, in some way, the tranquil evening had strained her. He felt, as he had felt before, that he was the one to kiss and she the one to hold out the cheek. He was also a little drunk and was glad that she had been the one to drive. 'A nightcap before you go,' he said.

'No, thank you, dear. You have one.'

He settled down with his nightcap and *The Times*, which he had not had time to read that day. 'You don't want all those lights on,' said Ann, switching on the reading-lamp above his chair and extinguishing all other lights. So he sat for quite a while in the comfortable half-dark of his own house and thought about his good fortune. It was a sizeable and very pretty house, furnished with care and without fuss. Ann had a great deal of taste, but it was not intrusive.

He wondered what his mother would think of it, and whether she would have an urge to redecorate it. He did not think Ann would let her. Meanwhile, the Dora Roberts pictures looked down from the wall, like updated Marie Laurencins. And she might lose her vogue as abruptly, Toby thought.

Then his mind inexplicably wandered to Amanda Ferrars's house, Haddesdon, in Suffolk, where she had held court. He wondered whether, now that he was married, she would ask him down again. She had known about himself and Maisie, and, not unnaturally, invitations had dropped off. What he missed most, he thought, with schoolboy greed, was not the string quartets, the writers, the painters, the pianist, but the superb food. It was a nuisance to have it uncomfortably out of doors, when the weather was clement; he much preferred to be indoors at a proper dining-table. Still, the pleasure was there all the same. The Haddesdon days seemed abnormally long ago. He began to feel lonely. Then unaccountably hungry. He went into the kitchen and made himself a sandwich.

He knew that Ann would be asleep when he went up, one long arm, as usual, flung out over the eiderdown as if she were hot. So he would not be lonely long. The kitchen clock seemed very loud; he looked at it. A quarter to one. He thought that he loved her more than she loved him, but not too much more. The strangeness of his situation would not leave him. Alone in the small hours, a husband, in this house that was still strange to him.

He crept up the stairs and into the bedroom. She was not asleep. She was lying on her back, her eyes wide open.

'Hullo, stranger,' she said. 'What have you been doing?'

'Making myself a cheese sandwich.'

'Pig. I slept for half an hour and then woke up. I've been trying to drop off ever since.' She added, 'If you still want me—'

'I do,' said Toby.

Delighted, he felt almost as if this was a reconciliation, though there had been no rift between them. He undressed hastily and got into bed beside her. She had left the bedside lamp on, and she glowed in the pinkish light. 'Now, you haven't too much drink taken?'

'Not to excess. I love you.'

'Bless you,' she replied, coming into his arms. When they were both satisfied, Toby fell asleep instantly. His last conscious thought was of being exceedingly happy.

The winter passed pleasantly. Percy Clover made a weekly call, and looked at Ann with longing eyes; to Toby he was an irritant, but not a serious one. They gave small dinner-parties, returning hospitality, and one night went with Maisie and Edward to see Edward's new play. It seemed to them both excellent, though at odds with the trend of the times. No news of Adrian.

They had several farinaceous meals with Mrs Roberts who, however, could not be persuaded to come to them again. Somewhat to Ann's irritation (she said so later) she had made the patchwork quilt into a cushion for Blackie, that stately animal with eyes like peeled grapes, and settled him in the kitchen. The quilt was, of course, covered with cat's hairs.

'I say, Mummy,' Toby said, 'we got that for your bed.'

'He wants a bed more. And I think it suits him.'

In March, Toby and Ann gave a small family dinner for Hairy and his wife. He was home on leave from Germany. Anneliese was German, but the least Teutonic specimen Toby could imagine. She had small, sharp features, a small chin and huge black eyes, slanting slightly upwards. Her hair was drawn tightly back into a knot, like a ballet-dancer's. Hairy, well-built and smart in his uniform, obviously doted on her. Her English was good, but slightly halting, and he would supply words when she needed them. Also at the party were Claire and Alec and the Llangains. For Moira, Toby had bought a bottle of vodka. The conversation was general. Claire talked much about her two sons and Llangain said, eagerly, but tastelessly, 'You next, Anneliese.'

'I hope to be fortunate,' she replied.

'Yes, you must give us a grandson,' said Moira fervently, downing her glass of vodka.

'You've got two already,' Claire put in, suavely. 'Don't be greedy.'

'Early days,' said Hairy, looking belligerent.

'Still, here's to good luck,' said his mother, now on her second vodka. 'You'll notice that the older we get the more we interfere. We believe that people don't notice us, like the ostrich with its head in the sand.'

'You've settled in nicely,' said Llangain to Toby. 'I like all the pictures.'

'They're mostly my mother's, of course.'

'Sometimes they're almost too familiar,' said Ann, 'and I think we could do with the challenge of a huge Titian, like the one in the Frari in Venice. But that's ungrateful.'

Toby was surprised she should have spoken like this, and attributed it to a touch of nervousness. 'Well, I can't buy you one, darling.'

'How's the work going?' Llangain asked him. 'They seem very pleased with you. How do you get on with all those takeover bids?'

Toby answered him, then turned to Anneliese. 'Will you like it when you come over to England for good?'

'I think I shall like it very well. I like England. I feel that not all people like Germany. I realise that there is much to forget.' She spoke firmly, in her soft little voice, and Hairy admired her with his eyes.

'Oh, that's all in the past,' said Moira. 'And, anyway, you weren't responsible for anything.'

'"Old, unhappy, far-off things,"' said Hairy, with his occasional lapse into literary expression. 'All over now.'

'Yes,' said Claire, 'and, Anneliese, you shouldn't have started that.'

'I am sorry,' she said. 'It is not quite knowing the language. I dare say I drop the brick.'

Alec leaned across to her. 'You shall drop as many bricks as you please. You're pretty enough.'

Anneliese bowed her head in acknowledgement.

'Ivor,' his mother said, 'you must bring her down to Glemsford again. It isn't very lavish, but it's nice enough, especially when the daffodils begin. I've become a great gardener, believe it or not.'

And so the subject raised by Anneliese was dropped. The dinner went on, Moira preferring vodka to wine. Toby felt that as a host he was doing very well, though he found the candour of Anneliese startling, and wondered that it didn't startle Hairy.

Then the telephone rang, and Toby went to answer it.

'Tim Thorold speaking. Is that you, Toby? I thought you were both coming down to take me out today. I've been waiting all the afternoon.'

'My God,' Toby said, 'we'd quite forgotten. I should have put it in my book.'

'Well, it doesn't matter now, but I thought you'd want to know.'

'Perhaps next Saturday—' Toby began.

'All right, if it's not a sweat to you. Good-bye.'

'Who was that?' Ann enquired as he returned to the table.

He told her.

'Oh, Christ,' said Ann, 'to do that to Tim! Is he furious?'

'He was quite calm about it. I told him we'd come next Saturday.'

'I wouldn't', she said, 'have had that happen for anything. Tim's my son,' she told Alec.

'We have to keep faith with them,' he answered, 'and we can't make excuses.'

Toby looked at his small-chinned, big-browed, intelligent face.

'No,' he said, 'we can't make excuses.' Since he felt rotten with guilt he had another glass of Sancerre.

'To think of him hanging about all day,' Ann muttered, and he saw that she was extremely put out and, like himself, feeling guilty.

'Well,' said Moira, 'they've got to learn to take it.' She nodded at Hairy. 'I'm sure we let you down often enough.'

'I'm sure you did,' he replied equably.

But from that moment the party never recovered verve. At half-past ten Claire and Alec left – to see that their own infants were all right, they said – and the Llangains left at eleven. 'Rotten with guilt,' said Toby after they had gone.

'Hush, pet, so am I.' She tried to smile. 'Well, if we cast a blight on Tim's day, he cast one on our evening. Let's talk of something else. Did you like Anneliese?'

'It's hard to say. She's gentle and pretty, but she nearly cast her own blight. I suspect that she's one of those appealing feminine figures with a rod of iron inside. She's not Jewish, is she?'

'Yes, but *pas pratiquante*. She and Hairy got married in church, with a triumphal arch of crossed swords. And she certainly doesn't bother with what she eats. Not having everything kosher, which is the gentile hostess's despair.'

'Do you suppose that worries the Llangains?'

'The whole marriage did, but they're putting a brave

face upon it. They don't seem especially anti-Semitic. It's the foreignness that sticks in their throats.'

But the question of Tim kept recurring.

Toby asked her whether they should not take Sam out, too, since the schools were not far apart. When she had agreed he said, 'Perhaps Tim would rather have you to himself. Certainly Sam would.' For Sam was still at the clinging age.

No, Ann said, that would not do. The boys had all too little time to get used to him. 'So I must work my passage,' Toby said, and Ann replied that in the circumstances he must. 'It won't be a hard day. There's a decent hotel near Godalming, with ping-pong and bar-billiards.'

'I'm rather a dab at bar-billiards,' Toby said. 'Perhaps they'll regard me as a hero.'

When Saturday came, it was grey, damp and blustery. 'Indoors for us,' said Ann, 'and with every conceivable excuse.'

They picked up Tim and drove to Sam's preparatory school. He was waiting for them in the rain, beneath the heavy trees that bordered the drive. 'Hungry?' Toby asked, and Sam replied that his stomach was quite empty. Tim smiled, and said, 'Fairly.'

Toby thought he was uncommonly silent that afternoon. 'But', said Ann, when the boys had gone to the lavatory to wash, 'it's perfectly normal with Tim. He likes to see what happens first, and then he talks.'

Toby beat them both at bar-billiards, and lost to Tim at ping-pong. Ann played against Sam, and let him win.

There was something all-embracing in that bare cellar room, with the wind raging outside. It was as though nothing else existed in time. But tea-time did exist, and when they went upstairs the boys made, even after a large lunch, a solid meal, Tim eating all the sandwiches, and Sam all the cakes. 'Aren't you having any, Mummy?' he said.

'Not for me. I'm going to keep my figure.'

'What about you?' The child turned to Toby.

'I've eaten enough for one day. You just go ahead and enjoy it.'

It was time to go back to school. Sam sat in front with Ann, Toby with Tim in the back. The wind dashed the rain against the windows of the car and made a roaring sound. They took Sam back first, and he clung to his mother. 'Don't go yet, Mummy,' he said. 'Supper isn't till seven.' She unclasped his hands, lifting his fingers one by one.

'Now, don't make a scene, Sam,' she said. 'We'll come again soon.'

'Just you come,' he said, and Toby flinched.

'Nonsense, we both love coming.'

He choked back tears, then got out of the car, turned his back on them and went briskly up the drive to the house.

'He gets that way sometimes,' said Tim. 'I know, because of the way he behaves at home. You mustn't pay too much attention to him,' he said politely to Toby.

When his own turn came to leave, he kissed Ann lightly on both cheeks, and shook hands with Toby. 'Thank you for taking us out,' he said. 'It was splendid.'

13

'So we have a young man in space,' said Amanda, 'and a re- markably good-looking little fellow, too.'

'Even the ranks of Tuscany . . . ,' Toby put in. He and Ann had received their first invitation to Haddesdon, but by themselves.

'You know what the ranks of Tuscany say?' asked Ann.

'No, dear. What?'

'Well, some Americans I know say it hasn't been done at all, but, if it has, not by Yuri Gagarin.'

'Idiocy,' said Amanda. 'If it has been done, why should this be the wrong young man inside the space-suit?'

'Yes,' Toby agreed, 'but our American friends just can't bear it. They wanted to be first.'

'I've seen him,' Ann said, 'when he was being driven through Kensington High Street. And he is a handsome young man, albeit small.'

'Bravo, Ann, I haven't heard the word "albeit" in years.'

'It seems to have been called for.'

Amanda was as handsome, in a gypsyish way, as ever. She still wore her hair in a great bun, now streaked with grey. Her dress was a caftan of many colours. She had great exophthalmic eyes, brown, but speckled with hazel. 'Oh, it is nice to have you two here! You must come to a biggish crush when the weather gets warmer; and Maisie and Edward must come, too.'

Ann said, 'We'd love to. We've heard all about your

crushes.'

'It's not really the right word. I seldom invite more than twenty in all. But, to return to Gagarin, what must it be like circling alone right up there? I can't think of a worse loneliness.'

Ann said, 'I expect pure excitement carries him on, don't you?'

Amanda assented. She appeared to like Ann.

'How are Edward and Maisie?' Ann asked. 'We haven't seen them for three months.'

'All right and happy, I think, but the press for his two plays disappointed Edward a lot, even though they're still running. It is unpleasant to outlive your vogue, but I wouldn't mind betting that he will strike another vogue in the distant future. He's sure to be put on in several years by the National Theatre, if it exists then. Maisie is a tower of strength to him.' Amanda finished her soufflé, reached towards a dish of sugared almonds. 'She has absolute faith in him, and that is what, in these rickety times, he wants. No space-hero could ever mean half as much to her.'

She spoke rather absently, as if Toby did not exist. Perhaps in her mind he was no more than a winding-sheet around a candle.

'Anyway,' Amanda said to him, 'how's your wonderful mother?'

He replied that she was happy and still working hard.

'I'm glad of that,' said Amanda. 'I wish I could see her again. Would she come here?'

'Well, she's so odd that I doubt it,' Ann replied for him, 'but if you'd come to see her I'm sure she'd love that.'

Amanda expressed astonishment. 'Do you mean that she'd receive me?'

Toby grinned. 'Certainly. And give you her special high tea, which I presume you don't know about.'

'I can't wait for it. Will you make approaches?'

Toby felt that all of them, Amanda and Maisie, Edward, Claire and Alec, himself and Ann, were all finding solid ground again, the ground provided by Amanda.

At tea-time Claire and Alec dropped in.

'If it isn't the old boy!' Claire exclaimed at Toby. 'And Ann. What a nice surprise!'

'Are you at Glemsford?' said Amanda.

Claire said yes, and that she had left the babies there with her mother. Toby wondered whether Moira would give them nips of vodka to keep them quiet. She and Alec declined anything to eat because they had lunched very late. 'We won't be a burden on you.' Amanda told her not to be silly.

'What have you been talking about?' Claire said comfortably. 'Gossip? Did you tell Amanda the dire tale of Adrian and Rita?'

Amanda looked intensely interested. 'But Adrian's a married man, after all our quite wrong prognostications. So what's he doing with someone called Rita?'

Toby explained that she was the ex-wife of his friend Bob Cuthbertson, and he told her the story.

'If I belonged to an earlier century,' she said, 'I'd have her whipped at the cart's tail, or wherever it was. Poor Adrian, and he's always seemed so vulnerable!'

'However, nothing more has been heard of her for months, now.'

'I haven't seen Adrian since his mother died. How is he getting along?'

Struggling against odds, Toby replied, but fortunately they were not financial ones. Ruth joined him in the visiting, and helped make up a quorum for early prayers. She didn't do the flowers, though, as there was a queue of women anxious to do that and to polish the brasswork.

Also, he had a willing young curate, though he wasn't very good.

'Poor dear,' said Amanda, 'and after that to be persecuted by a mad young woman! She is mad, I take it?'

'Nor-nor-west,' Ann replied, 'though I gather Bob says she was pretty wild when they were married.' She had not yet met Bob, who was a full professor now.

'I never thought strong melodrama was going to obtrude into our lives,' Amanda said, 'though it makes an exciting subject for conversation.'

Later, she said to Toby, 'Have you seen Maisie's daughter?' He wondered whether she said this out of a subliminal malice or whether she really wanted to restore everything to order.

He shook his head, but Ann said, 'I have. She's a beautiful child, and Edward's attitude is almost motherly.'

'Alec does put ours to bed occasionally,' said Claire, 'but sometimes says he'll enjoy them more when they're a bit older. That's an attitude I can't understand, myself, perhaps naturally. But I find them fascinating from the first moment they begin waving their hands about. They're like starfish.'

'Oh, come,' Alec said, 'I get enjoyment out of the starfish stage, too. But I like it when they begin to talk.'

Amanda said, 'Claire, you know he's an excellent father, so don't denigrate him.'

'Denigrate Alec? I'd as soon denigrate the Archbishop of Canterbury.'

'Whom I don't resemble, and you're making a silly comparison, darling.'

'A silly *analogy*,' said Amanda. To Ann, 'Did you like your boys when they were very small?'

'At all times,' said Ann, looking her straight in the face. 'They had something to contribute from the age of one day.'

Toby said, 'I like the boys very much now. Tim's just like Ann.' But his thoughts were on Maisie, ever since Amanda had mentioned her. He had made love to her in this house, and Amanda, finding out, had been outwardly liberal and inwardly condemning. In the room above this one, Maisie coming in in her nightgown to offer herself to him, thinking he was blaming her for a coldness. Then, Maisie in Paris, in the rain, enjoying herself like a child. He swept the thought of her out of his mind. It had been a stressful one.

'Toby,' Ann said, 'we'd better be going now if we don't want to drive after dark.'

He welcomed her initiative. The afternoon had become muddled in his mind, and he looked forward to being alone with her.

'Thank you so much, Mrs Ferrars,' she said. 'It's been lovely.'

'Call me Amanda. We have no surnames here.' She looked majestic, the caftan flowing out around her fine figure.

'Amanda, then,' said Ann.

'Alec and I must be going pretty soon, too,' said Claire, 'but first we'll want to talk you over. Don't you do that? Good-bye, sweeties.' She kissed Toby and Ann impartially.

When they were on their way Ann said, 'Darling, do you know you get all touchy at the name of Maisie? You're really no good at pretence.'

He was driving, and did not look at her. But at last he said, 'That was all long ago.'

'What? You and Maisie?'

'Yes,' he lied, 'but I never think about that.'

'Three of us under one roof.'

'Don't be cross. It's all such old history.'

The dusk was gathering, the delicate dusk of May.

Headlights were just necessary, and cut a sallow path through the greening mist.

'Well, I won't be cross. I can take anything about you.'

'Is it opening-time? If so, I think it would be nice to stop off at a pub on our way.'

'As you like, darling.'

But her air was fresh and springlike, nothing beneath it all. As it happened, they stopped at the very pub where, many years ago, Edward had spoken to him so gravely about Maisie. They had half a pint of bitter apiece, and played shove ha'penny. The smell of apples, smoke and beer was pleasant and comforting. Yet who needs comfort? Toby thought. I don't.

They arrived home a little after ten. When they were in the house, the drawing-room lamps lit, Ann said, 'Well, well, well. To think it of you. Give me a kiss.'

He gave her many. He was still too much in love with her to restrain himself. 'But I am not going to bed with you to-night,' she said, 'because I really am genuinely tired, not as I was the other night. Sleep well.'

And Toby knew what she meant. Nevertheless, he knew, or thought he knew, what had upset her. It was not the idea of Maisie; it was because he himself had only just admitted to his affair. If she loved me, he thought, she'd let all that go by. But her pride is hurt, and that is the only way one can hurt Ann. 'Pet,' he said, 'you know I love you.'

'I don't doubt it for a moment. Why shouldn't you?' and she smiled.

May passed with an invitation to a picnic, which Dora Roberts declined to accept, and Toby accepted rather doubtfully. As it happened, the day was one of dousing rain and the meal was held indoors. Much nicer, he thought.

The New Year's Honours List held a CBE for Edward.

'I'm so pleased,' Maisie said to Toby over the telephone.

'He was getting rather glum about himself. Now he will have a pretty ribbon and a medal, blue and pink, to wear whenever the occasion occurs. He says it won't ever occur. Is Ann there? I wanted her advice.'

'She's not home yet. Can I help?'

'I'm afraid you can't. This is a domestic matter. Shall I ring later?'

'Or she can ring you. I'll be writing to Edward, but congratulate him from me.'

As she hung up, he contrasted this airy call with her telephone calls of long ago. He fancied she had utterly forgotten him, and hoped that she had.

I4

Toby was half-way to Victoria tube station on a fine September morning when he realised that he had left some documents behind. He knew where they would be; he had been reading them in bed the night before, which Ann had not minded as she had her period. So he turned back, and let himself into the house. The fitted carpets were soft, and she did not hear him at first, even when he came into the room.

What he saw half-amused and half-staggered him. She was sitting bolt upright at the dressing-table, her head thrown back, her mouth wide open, pretending to bite into an imaginary apple.

'Darling, what on earth are you doing?' Toby said.

She spun round. 'And what are you doing back here?'

He explained. But he asked her again what her extraordinary exercise was for.

'If you must know,' Ann said, looking, for her, very put out, 'it's a way of strengthening my neck-muscles.'

'You've adorable neck-muscles. Why should you do anything of the sort?'

'This is preventive white man's magic,' said Ann. 'I am waiting for the day on which I begin to sag. It can't be long now.'

Toby told her she was ridiculous, kissed her, and went away.

But he wondered about her all the way to the office. It was unlike her to fear ageing, or to take steps to defer it. It dawned on him that he had never seen her looking absurd before, and the thought jolted him. In his eyes she was a perfect creature, stately in an easy-going way. He knew she was not getting to Bush House till about eleven thirty, and that she had had no fear of being caught. He had caught her, and she was glad when he went away. But all day the memory of that bedroom scene stayed with him. He loved her so much. How could he calm her idiotic fears? He decided to bring her flowers, and bought her some chrysanthemums, enormous-headed and golden, at Victoria Station.

When he got in, she had not returned. He asked Mary to put the flowers in a vase.

'I'm not much good at arranging them,' Mary said.

'They won't need arranging. Just stick them in a tall vase and they'll be fine.'

'I'll see what I can do.' Her performance with the flowers was adequate, and Toby put the vase where it would immediately catch Ann's eye.

When she arrived she exclaimed, 'They're beautiful! Who sent them?'

'I bought them,' Toby said.

She hugged him briefly. 'Bless you, how thoughtful.'

'I'm glad you like them.'

'Are they, conceivably, an apology for having broken in on my morning routine?'

'No,' Toby said, 'just love.'

'I must train you to knock at the bedroom door. I've trained Mary to do just that, and to knock nowhere else.'

'I could emulate Mary, but I'm not going to.'

'In that case, I must be dead certain that you won't appear when I'm doing my de-sagging exercises.'

'Don't say that,' he said. 'They're unnecessary and you're lovely. Any news?'

'Percy came round about six, according to Mary, but, as you know, I wasn't in.'

'Excellent. You ought never to be in to that ridiculous man.'

'I don't spy jealousy, do I? I should be so proud if I did.'

'I'm capable of jealousy but not over Percy Clover. Do you know, I believe he wrote me an anonymous letter before we were married?' Then he wished he hadn't said it. How was he going to explain to her? It had been said in a moment of absurd vengefulness.

'Percy? Nonsense. What did it say?'

'I can't remember now.'

'You can remember if you try.'

'It was some rigmarole about you having scads of lovers.'

'Oh, is that all?' she said. 'But I told you I'd had a few. Poor Percy, to accuse him of such wickedness!'

Yet nevertheless she did accuse him, when he paid them a visit again and, since it was a Saturday, found both of them in. She sat him down, poured him a stiff drink, then said, 'Percy, you sent Toby an anonymous letter. Why did you do that?'

He turned a dull, purplish red. 'I did no such thing. I wouldn't think of it.'

'Yet, nevertheless, you did think. Come on, dear, don't stall. You accused me of having scads – Toby's revolting word, not mine – of lovers. What were you expecting him to do?'

He was silent. Ann continued, 'Go on Percy, be a dear and confess. Neither of us will be down on you.'

There was no change in the Colonel, except that his flush had sunk from his forehead to his cheek-bones.

Then he said, 'What is this, a court martial?'

Toby said nothing throughout this exchange.

'So silly, Percy dear, so asinine,' Ann pursued him.

'Now, speak up. We can't have any dark secrets coming between us.'

Toby was pitying. He did not want the Colonel harried any more. 'Let it go, Ann.'

She said nothing, just waited.

Clover finished his drink and got up. From the mantelpiece he took a china figurine and played with it.

'And don't smash that,' Ann said.

He said at last, speaking out of a gasp. 'Never did anything like that before in my life. Don't know what got into me. I'm sorry.'

'Yes, but why did you do it? Toby's never harmed you.'

The Colonel replaced his toy. When he spoke again he seemed on the verge of tears, but his voice was steady. 'I didn't want him to marry you.'

'But I wanted to marry him. Weren't you being a bit inconsiderate?'

'Didn't want anyone to marry you.'

Toby said, 'That's quite enough. We're going to forget about the whole thing.' He refilled Clover's glass. 'Now sit down again, and I'll keep Ann at bay.' Toby had, indeed, been alarmed at her insistence. He had never believed her as formidable as this.

'Never mind, Percy,' she said, '*silence à la mort*.'

It was hard to get the talk going again. Toby asked a trivial question, to which Clover replied mechanically. Ann began to talk about a play they had recently seen, but after a short while Clover took his leave. He did not kiss Ann, as was usual with him, but instead she kissed his cheek. 'Silly old man,' she said, 'come again soon.'

When he had gone she said to Toby, 'Quite a scene.'

'Yes, and a bit cruel. You shouldn't have chased the old boy like that.'

'Were you cross with me? But I wasn't hard on him in the

light of what he had done. Men have been cashiered for less. He won't do it again.'

Toby said he doubted whether anonymous-letter writers in the Army would have been cashiered — simply dismissed the service.

'Anyway, you were annoyed with me.'

'Not that, darling, but because Percy was forced to fight so much below your weight.'

'I promise that you shall never see me fighting above yours.'

Toby said that the one good thing about it all was that they would never see Clover again.

Ann laughed. 'You don't understand poor Percy in the least. He would rather have a scene with me than nothing at all. He is the most faithful swain I have ever had. Besides, Mike, for some incomprehensible reason, was devoted to him.'

'Did he pursue you when Mike was alive?' The moment he had asked the question, Toby was sorry. Indeed, he did not often like to ask questions, but to let information come his way in its own sweet time.

She said, her tone faintly irritable, 'I told you you didn't understand Percy. He was too much of a gentleman to pursue me in Mike's day. It was only when I became a widow that he let himself go.'

'If he was a gentleman for Mike's sake, I don't see why he shouldn't be for mine.'

'Because he is older and no wiser. Not nearly so wise as he was, in fact. Now let's forget all about him and have dinner.'

Toby did his best to forget, but not with conspicuous success. To be jealous of Clover would have been absurd, but he was touchy about anyone in Ann's past.

'I might as well be jealous of Claire,' she said, having

followed his thoughts, 'and have more reason. But I'm not.'

'I thought we were going to forget Percy.'

'So we are! And so we shall.'

She told him, rather in the way of a mother placating a child, that he was having whitebait that night. She couldn't cook them herself, but Mary had taken on the task. 'All for my infant husband.'

'Don't,' he said. 'You know I hate it.'

'You mustn't be squeamish. I shall make jokes about you just as I please. And it's good for me to remember my mature years now and then.'

He was mollified, and the evening passed peaceably, with no more strain. They listened to a concert on the radio and Ann was absorbed, but Toby never could listen to music without reading. 'Philistine,' she gibed when it was over.

'I agree.'

As Christmas approached, a season Toby cordially disliked, and the boys were due home, Ann threw herself into seasonable things. She decorated the house with holly and mistletoe, bought presents and wrapped them elaborately. 'I've bought Tim a sweater from us, and Sam a train set. That means we shall have obstruction all over the drawing-room floor.'

'If you don't mind, I'd rather give the boys something by myself. Otherwise they'll think of me as a mere cipher.'

'Suit yourself,' she replied. 'But I think you'd better pay half of the train set. It was pricey. What are you going to give me, by the way?'

'You must wait till you find out,' said Toby, having not the slightest idea of what he was to buy her. He thought that one of the things he might give her was the large silver and green turquoise ring he had bought for Claire, and put back in his pocket when she rejected him. And

117

then, perhaps, expensive scent in an atomiser. He would have to see.

The boys returned in high spirits. Even Tim, who was far quieter and more adult than Sam, seemed pleased and happy. Toby hoped he would like his gift, the reproduction of a Book of Hours, and whether Sam would enjoy a gigantic jigsaw puzzle. If he doesn't, I will, he thought.

Tim was getting taller and more handsome. He had a long neck, like Ann's, and dark curling hair. Sam was nothing like his mother to look at but was, as Toby could see from Mike's photograph, very like his father.

Toby and Ann gave a party on Christmas Eve, at which the boys were allowed to serve kickshaws. As Ann had predicted, Clover was there, moister of eye and a little stouter. Facetiously, he drew Ann under the mistletoe and kissed her. Toby guessed that he would feel that kiss on his lips for years to come. He didn't, however, resent it as he had imagined, but was a little proud that someone who was his could inspire such devotion.

'What are you drinking, Tim?' he said.

'Only sherry. Sam's drinking coke.'

'Harmless enough,' said Toby.

'My mother would have something to say if it wasn't. She's terrified of the demon drink, though I notice she doesn't go short herself.' Toby thought he was growing up. He had not failed to notice the 'my mother', instead of 'Mother', which seemed to force a space between Ann and himself. Sam came up with a plate of cheese éclairs. 'These are wizard,' he said. 'You must try them.'

The visitors came and went. Claire came without Alec and stayed to the end. So did the Baumanns. Sam grew more and more sleepy, but shook his head at any intimation that he should go to bed. The ashtrays were filled with stubs, some of the holly berries shrivelled in the heat. Moira

Llangain was there alone. 'When I get up to go,' she whispered to Toby, 'just help me to get out of my chair. I shall need a strong arm to the car.'

'You're surely not driving?' said Toby, appalled. He had watched the contents of the vodka-bottle going down and down.

'Certainly I'm driving,' she said, in a voice of queenly reproach, 'and, if you mean I've had too much to drink, that's when I drive really well.' She tried to get up, fell backwards and was hoisted from her chair by Toby and Tim. 'Thank you both very mush,' she said, blurring a single word. She went round the room very straight and very careful, making her good-byes.

'Look, I'll drive you home,' said Toby at the door. 'I never drink much at my own parties.'

'You will not drive me home,' said Moira, stately. 'I am perfectly all right.'

He helped her into the car and watched her go with misgivings, but saw that she was genuinely one of those who drove better when she had been drinking. The car negotiated a cunning U-turn and went on its way. 'Happy Christmas to all!' she cried, leaning out of the window.

When all the guests were gone, Ann said joyously, 'Now let's sit down and talk everyone over. Boys, you go to bed.'

'Not me,' said Tim. 'I'm a big boy now. I want to talk them over, too.'

'That's as maybe,' she said sternly, 'but Sam goes up right now, or Father Christmas won't visit him in the morning. Now, Sam, do as I say and I'll come up to tuck you in.'

Sam obeyed with feigned reluctance; he could hardly keep his eyes open.

'And now', said Ann when he had gone, 'to clear up the mess. Mary won't be there in the morning.'

Mary was on leave Christmas Day and Boxing Day, and it was Christmas Day already.

'You can help me a lot, Tim,' Ann said.

'What shall I do?'

'Take up all the used glasses for a start and put them in the kitchen. I'll wash them later.'

She herself went collecting up the piled ashtrays. 'And a wash for these, too. Also, a brief run of the Hoover over the carpet.'

'When do you talk about the guests?' asked Tim.

'When your stepfather and I—' He frowned. 'Have got the clearance under way.' For fifteen minutes she was very active between drawing-room and kitchen. 'Does anybody want the last catered-for scraps?'

'I'll have some,' Tim said. 'I thought dinner tonight was rather scrappy. Are there any sausages left?'

When at last Ann settled down, Tim said, 'Now we do the talking. Lady Llangain was half-seas over, wasn't she?'

'Yes,' said Toby, 'but I tried to drive her home. In the event she went off by herself with great *éclat*.'

'And Mr Baumann drank quite a lot.'

'That would not discompose him, dear. Nothing does.'

'Why weren't the Cranes here?'

'They'd another engagement.'

'Everything ought to be made way for but ours.' Tim was lordly, and had drunk a good deal of sherry – a dreadful drink, Toby thought, for anyone making an evening on it.

Tim said, 'I admit I'm tired. I'll go up now. Shall I look in on Sam?'

'Do, darling; and, if he's still awake, call me. I'll be coming up myself soon.'

'He won't be asleep.'

But he was. She was able to hang up his stocking at the

foot of the bed without awakening him. It was a stocking designed to appeal as much to Tim as to Sam. When she went to join Toby in the bedroom, she was very tired.

'But a nice party anyway,' she said.

15

In February, Edward Crane died in the foyer of the Haymarket Theatre where he and Maisie had been watching the dress rehearsal of his new play. As Toby learned later from Ann, he had suddenly whispered to Maisie that he felt hot and must get some air. So they went out together, and he sat down on a bench with his eyes closed. Then he leaned right forward and toppled to the floor. Maisie, distraught, tried to turn him over, but he was too heavy. She ran back to the rehearsal to look for help and, when she returned with the director, asked him to send for a doctor and an ambulance. Edward must have heard these exchanges, because he said to her with difficulty, 'Too late, my love, and too old.' The director, himself a large man, attempted to get him back on the bench, but Edward died in his arms.

'Maisie said he seemed to have no pain. Thank God for that, anyway.'

'I can't thank God for anything. Edward was such a good chap.' And Toby meant it.

'She's bearing up wonderfully, but she seems to need people all the time. Amanda's with her, of course. And Claire came in when I was there. I think Maisie would like it if you went.'

It was with mixed feelings that Toby did as she suggested. Edward, of whom he had been jealous, was dead, Maisie alone again.

Maisie herself opened the door to him. She was all in black. He kissed her and she wept. 'Sorry, Toby. Come along in.'

Amanda greeted him, Amanda who knew all of their past. 'Poor girl,' she said, 'poor Edward. The world won't be the same place without him.'

Toby was jolted into remembering the old sick joke: 'That's all very well, Mrs Lincoln, but how did you like the play?'

He asked about it, not knowing what else to say.

'It's a success,' Maisie said. 'He would have been so happy. It's queer,' she added, 'but I used once to be so jealous of his actresses, though he never gave a look to any one of them.'

'All his looks were for you,' Toby said. 'Why shouldn't they have been?'

'I know, but it was different at first. I couldn't bear going behind to meet them.'

'When is it going to be?' Toby asked Amanda when Maisie left them for a minute.

'Friday, at Golders Green. Funeral private. There may be a memorial service later.'

Maisie returned. She had been powdering her face. 'Does it hurt you to talk about him?' Toby asked.

'It hurts me not to. It makes me feel that he's still somewhere around. Only I cry when I see Clemency. She's just old enough to ask after him.'

'May I go and see her?' Toby asked. She nodded towards an inner door. 'She's in there with Nanny.'

Toby went into a room where a pretty little girl sat threading bright-coloured beads. The nurse was helping her. 'I'm Toby,' he said.

'Where's Daddy?' she asked. She had her mother's curling hair, golden, damp-looking.

'He's away for a while,' Toby said, wondering what she was being told.

'A long time?'

'Rather a long time.'

'I don't want him to go away.'

'No, of course you don't. Those are pretty beads.'

She held up a string triumphantly. 'Clemency did it.'

'Clemency was very clever.'

'Would you like it?'

'Well, I've nowhere to wear it, have I? Why don't you give it to Nanny?'

'Because it's special. I'll give it to Granny, then.'

'That's a sound idea.'

'You ask Granny to come, then.'

He promised he would, and escaped. He told Maisie how pretty the child was, and she nodded almost indifferently. Ann had said she was bearing up well, and so she was; but the tears still flowed very easily. 'Come and see me again,' she said as he rose to go, 'and bring Ann. I hate being alone.'

He said he would. He did not kiss her again, but held her hand for a minute. 'We're all for you,' he said, 'all your friends are.'

As he walked away down the street, he thought that he was still moved by her, but suppressed the thought out of loyalty to Ann. He could remember Maisie on the lawns at Haddesdon, her skirt spread over the grass, her face peaceable as though she, too, were stringing beads. Amanda's poet, her painter, her string quartet. And Edward, sitting up, his eyes upon Maisie. In those days Toby had had no idea that Edward was in love with her. He had even wondered whether he came to see Amanda. Mrs Roberts's picture, portrait of a smile in a meadow. It now hung over a console table in Maisie's drawing-room.

The whole thing seemed to him in retrospect something like the Forest of Arden. And, indeed, there had been one great tree which gave a lavish shade. They had sat beneath it, at one of Amanda's lavish picnics, each one of them her own choice. He thought there would be no more Amandas in this world for a long time, if ever.

Ann wanted to know how his visit had gone, but he answered briefly. He told her how Maisie had been hard put to it not to cry and, indeed, had not wholly succeeded.

'She must have loved him very much in a filial way,' said Ann.

'I hope you don't love me in a too motherly way,' said Toby, his spirits rising, 'because I should never stand for that.'

'No,' said Ann, 'except with the boys, and often not with them; I haven't the motherly gift. I like you as you are.'

'Only like?'

'Some days I love you and other days I like you. So you see, you perform on two levels. It is very nice.'

And with this kind of thing he had to put up, that evening. Her cool and refreshing presence generally pleased him, but there were many times when he wanted more than this. There were even times when he wished her, in some respect, to be helpless.

Claire telephoned and asked to speak to Toby. 'I gather you saw Maisie today. How was she?'

'Brave, but lachrymose.'

'Don't be beastly!'

'I didn't intend to be. She likes visitors, by the way; she implies that they stop her thinking.'

'My poor little Maisie!' said Claire, referring not to her age, but to her height. Claire was a strapping girl. 'Now may I talk to Ann? She may be more vocal than you are.'

The women talked for a long time. Toby did not even listen to Ann's answers. He was rereading Chesterton's Father Brown stories, and believed he was absorbed in them. No thoughts of Maisie, no thoughts of Claire, seemed to be intruding.

The memorial service, in March, was excellently attended. Actors and actresses were there, directors, lessees of theatres. A man Toby did not know gave the address. The music was well chosen, – he suspected by Amanda who, in a great black hat, looked the perfect *salonnière*. Maisie was out of mourning but wore a black coat over a white wool dress. (Toby always noticed such things.) He guessed she did not enjoy all the hand-shaking afterwards.

That same day he had received a letter from Bob, at whose shotgun wedding Maisie had been present. Lunch at the Dorothy Café, drinks in a pub afterwards. Only Maisie seeming secure and unembarrassed.

Bob wrote: 'Dear Tobe, I was upset to hear of Crane's death. Give all my love to Maisie. I am writing to her, but I am no hand at this kind of thing. How are you? Is Adrian putting up with anything from Rita? Really, I think she is dotty. Come and see me soon, and bring your wife.'

Adrian, however, wrote in a different vein. 'Do tell Maisie how deeply sorry I am – or, rather, amplify it – because I am not much good at writing letters of condolence, which I suppose ought to be my *métier*. Ruth and I are both well, but the letters have begun again. I am not burning them this time but am treating them as evidence if I should ever need it. Ruth and I both feel as if she were a ghost who haunts us. Are you ever coming down to Lincolnshire with Ann? We can make you quite comfortable for a week-end.'

'Do let's go,' said Ann. 'I long to meet the *dramatis personae* of the Rita story.'

'Not till it gets quite a bit warmer. Adrian may think his rectory is cosy, but I very much doubt it.'

When they went to bed that night, Toby traced her bones from her spine to her neck and said, 'You beautiful white bitch.'

She reacted as she always did to an occasional coarseness. 'Watch your tongue, or I shall think the cat ought to have it.' But she softened in his arms. 'Randy,' she said.

'Yes, I am. What about you?'

'Not especially, but enough. Come along, then.'

He enjoyed her delightedly, feeling that he was compensating for the strains of the day. She responded more energetically than usual, crossing her ankles behind his back and staring at him with eyes wide. Maisie and other things drifted away. He was with Ann, miraculously his wife. When it was over she laid her head on his breast. Toby turned out the light.

'Do you know what I thought?' she said.

He replied no.

'That you weren't thinking about me until tonight.'

'I'm always thinking of you, unless I have one of Clive's beastly takeover bids. I can't do more.'

'Cold man,' she murmured, and almost at once went to sleep, which meant that he must gently lever her off him if he were to get any sleep himself.

They went to stay with Adrian in April. He lived in a small village with scrubby country all about, but the rectory was sizeable.

He came out to greet them. 'God, he's all you said,' Ann murmured as he led them in to a dark hall smelling of floor polish.

Ruth came out to them. She was small, rosy, brown-skinned and with modest bustline, just as Toby imagined Ruth Pinch must have been. But her eyes were very sharp and bright. 'Hullo, Toby and Ann,' she said, 'you're not strangers, because I've heard all about you.' He reminded her that they had met for a few minutes some time ago. 'Shall I show you your room? It's nice and warm up there.

We've got convector heaters all over the place, but even they didn't help much in January and February.'

'It was the coldest since 1740,' said Adrian, with an air of solemn knowledge.

'Was it forty or fifty?' Ruth enquired.

'Forty.' He was looking as owl-like as it was possible for so handsome a man to look.

'Give me your bags,' Ruth said, but Toby would not let her take them.

She told them they were on the first floor, and led them up some wide stairs and along a brown-painted passage, where a bunch of honesty in a brown vase rattled in the draught from a window. 'I should have had that done, but I forgot. The window's stuck.'

Toby put down the bags and wrenched at it. It shut. 'You are strong!' Ruth cried, in admiration of this feat. She led them into a big room on the right. There was a large double bed and a washbasin. 'Your bathroom's right opposite. It's all yours. Ours is farther back.'

She told them to make themselves comfortable then come down for some sherry. She said to Ann, openly, 'Aren't you pretty?'

Ann was taken aback by this directness but she looked pleased. 'Thank you very much, but I don't deserve it. This is a very nice room!'

When Ruth had left them, she came to Toby and kissed him. 'You didn't exaggerate. He takes one's breath away. I can't wait to hear him preach a sermon.'

'So you shall, tomorrow. We'll have to go to church.'

They went down into the sitting-room, which was big and ugly, but comfortable. 'What it wants is a coat of paint,' said Adrian, 'but we can't afford it at present. Besides, it would startle the parish if we suddenly became smart.'

Toby thought it would be a long while before the rectory could be described as such, no matter how many coats of paint it had. The very young curate came in and was introduced as Billy Stevens. He was rather fat.

After lunch, which Ruth had cooked well, the curate went off on parish business, leaving the four of them to talk.

'I've told Toby all about Rita, of course,' he said. 'It still goes on.'

Ann exclaimed. 'Can't anything be done?'

'I did write to her once telling her to leave me alone, but it didn't stop her.' He got up and went to a roll-topped desk. 'Here,' he said, flushing, 'you'd better look at some of them. They're the most ghastly trash.'

He handed over a stack of letters, twenty or thirty of them. 'I burned all the earlier ones. I'm just keeping these so I shall have something to show anytime I want it.'

Toby took up one of them and read it. He didn't wonder that Adrian had blushed. This one began, 'You beautiful man, why are you so cruel? If you knew how I feel inside me you'd write. Tell that silly little wife of yours that she can't have you all to herself. I want you and I'm going to get you.' Ann looked over his shoulder.

'It's *Peg's Paper* sort of stuff, isn't it?' she said to Adrian. 'You must get angry.' Ruth was out of the room clearing the dishes. 'Angry because of Ruth, I mean, too.'

'I always show them to her. To hide them would be like a sort of complicity with Rita. Oddly enough, she takes them very lightly. It makes me sickeningly embarrassed even to show her.'

'If I were you,' said Ann, 'I shouldn't open them. I expect they're all the same. I agree that you should keep them, but don't see why you want to torment yourself by reading the rubbish.'

'I know you're right,' Adrian said, 'but they have a grisly fascination. All the same, I won't open the next one.' He paused. Then he said, 'Do you know what terrifies me? The thought that she'd write on postcards, for the postmistress to read and put the whole rotten affair all over the village.'

'Adrian,' said Ann firmly, as though she had known him for years, 'you must have had some of this before. Quite a bit of it. But there is no reason why you should endure it if it comes to postcards. You'll have to make the police take you seriously.'

'If I took Rita to court, think what the headlines would be. "Parish priest sues woman for writing letters." I should look so wet I'd never hold up my head again. There would be pictures, too.'

'We'll consider that,' she replied, 'if you actually get a postcard. Let us know at once.'

'But I don't actually know what you could both do.'

'I know,' said Toby. 'I should go to see Rita. Give me her address, will you?'

Adrian produced it and he wrote it down. Then the letters were restored to the desk just as Ruth came in. 'This is lovely,' she said, holding out her hands to the small log-fire which augmented the convector heating. It was a cold spring. 'We don't often have guests. It's rather a way to come.'

Toby thought again of Ruth Pinch. He could almost hear the fountains of the Temple Gardens playing. She was one of those essentially comfortable women who manage to make comfort all round them. 'Yes, but not impossible. When you can both come up to London you must stay with us.'

'*When* we do,' said Adrian. 'We can't really both get away together. There's Billy to look after; he can't do a thing for himself.'

'Still, it's very kind of you to ask us,' said Ruth. 'I haven't been in London for years. I should hardly know myself.'

After a while Toby grew drowsy. It had indeed been a very long drive. 'Do you mind if I have a nap?' he asked Ruth.

'Not a bit of it. Perhaps Ann would like one, too.'

'I'm not tired. You go on up, Toby.'

'There are nearly two hours till tea-time,' Ruth said, 'and I hope you like crumpets.'

'I'll go up with you,' said Adrian. 'I must work on some notes for my sermon.' He took Toby up to a small study. On the bookshelf was very little but a *Crockford's*, a medical dictionary and a dozen battered Penguins. 'It's quieter for me upstairs,' he said. 'I get interrupted by callers if I stay below. Ruth and I love crime stories,' he added, 'and I've got all the Penguins of Famous Trials.'

Next morning they all went to church. Ann had been right about Adrian's appearance in the pulpit. The church was fairly full, mainly with women. He preached a brief, dull sermon, not exceeding fifteen minutes. He had no gifts as a preacher, but the women did not seem to care. They sang the hymns ardently, led by one strident soprano voice that came from a back pew. 'Mrs Hart,' Ruth whispered. 'She has to be asked to sing at parish concerts.'

She told them that there would be cold roast beef and jacket potatoes for lunch. 'I hope that will be all right for you. I'm not one of those clever people who dare leave the oven all by itself.'

They were now in the porch, waiting while Adrian shook hands. Lovely sermon, Father. Cold day, isn't it? Are you preaching tonight, Father?

The church was right in the centre of the village, so they had only a short way to walk back. They came to what

131

seemed to Toby a rather sumptuous pub, and he asked Adrian if he ever went there.

'Now and then, to have half a pint with the men. Not on Sundays, though. It would seem to them all very improper just after a sermon. And it would be improper if Ruth went there at any time. Would you and Ann like to look in while Ruth's getting the dinner on?'

Toby looked at Ann, who said, 'Yes, if you don't mind. It would be nice.'

They went into the warmth and the glow. 'Only beer would be appropriate here,' he said to Ann. 'Half-pint?'

They found seats in an ingle-nook. Horse-brasses were bright on the walls, and hunting-pictures also. 'Love you,' he said, drawing on his beer. She smiled. 'Good,' she said.

'Not reciprocated?'

'Oh, reciprocated. Aren't you rather enjoying yourself? I am. Even in April there's a Christmasy flavour, here and in the rectory. Ruth's a proper homemaker, not like me.'

'You're good enough.'

'With Mary to back me up. When she has her holidays you will suffer the full rigours of my cooking.'

Toby had a most peculiar feeling that someone was staring at him. He felt it across his shoulder-blades.

He turned round. There was a young woman in a dark corner directing her gaze upon himself. At once she got up and came forward. It was Rita.

16

Toby stood up, not out of courtesy but out of a reflex action. He said to her, 'What are you doing here?'

'Free country, isn't it? One can spend a week-end where one likes. Who's that?' She pointed to Ann.

'My wife.'

'Pleased to meet you,' Rita said mechanically. She pulled up a chair to be near them. She was wearing a fake fur coat over a very short red dress, and dingy white boots. 'I was in church this morning. You didn't see me. I was sitting right at the back with a fat woman with a voice like a train-whistle, and I slipped out before the end. But I saw *him*, and he was marvellous. You going to buy me a drink?'

'No,' said Ann, 'we're not.'

'Someone's been shooting off their mouth, isn't that it?'

'Look here,' said Toby, 'we know all about your antics with Adrian, and you've got to stop it. This is monomania.'

'Oh, don't you use long words! I don't know what the hell you're talking about. I only write letters. That's not criminal, is it?'

'I want to say something,' Ann put in.

'More meddling?'

'You may call it that. But Adrian has an idea that you might start writing him postcards, in which case the business would be all over the parish. And in which case he would go to the police.'

Toby shot her a startled glance.

'You're putting ideas into my head,' said Rita with a

guffaw, but her eyes were wary.

'And that *would* be an offence,' said Ann.

'I know all about offences. My dad was a policeman. He's dead now, and so's my mum. Now all I've got is *him*.'

'But where do you think you're going to get?' Ann went on. She was pretty sure that Rita would write no postcards. 'You only make him angry.'

'Soppy old Adrian getting angry? Don't make me laugh. And as for what I'm going to get for it, he'll answer me one of these days. As for that tatty wife of his, I'd throw acid at her if it could make her any uglier than she is.'

Toby knew she could be dangerous.

'Then it would be a good long jail-sentence, wouldn't it?' said Ann.

'Oh, don't talk balls. I can look after myself all right. I'm in love with him, do you see it? I have been for years. I think of him day and night.'

'And he probably thinks of you,' said Toby, 'but not in a way you'd like. Now you get out of here.'

'I'm staying here, so I shan't.'

'Then we will get out of here,' said Ann, 'and give good warning to the Stedmans. Come on, Toby.'

Without glancing at Rita again, Ann made for the door and he followed. Neither of them spoke for a few minutes. Then Ann said, 'She chills my spine. And to think of it – all this for a silly, hopeless love. Sometimes I hate love.'

'Don't say that.'

'When I think of all the earthquakes it can cause.'

'Ann,' he said, pausing outside the vicarage, where some crocuses bloomed randomly. 'Do you think it was wise, about the postcards?'

'I took a risk. But I'm sure she had that in mind, and I'm equally sure she won't act on it. Any more than she's going to throw vitriol at Ruth. She isn't afraid of hell, but she is of

134

jail. Now, alas, we'll have to go inside and tell them all about it.' They went in.

Toby said, 'I'm sorry we're a bit late, but we ran into an old nuisance of yours. Rita's in the village, staying at the Bull. We've been talking to her. And I'll tell you what was said.'

'She was in church this morning,' Ann put in.

'Oh, God,' said Adrian, pausing in the carving of the meat.

'Now, listen,' said Ann. She waited till they were all seated. Fortunately the curate was absent in an outlying part of the parish.

She left them aghast. Adrian said, 'It makes me look such a fool.'

'That's the least of it. But I think you won't get post-cards.'

'Was she serious', said Ruth, 'about the acid?'

'I don't think so for a moment,' said Toby, 'and neither does Ann. She'd be too scared. But even to talk about it shows how disturbed she is. She's got no one to go to. Both her parents are dead.'

'Now, it's better not to get sentimental about her "we're all guilty" nonsense,' said Ann.

'I feel guilty,' Adrian said, 'and I don't know why I should.'

'You feel guilty', said Ruth unexpectedly, 'because she only wants one thing in the world and you won't give it her.'

Toby expostulated.

'Well, it's true. But I could see Adrian was thinking about her orphaned state and wondering what he could do to help her.'

'Perhaps I ought to see her if she comes here,' said Adrian. 'That is, with you all here it wouldn't be so bad.'

135

'She'll ask for the seal of the confessional,' Toby said, 'and then she'll get you alone in your study upstairs.'

'No,' Adrian said, 'you may think I'm a feeble type but I'm not as feeble as all that. Will she come up here, do you suppose?'

'With Toby and me here, I doubt it. But one must plan for contingencies.'

'Let's all cross our fingers and pray that she won't,' said Ruth calmly. 'Ann, another slice of pudding? No?'

'Let's have a plan of campaign,' said Adrian. 'I do feel I have a pastoral duty towards her—'

'Rubbish,' Ruth said.

'And I'm going to do what I can. I shall want only Toby to stand by. You girls must go to the morning room.'

They sat after lunch looking anxiously out of the window. At three o'clock she came.

'Morning room, Ruth,' said Ann. 'Just lead the way.'

Rita rang the door-bell.

Adrian, when the coast was clear, went to open it, Toby close behind.

When she saw him her whole face seemed to blossom and to become beautiful. She said, 'At last!' and, stepping across the threshold, stood up on tiptoe and, before he could check her, kissed him on the lips.

'Now, stop that,' said Adrian.

'Why should I? We're old friends. Don't you remember coming to see me in hospital after Estella was born? You brought me white flowers.'

'Yes, I do remember, but come along in.'

In the living-room she said, nodding at Toby, 'Do we want him? I want to see you alone.'

'Toby will stay,' Adrian said. 'Now, sit down. Yes, I've known you a long time, but never closely.'

It was as though no one was in the room but herself and

Adrian. Toby might have been a mile away. 'You don't know how wonderful this is. Just to see you. How do you feel about me?'

'Annoyed, rather,' Adrian said. 'Your letters are by way of being a persecution.'

'They're love-letters, all of them. And I don't even suppose you read them. How gorgeous you look in the pulpit! And you don't realise a bit of it.'

Adrian said, 'You were uttering threats this morning, according to Toby.'

'I'm damned if I was! I only made a joke about throwing acid at Ruth.'

'Look, you're not well. Will you see a psychiatrist, if I can find one?'

'A trick cyclist? No, I will not. I'm not mad. Only just to sit here with you—' She dissolved into tears. Toby gave her a handkerchief. 'It's wonderful, wonderful.'

'I'll do everything I can to help you, but these letters must cease.'

'You've no idea how wonderful you look when you're being stern,' she sobbed, barely audible between the gasps for breath.

'Pull yourself together,' said Adrian. 'This kind of talk won't do at all.'

'Do you remember Bob? He battered me once. And now he's a professor and an FRS, whatever that may mean. He's bringing up Estella. I couldn't bear to do that.'

'Well, for the child's sake—' Adrian began ineptly.

'What do I care about the child? Or about Bob and his wretched career? All I care about is you, and just seeing you will last me for months.'

'You'd better go now,' said Toby.

'It's Mr Interference speaking. You're not the one to tell me to go.'

'I tell you to go,' said Adrian. 'And don't forget, if there is anything I can do for you—'

'There is, and you won't.' She had dried her tears and mastered them. 'So I won't ask for any help from you.'

'You can do one thing for me, if you like to,' said Adrian. 'You can stop writing me letters.'

'I can't. It's the only way I have of being a little in touch with you.'

'Then I shan't read them. Now, go away, Rita, there's a good woman. Your time's up.'

She rose, and in the mirror looked at her pony tail of hair which she had scraped into a rubber band. 'OK, then, see me to the door.'

'Toby will let you out.'

She gave Toby a look of pure hatred. 'I can see myself out.' Defrauded of a chance to kiss Adrian again, she left with scarcely a backward glance at him.

'Well,' said Toby, 'that was relatively painless.'

'You must have a funny idea of pain,' Adrian replied.

Toby was discomfited.

'I ought to have done more for her,' Adrian said.

The women came back. 'What happened?' Ruth said eagerly.

'Oh, it went off all right. I'll tell you the details later, and Tony can tell Ann on the drive back. We've only got a bit of the afternoon left, so let's enjoy it.'

Adrian, Toby felt, was coming on. Priesthood had matured him somewhat.

He and Ann replied that that would be best, and they settled down again. But the afternoon was not an easy one, and Toby was glad when they were on their way.

He said, 'Adrian thought he ought to have been gentler with her.' She was driving as far as Wragby, when Toby would take over.

'Fine words butter no parsons,' said Ann. Toby grinned but was at once serious again. 'She is a poor devil, I suppose, but she's enjoying her devilry. Adrian is really more upset than he looks. For a moment I thought he'd offer to pray with her, but common sense prevailed.'

'I like the Stedmans,' said Ann, 'especially Ruth. She's got more guts than her husband. But neither deserves to have this to endure.'

'I'd have enjoyed the week-end otherwise,' he replied, 'but for the strong drama. And, to tell you the unvarnished truth, I couldn't help enjoying that. It must be a sad weakness in me.'

'You're not weak, darling, only caddishly human.'

'Didn't you enjoy it rather?'

She said that she had, but was ashamed to admit it.

As they neared Wragby, they saw Rita alighting from a bus near the station. She looked very small in the cold and overcast afternoon. When she was out of sight they changed seats.

'I don't like her being alone all the same, do you, Toby?'

He said that if she wanted to go back to Bob he would take her like a shot, though he would hate it. However, there was no fear of that. But as they drove through the bleak khaki countryside, where the spring was late, he thought how decisive Ann was becoming, and he wasn't sure that he liked it. He loved her, of course, but he didn't want her taking all the decisions.

'What is it, pet?' (The rather belittling endearment he had used to Maisie, all those years ago.)

'Nothing's the matter. I suppose I'm just a bit tired.'

'You'll be more tired when we get home. Somewhere near Peterborough we'll find a nice pub and have some food there. Are you sure you don't want me to drive?'

He said he was quite sure. As night was falling and

Sunday opening-time had come into operation, they did as she had suggested.

17

Later that month, Maisie came for a drink with them. She still wore black, but it was smart black, not oppressive.

She said before she could stop herself, 'Oh, you've still got my lamp.' Then her colour darkened.

'Yes, we have,' said Ann, not knowing before that it had been a gift from her to Toby. 'It's very pretty. I love those converted oil ones.'

'Mother has some real ones at home, oil-filled. They're still prettier. They give a lovely light, but I'm sure they're a fire hazard. Toby, how's the bank? You can't think how awed Mother and I are.'

'Oh, I'm a very small fish in a very large pond,' he answered. 'I get on all right.'

'Ann says you were in New York.'

'Only for six weeks. I was supposed to see just how the firm was running there, but in reality they were testing me out.'

'You got the job from Llangain, isn't that it?' said Maisie. Toby said he had been very kind and that he was grateful.

'I like Claire,' said Ann in all innocence, though Toby knew she would bring up the question of the lamp later.

'Yes,' said Maisie, 'everyone does.' She had a graceful way of sitting, with just her ankles crossed.

Toby, to avoid dangerous ground, told her the story of Rita.

Maisie, who had been at Rita's marriage, was much

disturbed. 'It's hard not to laugh, though, to think of Adrian getting himself kissed,' she said, 'though it's all pretty horrid. And, of course, you can't help pitying her. Where's she living now, do you know?'

'Notting Hill.'

'Have you got the address?'

'Yes,' said Toby, 'but I'm not sure I shall give it you – not if you have any idea of looking Rita up.'

'Not really, but I might write to her. So do give it me.'

Reluctantly, he obeyed. He knew her loyalty to the Cambridge group, and was still prepared to consider Rita one of it. He could still see Maisie as an undergraduate, riding her bicycle in the town, and could not restrain a faint echo of feeling for her.

'Now, don't be an ass, Maisie,' said Ann. 'We all know how kind you are, but we're not prepared to see you making an ass of yourself, which you would do if you looked Rita up. She isn't at all your type these days, though she may have been in the past. She's become sluttish.'

'Perhaps she can't afford to be otherwise,' Maisie said.

'Oh, yes, she can. She's got white boots but she never cleans them.'

Toby, to change the conversation, mentioned Edward. 'It must be hard for you without him,' he said.

Her eyes did not fill; she was over all that. 'Yes, it is hard sometimes. He was so good and so wise. But I have Clemency as a reminder of him. She looks like me, rather, but she has all his placid ways. Not that he was always placid, though he was with me. He wasn't placid towards theatre critics, for example. He said they came to his plays hoping to damn, but they were usually so riveted that they had to find something agreeable to say.'

'He was the wise old man of the tribe,' said Toby, hoping she would not mind the reference.

But she said, 'Certainly he was. When I think of the bricks I might have dropped without Edward!'

But Ann protested, 'You've never dropped a brick in your life.'

'You just don't know, Ann.'

But Ann could think of one brick that Maisie had dropped that evening, though of course she said nothing.

'Don't go to Rita,' she said abruptly. 'She is mad. And she makes things very unpleasant.'

'She seems rather deprived,' Maisie said. 'Do you suppose it can be that?'

'No,' said Ann, 'I damned well don't think so. In a way, she's fulfilled. Adrian fulfils her.'

Toby was watching the green light on Maisie's hair. He said, 'You'd put yourself at risk, I'm sure of it.'

Maisie said serenely, 'She won't throw vitriol at me.'

'I hope she won't throw it at anyone. But she's a risk to know. Keep out of it, there's a good girl.'

'I expect I shall. But if I thought there was anything I could do—'

'You mustn't. It is all Adrian's fault in a way, for looking like a film star in the pulpit. Not that he can help that.'

Maisie said, 'Of course he can't. Adrian is Adrian. I remember when he first came to Haddesdon, and my mother said, "Don't for God's sake fall in love with that one." And I didn't.'

'He never took much part in proceedings at Haddesdon,' said Toby rather recklessly. 'He never played paper-games, and though he was so polite he never played other games, either. He only knew Amanda through his mother.'

'Is his mother still alive?'

Toby said she had been dead some time, dying in the vicarage while the old vicar was there, in as much comfort as anyone could bring her. 'I never met her, but she sounded a wonderful woman.'

'You exaggerate, of course,' said Ann, 'but I'm sure she was excellent.'

'You don't know about it,' said Toby, causing Ann to look at him with penetration.

He realised that this was the very first time he had nearly snubbed her, and took rather a craven view of what would happen later. But she had been asking for it, all the week-end with the Stedmans.

'He was so beautiful,' said Maisie contemplatively. 'He had what they call *le beauté mâle*. But to me he was never lively enough to be attractive.'

'Ruth finds him so,' said Ann, 'but she is so plain and he is so much the reverse.'

'His *curriculum vitae* is interesting', said Toby, 'only when Rita enters into it. Otherwise it's pretty stolid.'

'Did you ever realise', said Maisie, 'that one finds it difficult to continue a conversation about Adrian without bringing Rita into it? There was so very little to say before.'

Toby remembered him under the great tree at Haddesdon, answering politely any question put to him, but otherwise immersed in his thoughts. He put this to Maisie.

'I shouldn't think he had many thoughts of an enlivening or enlightening nature,' said Ann. 'But my experience of him is small.'

When Maisie had gone away, Ann said at once, 'She gave you that beautiful lamp. Did you go to bed with her? I think you did.'

'A long time ago,' said Toby, fencing off the worst.

'I feel overwhelmed by your lovers. First Maisie and then Claire. Then, of course, me, but only once out of wedlock. Dear me, dear me.'

'Look, darling, this doesn't matter anymore. I'll throw the lamp away if it irritates you.'

'You underrate me. When did I ever throw away anything that was pretty, whatever its provenance? But I still think you might have told me about Maisie.'

Toby said, 'I didn't care to. It wasn't a long affair, and it ended miserably. I was only glad', he said, lying, 'when Edward came along.'

In fact, she had been the worst loss of his life and it had all been his fault. Ann was watching him closely, and for the first time he felt that she had intruded upon him.

'Did you go to the wedding?' she said.

'No. It was all quite quiet.'

'I'm glad we had flowers and that I wore a white dress. I don't know if you noticed.'

'Darling, I notice everything about you. And I have always noticed women's clothes. I don't know what that makes me.'

'A suspicious character, but never mind.'

He got up and kissed her. 'That's for you. And now stop worrying about me. My wild oats are all sown. We grow old, we grow old, we shall wear the bottoms of our trousers rolled.'

'Grow old on your own account, if you must. I'm going to try not to.'

'And yet you're obsessed with age.'

'I am, after seeing Maisie. The Primavera.'

'Don't be obsessed,' he urged her. 'You make me uncomfortable when you are.'

She made a graceful turn of her beautiful neck and closely regarded him. 'Could I be jealous, do you suppose?'

'It would be insane. Still, one isn't always at one's psychological best. I was rather jealous of Percy, just because he had known you much longer than I have.'

'Percy has known me for many years, and knows nothing whatsoever about me. Toby, did I propose to you or didn't

I?'

'In a way, you did. It was a wonderful thing to happen to me.'

'And I wouldn't have done that if I hadn't felt sure of you. And, despite your new revelations, I still feel sure.'

'Good girl,' said Toby, who had been thinking about her a lot that day. He could have wished sometimes that she would be less cool, less composed in the face of everything. He never felt that his own love was quite reciprocated. She always held a little back from him, or so he told himself. He would have liked her less efficient and more compliant. Still, she never disappointed him in bed, where, Toby thought, they would soon be going.

A letter from Maisie.

'Dear Ann and Toby, I have done what you thought I ought not to have done and called on Rita. I called about six, and she was in. She didn't seem surprised to see me; she doesn't seem surprised at anything. I think she is in a sort of perpetual trance. She offered me coffee and asked me to sit down. She has rather a nice flat, since I gather she is living with a Jamaican who is doing quite well and who seems complacent. I expect he pays for her Lincolnshire trips. When I told her what I had come about she said "Oh, that. Another of them." She said all the obvious things about her life being her own and she didn't want any meddling. I said I thought she could do with some advice, and she said, "Well, buck up with it, then, as Len will be home soon." I told her quickly that she must wipe Adrian off the slate. She only succeeded in upsetting him. Then I said, "I wish my husband were still alive. He was so kind and wise, and he'd have given you the best advice." She said she'd never met him, but she didn't need advice. Then she asked me to drink up my coffee and go. So you see, dears, as you expected, I didn't have a very fruitful evening, except for finding out

146

about the Jamaican. I gather she does no work and that he maintains her utterly. I thought Rita was looking tense and run-down, and, though I hate to say it, rather dirty. I remembered her white hat and flower at her wedding. She was dainty then. That's all I have to tell you. Love from Meddling Maisie.'

'I'm surprised that Rita told her so much, or at least gave her so much to infer. Do you suppose that talking Adrian over with *anyone* is better than nothing?'

'I'm inclined to think so,' Ann said. 'I'm glad Len is kind to her.'

'Does the poor chap realise that he has a mental case on his hands?'

'I haven't the least idea. But I doubt it. He seems to be very innocent.'

'I wonder which one, in that household, is going to use the flick-knife on the other?'

'Oh, don't. There are things you mustn't even think.'

'I was only joking,' said Toby.

'Mental cases with knives are nothing to joke about.'

That evening he went to see his mother. Ann was dining with a fellow-producer.

Mrs Roberts, told the whole woeful story of Rita and Adrian, was angry.

'How you dared to let Maisie call on that woman I can't imagine.'

'But, then, you could never see that Maisie was unstoppable the moment she got the bit between her teeth.'

'It's nothing to do with Maisie's teeth. It's just that she's a thoroughly nice girl and shouldn't be used. She's had her share of sorrow, too.'

'That's what I was trying to tell you. We couldn't stop her at all.'

'And what did Ann say?'

'The same as I did.'

'Well,' said Mrs Roberts, cutting a raised pie of her own making, 'you should have tried harder to stop her. Both you and Ann. If ever I heard of a more dangerous young woman—'

'It's probably all talk.'

'Don't you believe it,' Mr Roberts put in. 'You never know with those types.' He sounded as if he had an infinite knowledge of them.

'Maisie doesn't deserve this,' said Mrs Roberts, 'and I'm still surprised that you didn't forbid her to go.'

'Mummy, you never have understood, all these years, that Maisie is her own boss.'

'Does she ever ask after me?' said Mrs Roberts, in a tone that in another woman could have been described as wistful.

'Of course she does. You would have been interested to see her flat. It is rather fine and handsome, but one of the sofa-springs has broken, and that reminded me of Edward. He simply didn't care about things like that.'

'No, but he cared about Maisie. You ought to have thought of that.'

'Come on, Dora, it's not Toby's fault,' said his father.

'No, it's not my fault, Dad.'

Mrs Roberts meditated for a full minute before changing the subject. 'I expect you and Ann lead rather a grand life.'

'Oh, not really. We're quiet people.'

'But you do,' Mrs Roberts persisted, 'and at first I thought it was what I wanted for you. But I was disappointed that you didn't become a don.'

'I had no ambitions in that direction. Can I see what you've been painting?'

'I think the fashion for my work is over and done with.'

'No, it's not. Let me see.'

She took him, as usual, upstairs.

On the chair that served as an easel was a larger painting than usual. It represented the Backs at Cambridge, which she had painted before, but now in full springtime. Young men and women lolled on the grass, and in the middle of them was a likeness of Maisie, lap full of daisies, smiling.

'Mummy, this is really good.'

'I'm glad you think so.'

'Maisie would love it.'

'Do you think she'd accept it, as a present?'

'I haven't the least idea. But I don't think she could buy it. After Edward's death she seemed well placed, but she's been unsure of that. Of course, she has all his royalties.'

'Silly,' Mrs Roberts said with some scorn. 'As if I'd ask her to pay!'

The cat strolled in, presented his head to be stroked and jumped on the bed.

'Maisie's free now,' said Mrs Roberts thoughtfully.

'And I'm not. Is that what you meant?'

'Of course I didn't. I only thought for a moment—'

'Mummy, Ann and I are very happy. Is that good enough for you?'

'Do you mean I'm prying?'

'Don't sound too lofty. It doesn't suit you. Besides, if I were free as the winds of heaven, Maisie wouldn't look at me.'

'I remember, when you and she were both so young—'

'Stop remembering, Mummy. It's what we all have to do several times in our lives. Come on downstairs and give me a drink. I've brought you a bottle of whisky, by the way. From Ann and me.'

They went down. The black cat uncoiled and, with an easy jump from the bed nearly to the door, came with them.

Mr Roberts said, 'Well, son, how are you? And why

haven't you brought Ann with you? I like Ann.'

Toby explained about Ann's absence. 'Another time,' he said.

'We've been talking about Maisie,' said Mrs Roberts, who to Toby seemed to have the devil in her that night.

'Maisie. That was a good girl. Mummy wrote to her when her husband died. How's she bearing up?'

'Very well,' said Toby, 'but she took it hard at first.'

'She liked to have a smoke with me.'

'Don't talk as if *she* was dead,' said Mrs Roberts distinctly.

'She does seem part of the old days. Ten years, isn't it?'

'About that,' Toby replied. For once in his life his mother was making him feel uncomfortable. He humped Blackie on to his lap and stroked him. 'How's a beautiful catto? "There never was such a pussens as the pussens,"' Toby quoted Leopold Bloom.

Mrs Roberts went into the scullery. 'Food's ready whenever you like,' she said. 'Finish your drinks first or bring them with you.'

'Did your mother tell you we were making a great change?'

Toby said she had not. She came back to them. 'We're having the telephone put in,' she said.

'Wonders will never cease! Do you think you'll learn to use it properly at last?'

'Of course I can use it. But so many people ring up your dad's shop that I thought it wasn't fair on him.'

'You'll be changing house next.'

'I shan't,' she replied firmly. 'I'm only going out of here feet first.'

'That's enough of such talk,' said Mr Roberts. 'Morbid, that's what it is.'

Toby said he felt she was immortal, and she replied

briskly that, give her another fifteen years, she'd be likely to prove he was wrong.

'Anyway,' he said, 'you can't think of dying when you've had the telephone put in. When's it going to be?'

'Early next week. If it means that you won't be writing me letters again, I shall wish I hadn't agreed to it.'

'I'll go on writing you letters,' Toby said, 'and Ann will telephone you. It's time you came to us again.'

'You know I don't like to go out much.'

'But haven't you been improving in that respect?'

'I don't think so. I'd rather you brought Ann here.'

This was early May. In June, the Birthday Honours brought Mrs Roberts an OBE. 'Now you'll have to go out,' said Toby, when, in a bemused way, she told him this on the telephone.

'The coat I had for your wedding will do, won't it? I can't stand another shopping jaunt.'

'You shall go in your apron if you're more comfortable that way. Now, hang on and I'll get Ann to talk to you. It's great news.'

And, indeed, Mrs Roberts seemed to be delighted for once. She was full of her plans for a visit to the Palace. 'Though they say the invest-whatever-it-is may not take place for a couple of months or more.'

18

The Investiture did, in fact, take place in August. In the bright, huge, golden ballroom, Toby and his father sat side by side. On the dais before them were the Yeomen of the Guard flanking the Queen, who was wearing dark-blue silk with diamonds. Toby had his father get there early, on Ann's urging. 'Then you'll get a seat near the front, and really see what's going on.' When the whole thing was over, they were returning to her for lunch, and, furthermore, to her special aspic, which he hoped would not be thrown in a semi-liquid state on the nearest innocent guest.

The band was playing selections from *Oklahoma* and other musicals. The Knights Bachelor in their ranks could not forbear to take something of a waltz rhythm to 'I'm in Love with a Wonderful Guy'. The room was rather hot and it all went on too long. Toby wondered how his mother would comport herself, but he believed she would be entirely efficient. She had refused Ann's attempts to instruct her in a proper curtsey. 'I shall make a decent enough bob when the time comes,' she had said.

And the time had come. She was waiting beside a very large official to take her turn. She looked very small, but neat, in her wedding garments, which had become quite appropriate to a cold day.

She performed the drill beautifully. Three steps forward, bob, and one more up near the dais. The Queen said something to her and she replied, in an interested way. Then three steps back, curtsey, and retire.

'She's got what it takes, your mum,' said Mr Roberts. 'And now we'll have to wait and wait till the other ones are done.'

In due time they saw Mrs Roberts slip into the hall behind them, bearing a dark box with her decoration inside. She could not get right near them, but was content to sit at the back, while the ceremony went on.

'What was the worst of it?' Toby said to her afterwards.

'Having to leave you both and go in on my own. Then we had instructions given us as we sat in a sort of pen. I was pretty nervous. But once it all got under way I wasn't.'

'What did the Queen say to you?' asked Mr Roberts.

'Oh, she was very pleasant. She said she liked my paintings and that her husband had one. That was all.'

'You were fine,' Toby said. 'Not a bad curtsey, if I may say so.'

'Yes, you may say so. I was scared of it until I tried to do it, and then I found a bob would do.'

Outside the Palace photographers were waiting. Mrs Roberts was posed showing Toby her decoration. This she did not like at all, but she went through with it. Toby thought she was telling herself to be steady and brave, since one didn't visit Buckingham Palace every day. But he was glad when they were allowed to go off in search of a taxi.

Ann had planned a larger luncheon than he had expected. Here was Maisie, here were Claire and Alec.

'And how did it go off, darling Mrs R.?' Ann said, when greetings had been made.

'Dora was grand,' said Mr Roberts, beaming pride. 'She did everything just in the right way. Now tell them what the Queen said to you.'

When this had been done, Mrs Roberts declared how sorry she was that Maisie and Claire could not have been present at the ceremony. Toby was pleased that she had included Claire, never a favourite of hers.

'Now you must all have some champagne – and you, too, Mrs R., even if it's a sip. I heard all about you at your first show.' Ann removed Mrs Roberts's hat. 'You look splendid, but we mustn't be too formal.'

'That first show', said Mrs Roberts, 'was all Maisie's doing. She ought to have a medal, not me.'

'I was selling on a buyer's market,' said Maisie, and kissed her.

Mrs Roberts did, at Ann's urging, drink a half-glass of champagne. 'Isn't this fun?' said Claire. 'I am enjoying myself.'

'Fine,' said Alec. 'Well, congratulations. I'm sure I could never have gone through with it.'

'Yes, you would,' Claire said, 'because you'd only have had to bow and not curtsey. But why anyone should give you a decoration is more than I can imagine.'

Mrs Roberts was asked again to show them the contents of the black box, on which was written, 'OBE, LADY.'

Then Ann brought in the aspic, which was firm as a rock and finely marbled with slices of egg and cucumber.

'You did that yourself?' Mrs Roberts said, quite awed.

'But it's really the only thing I can do, and it's no good as a staple diet. Praise from you, though, is praise indeed.'

'It does look lovely,' said Maisie. She was out of black now and wearing blue. 'It seems a shame to cut into it.'

'We must, though,' said Ann, 'or we'll starve.'

Toby thought how composed his mother was. This was her great day and she was unused to luncheon-parties, but she was serene and appeared to be enjoying herself.

During the meal, the conversation turned to general topics. Claire was fascinated by the Profumo scandal of the previous year, by the story of the call-girls and the suicide of the pimp, Stephen Ward.

'You'd think people like that would know better, wouldn't you?' said Mr Roberts.

'But they never do,' Claire said sagely. 'I'm sure I'd have been more careful than that.' She added, 'I'd hate to be a call-girl. I'd be so scared that nobody would call.'

'You're a disgrace,' said her husband, 'and it's high time we were going.'

But then the talk turned to children, Ann's two sons and Claire's also, Maisie's daughter, and it was past three o'clock when Toby said he must take his parents home.

'I thought when you first drove that I'd never drive with you,' said Mr Roberts, getting up. 'But now you seem very good to me. I trust Mother to you, don't I?'

'It's been lovely, Ann,' said his wife, 'and lovely to see you all again. Now I must put off my glory and get back to the job.'

'Your job is your glory,' said Maisie, and Mrs Roberts coloured, both with pleasure and champagne. Toby guessed that she would not be persuaded into other social engagements for a month or so.

So the party broke up, and the great day was over.

The next week began with a telephone call from Bob. He would be in London over the next few days. Could he and Toby meet?

Toby said that he would be delighted but that he wanted Bob to meet Ann. He suggested a drink on the following evening.

Ann was pleased. 'That's the husband of the famous Rita, who once found himself in the dock for bashing her.'

'It was only a black eye,' Toby said, 'and only one blow. And he's had so much to bear. Don't forget to ask after his daughter, Estella. She's the light of his life.'

'I won't.'

'And let him off lightly. He'll be paralysed by you.'

'Good God, do I paralyse people?'

'Some. Because you're so beautiful and so much on top of everything.'

'I don't know whether that's meant to be praise,' Ann said doubtfully, 'but I shall take it as such.'

She liked Bob at once, though he was a little nervous with her. His scientific eminence had not quite obscured his class-consciousness. But he heard compliments being paid to his daughter with the utmost pleasure. After all, Toby knew her and Ann had been told.

Bob told them that he expected to be offered a Chair, and Toby congratulated him.

After some time Bob said, 'I don't suppose you've heard anything of Rita.'

'Oh, haven't we?' said Toby. 'We'll tell you. Do you know she chases Adrian down to Lincolnshire, and lives with a handsome Jamaican?'

'Good God, she doesn't!'

'Yes, she does. She has really been an awful nuisance.'

'But if she's living with her Jamaican', Bob put in, 'what on earth does she want from Adrian?'

'Love,' said Ann, 'absolute and all-absorbing love. It is like expecting the princess to spin straw into gold.'

'What princess?' said Bob obtusely.

'Oh, any old princess. But you mustn't blame yourself for anything. She's ungovernable. Maisie looked her up the other day, and learned of her circumstances then.'

'Does she still go around with a flick-knife?' Bob asked Toby.

'No, I think not. But she's rather a dangerous girl. If you don't mind me saying so, you were lucky to be rid of her.'

'I know I was. But I don't like to think about it.'

'Sorry. I was only thinking aloud.'

Toby wondered what Ann thought of him, with his faint Sheffield accent, his untidy nibbed pullover a little too short in the arms, his lack of a tie. Not much like the idea of a professor, really. Yet he had made his rooms in college neat and agreeable. He had been quick to learn about glass, about silver, about wine. He was on the whole a happy man.

'Oh,' Bob said, 'I saw that picture of you in the papers, with your mother. Congratulate her from me.' He added as if it were not a *non sequitur*, 'I may be getting married again. I don't really feel sure of it. Once bitten twice shy. But Carol's a nice girl and she's mad about Estella.'

They expressed joy at this news, and Toby said he was sure he would rather not be alone. It would be nice to come home to someone other than Mrs Flax. Marriage, he assured Bob, when it was a good one, was a great thing in life.

'We shall see. If I am going through with it I'll let you both know.' Carol was, he said, the daughter of old Branch, a classics don. She was tall and strong, and she took an interest in his work at the Cavendish. 'Rita used to hate me going to the lab., especially in the evening.'

'But that's all done,' said Ann, 'done with and over. We shall wish you to be very happy with Carol.'

At that, Bob took his leave, saying that he would keep in touch.

'Did you like him?' Toby asked Ann when he had left.

'Very much. He'll become a favourite of mine among your friends.'

'I don't wish many of them on you, do I?'

'But I like it when you do. I like Maisie, too, though I feel inclined now to give her a look askance. But she's your friend rather than mine. I only met her through Claire.'

'There's no need for any looks askance. Come and kiss

me.'

'It's Wednesday and I've got to get dinner on.' She eluded his embrace and left the room.

When she came back, she said, 'I suppose Bob's in line for a knighthood one of these days. I expect Carol would like that. Most women do.'

'I shall never make you a lady,' said Toby, 'and furthermore you don't deserve to be, snubbing me as you did just now.'

She laughed at him, and for a minute laid her cheek against his. 'All right on the night,' she said. 'But you mustn't impede me when I've got the cooking to do.'

19

One fine misty morning in September, Toby ran across Maisie in the Burlington Arcade. He was returning from a visit to his tailor. Maisie was staring into a window full of jewels, and the glaucous light from the overhead lamps was on her head. 'Hullo, pet,' he said automatically. She jumped.

'What are you doing here?'

'Fetching a suit,' he said. 'And what about you?'

'I've been going round the Bond Street galleries,' she replied, 'always thinking that I might buy something. But I don't seem to.'

He thought he had never seen her looking prettier. In a grey suit, her head bare, she seemed delectable. (He often thought of Maisie in terms of eating.) Her damp-looking hair caught all the colour there was from the filtered daylight, too.

Now he said, 'If you had an infinite amount to spend, what would you spend it on here?'

She returned her gaze to the shop window. 'I'd take sapphires, only Edward gave me those. No, I think emeralds.' She pointed to a necklace of diamonds and emeralds. 'But it wouldn't worry me if I never had them.'

'I wish I could buy you an emerald,' said Toby.

'But you'd have no call to do so,' she replied, putting him off. 'Or this more available item, the topaz bracelet.'

'I could afford about as much as that,' said Toby. 'Only I have no right to.'

'I know this is all a game,' said Maisie, after a silence, 'but it's about time to stop.'

They walked together towards the thunder of Piccadilly.

'I may at least take you home?' he asked.

'Certainly not. We're miles apart.'

'Not miles. But, anyway, let me get you a cab.'

'You can do that,' she said.

As they waited, he said to her, 'It's been a very long time.'

'I know. But time is a great thing.'

'A great healer?'

'Yes, I was thinking of Edward.' But she had not been.

'Pet—' said Toby.

'You musn't call me that. That's for an earlier day.'

They had left the Arcade, the precious things – jewels, men's cashmere cardigans, leather goods, hand-sewn underwear for women.

He said, 'But they were good earlier days, weren't they?'

She made no reply.

'So don't let's pretend that they weren't there.'

The sunlight made embroideries in her hair.

'You're being silly, Toby.'

'Admit that they existed, though. Think of Paris in the pouring rain.'

'Ann wouldn't like you saying all this to me.'

'Nonsense. Ann's a wonderful woman and hasn't a single streak of jealousy in her whole composition.'

'Taxi,' said Maisie, and he hailed it. As he helped her in he said, 'It's been good this morning.' She did not reply. He watched the cab drive off and then turned towards Green Park tube station.

To Ann he said, the moment he had got into the house, 'I met Maisie today in the Burlington Arcade.'

'And did ye now?' she gibed, in an approximation to an

Irish brogue. 'And phwat had she to say?'

'Oh, we talked of jewellers' shops, and about Edward. She was pleased by the size and tone of his obituaries. I think she's still missing him badly, though she doesn't let it show much on the surface.'

'If she doesn't let it show, how on earth do you know?'

'My feminine intuition. No, I said she doesn't show it much, but I meant not quite. She's no Merry Widow, not like others one meets.'

Ann seemed satisfied by this, but when he surprised her in the bedroom an hour later she was doing her munching-the-apple act, and looking as plain as she could do.

'I wish you'd stop that,' he said.

'And I wish you'd stop coming on me so suddenly. I am only taking precautions.'

'Rubbish,' he said, but when he peered at her in the mirror he fancied he could see a slight slackening of her jaw-line. But it was impossible to believe, or Toby found it so, that she could ever age. 'There's nothing wrong with your neck that a stiff gin can't cure.'

But she was not to be induced to drink in the mid-afternoon and, to tell the truth, he hardly expected her to do so. 'There's something you could do, in the mid-afternoon,' said Toby, 'and that's come to bed.'

'If you like,' she said rather feverishly, 'so come on, my pet.'

Maisie's word again, or the word he had used for her.

He took her very gently, as if afraid that she might break. For her part, she had recovered her high spirits (had she ever lost them?) and pleasured him extremely. 'You are a marvellous girl,' he said. She rose and went into the bath-room, where there was a bidet. He heard the run of water.

'No one's as good as you,' he called out, to receive the reply, 'I can't hear, so wait for me to come out.'

She came out in the mulberry-coloured robe that he had much admired. She had let her hair get wet under the shower, since it would dry into its normal shape rapidly. She came and sat on his knee. 'Right, darling?' she asked him.

'Very very right. And nicest of all in the wicked afternoons.'

They were dining out on a November evening of that month, when the proprietor of the restaurant came with bad news, the news that was to send a shudder through the world. John F. Kennedy had been assassinated.

'I can't believe it,' Ann said. 'He was so young and, from all I've heard, so vigorous.'

A gloom settled over the whole room, and fresh orders were given in whispers.

Far too many American presidents had been assassinated, said Toby. He himself had never been a Kennedy enthusiast, certainly not over the Bay of Pigs and probably not over the missile crisis, though Toby had been far from disturbed by all the sensation – Kennedy appearing before the American flag to assure millions of listeners that if he had to fight he would be ready. Toby set stock by the wily Krushchev.

'It seems like the end of an era, somehow,' said Ann, 'though what era I can't imagine. Poor pretty Jackie, so much unmade for tragedy.' They went home to see television.

The police arrested a man called Lee Harvey Oswald, who was himself assassinated not much later, by a night-club owner called Jack Ruby, in full view of the television cameras. Toby said he found something very odd about the whole thing. Why was Ruby permitted to fire point-blank at the man held by the police? 'Stranger things happen in Houston than either you or I could dream of. Don't turn the TV off,' Toby said quickly. 'There may be news-flashes.' There were, and they went to their beds sated with drama.

'It's melodrama really,' Ann said. 'I expect to find that it's all happening in the Red Barn.'

But she was more moved than she cared to show, and Toby, who was quick at divining her thoughts, was well aware of it. To him Kennedy did not seem so young, but to Ann he did. Her hands were less precise than usual as they moved through the creams and lotions on her dressing-table. 'Poor pretty Jackie,' she said again.

'Pretty, but I bet you she's as tough as old boots. Now it will be fascinating to see whom she marries again.'

'Oh, don't! That's far too premature. If I were in her place –'

'Impossible. You're different animals.' He kissed her nape. At once she turned and hugged him.

'Well, that's very nice,' he said. 'Do it again.'

Then she laughed. 'Oh, no. That was just for once. I've never been cuddly.'

Yet, in this second year of their marriage, he thought that she seemed more fond of him than usual, and was certainly more demonstrative. He remembered Maisie, who had been very demonstrative. When he was with both of them, he felt rather like Macheath. Next day he gave her the ring he had meant to give to Claire.

She was pleased. 'Where on earth did you get that? It's not English. Or French.'

'I just ran it to earth. You really like it?'

And, indeed, on her beautiful fingers, it looked admirable.

'But I must buy you diamonds one fine day,' he said, touching the zircon and the turquoise rings.

'I don't want diamonds. They're such frigid things.'

163

They were busy till the end of that year, entertaining and being entertained. Toby was delighted to play host, with Ann at the other end of the table. He felt (though he did not know it) like the young Rastignac starting on the conquest of Paris. Ann had somehow conferred status upon him. Life was balmy, pleasurable, entirely liveable. He began to feel that it was like that for all of his friends – until he received a long letter from Adrian. This he passed across the breakfast-table to Ann.

'Dear Toby, I think I shall go mad. She was here again last Sunday, but sitting in a front pew so that she could keep her eyes on me all the time. I don't know how I got through the sermon. When I was doing the greetings at the porch she hung back, until only Ruth and I were there. Then she said something like "Cornered you at last. That's your wife, isn't it?" and Ruth said, "I am. What do you want?" then Rita said, "Let me come back with you and I'll tell you." I was just about to say "Certainly not," when Ruth said, "Oh, let her. I'm tired of the thing going on so long a time."

'So we moved off, and she followed us like the shadow of a Schlemiel.'

Toby gave Adrian full marks for this. If the persecution by Rita had stirred his imagination at last, perhaps there was something to be grateful for.

'Anyway, we got home and damned if Ruth didn't ask her to stay for lunch. "And be patronised by you?" said Rita. "No fear. But I'll tell you what: you'll have to move over. I want Adrian." "You can't have him," said Ruth, "and it's high time you realised it. I'm his wife."

'This all made me feel an absolute fool, going on, as it were, above my head. "Yes," said Ruth, "I'm his wife and we've no room for anyone else. Why don't you drop the whole wretched subject and share our meal?"

164

'"I can't forget it," said Rita. "He's in my mind by day and night. Day and night, night and day," she sang as if to herself. Ruth said, "But you really must put a stop to all these letters and these visits." "Easy for you to say, bun-face," she said offensively. Then Ruth began to show her the door, but she came and hung about my neck. It was awful. I picked her off, finger by finger and said, "You must stop this for good and all. I can't reciprocate your feelings at all. Get that into your head and go back to London." "If it wasn't for Len," she said, "I wouldn't be able to come. He's a good man to me, but he's not you."

'Somehow we got her to leave, but not before she had kissed me forcibly several times. As I told Ruth afterwards, if it wasn't for chivalry I'd have left her lying in the pass-age. So here's my news, and I'm frightened that something will break soon.'

Toby read this without grinning and then, handing it to Ann, he did grin. 'Poor old sod,' he said, 'poor old sod.'

She shouted with laughter at first, then grew grave.

'You do realise', she said, 'that nothing can help him now? If he had the police in, it might start a scandal and would almost certainly get in the papers. That would show him in a ridiculous light, which he couldn't afford. Clerical scandals are about the last thing one wants. No, he's got to live with this and nobody could do anything. Poor Adonis, he'll never get rid of his Venus. When you write to him, tell him he just has to wait this thing out.'

'I only hope that she doesn't get up to any more tricks in Lincolnshire, because next time it might be very hard to keep this under wraps. I shouldn't be surprised if the par-ishioners had already noticed the stranger who goes off home with Father Stedman and wife.'

'Father Stedman', said Ann, 'is very lucky to have a wife in these circumstances. Oh dear, I'm sorry I laughed. This is ludicrous for us but isn't so to him. If I saw Rita I think I'd beat her. A little rhyme. I suppose it's no good telling Bob?'

'No good at all. After all, you must remember that Bob was prosecuted for – mildly – beating her up. None of this ought ever to come to light again.'

'And it all makes Adrian seem less dim than he really is.'

'I thought even his letters showed a degree of point. He is really angry, or as angry as it was in him to be.'

'And it is not in the least an eternal triangle, since Ruth doesn't make a third angle at all. I haven't beeen to church for years, until we went that once to hear Adrian, but I shall pray for him. I don't see anything else doing the slightest bit of good. Does Rita seem to you extremely sinister?'

Toby said, 'Certainly she does. It's impossible to follow her to her next move.'

That evening they dined with Maisie. The Llangains were there, and Claire, without Alec. Toby told the story of Bob and Rita, and was listened to in silence.

'Poor Adrian,' said Maisie. 'When I think of how he used to come to Haddesdon, almost mute, but looking so beautiful. Like a film star – no, more than that. Like an Italian painting of a young man unknown.'

She spoke of Haddesdon lightly, as if it held few special memories for her. He – and Claire – might not have been in the room. He supposed it was what this generation called civilised.

When he rose from the sofa, Toby realised again that one spring was broken; this reminded him of Edward, who had never cared much about comfort. He wondered when Maisie would have it repaired.

'Dear old Haddesdon,' said Claire. 'How's Amanda, Maisie?'

'Abroad, of course. At this time of year she always is.

She's worried a bit about going deaf. I tell her her ears only want syringing.'

On this practical note, they went in to dinner.

20

Towards the end of the meal, Toby began to feel frustrated. Here he could not flirt with Maisie in a jocular fashion, meaning no harm.

Llangain asked him if all was well. He felt, he said, responsible for him.

'Very well, sir.'

'Remember when you used to come down to Glemsford?'

Toby said yes, and thought the question had taken Maisie away from him again.

'All seems very long ago.' Moira lapped at her wine as if she had just struggled through the Sahara to an oasis. She was a big woman, who had been tippling for years, showing no more sign as yet than a slight blurring of speech. Toby thought that the wine might be acting only as a chaser after the vodka she had drunk. 'Very long ago. And to think', she said, slightly maudlin, 'that there was a time when we didn't know each other.' She spoke as if Toby had been her partner in an *affaire*.

'Do you remember Mother's string quartet?' Maisie said on a burst of laughter. 'They were so active and so very dull.'

'I remember,' said Claire, 'and dull they were. Of course I'm no musician, so I can't remember what they played.'

Toby asked about her infant son, and heard for the first time that he was called Christian. 'Decorous,' he said.

'Not my choice,' she said. 'Alec's. Did you know he was a bit godly? Well, he is, and I'm not.'

Her manner of speaking grated on Toby, who changed the subject. He asked about her brother. 'Hairy?' she asked. 'He's still in Germany with Anneliese. He ought to be home this spring.'

'And no sign that they're breeding,' Moira grumbled crudely, the drink beginning to take effect at last. 'I suppose she can't.'

'Or that Hairy can't,' said Claire, with a touch of acidity.

'What nonsense, blaming it on Ivor,' said Llangain.

'Anyhow,' said Claire, 'it's not a topic for us.'

Ann, who had been rather silent, put in a word about Haddesdon, in Mrs Ferrars's great days.

'Oh, you should have been there!' Claire cried. 'Such picnics, such games, and such food!'

'I believe you only came for the food, Toby,' Maisie laughed. Then she flushed.

'Well,' he replied easily, 'my undergraduate days didn't do much in the way of feeding me. But that wasn't all of it, you know.'

He thought how a vast tactlessness became them all. Nevertheless, he would have to warn Maisie not to give Macheath parties again. Of course, everyone was remembering the 'old days' of thirteen years ago, and Maisie not the least of them. He even wished Edward was there to muffle the tactlessness, becoming as it might be.

Maisie was beaming down the table. 'Shall we have some coffee in the sitting-room? We won't separate the men tonight; there aren't enough of them.'

She rose and opened the door. Moira preceded her, then Ann, then Claire. Toby and Llangain followed. 'Are we being done out of our port, Maisie?' he said.

'Certainly not. We are all going to have port.'

'Claire used to say that it was cruel to women to shut them out of the port,' said Moira.

'So it would be,' Maisie agreed. She lit a cigarette. 'Ann? Oh, no, you don't. I remember. Is it because of propaganda, or do you just not like them?'

'When I try, they choke me. That's all there is to it.'

'I always imagine you with a long, onyx holder, smoking with grace, as you do everything,' said Claire.

'Thank you. I'm flattered. But I should just swallow the holder. Yes, port, please.'

Toby thought he might bring them to the saga of Adrian. Maisie listened enthralled, Claire with interest, though she had barely met Adrian twice, and the Llangains with puzzlement.

When Toby had done, he said, 'I hope nobody will tell Bob, because he'd go at her like a bull in a china-shop. And he wouldn't be granted a *locus standi*.'

Maisie said, 'Is there nothing I could do?'

'No, pet,' he said rather absently, 'nothing but stay out of things. She has us by the hair of our heads.'

'But she can't be allowed to go on—' Maisie began. She appeared not to have heard the slight brushing endearment of old days.

'It can't be stopped,' Toby said, 'and anyone attempting to stop it would only do Adrian harm.'

'But, as I remember him, he'd be incapable by himself—'

'Nevertheless, don't, Maisie,' said Ann. 'I assure you I've seen her in full cry, though perhaps not so full a cry as Adrian saw last week.'

'But you can't have a woman like that badgering the parson,' Llangain exploded. 'What do you think, Moira?'

She looked at him, then at her glass, which was empty. Maisie hastened to fill it. 'I think Toby's quite right,' Moira said. 'He's in an untenable position,' she added, slurring her words rather badly.

'Why doesn't he write to his bishop?' Llangain pursued.

'I don't know why,' said Toby, 'but that's about the best idea I've had given me.'

Llangain looked gratified.

'I'll write and suggest it,' said Toby, 'or Ann will.'

'I'll write to Adrian gladly,' she said, 'if he won't seem to think I'm intruding.'

'Do you think that's what he wants?' Claire cried. 'Isn't he mutely begging to be intruded upon?'

'I suppose he is, really,' Toby said, 'but I think intrusion ought to be cautious.'

'Nothing more cautious', she said, 'than writing to suggest him getting in touch with his bishop. Who is his bishop? Does anyone know?'

Nobody did.

'He'll know, at all events.'

'I hope he does. From all you say, he sounds a bit muzzy,' said Claire. 'Maisie, you're not to start do-gooding. Do you hear?'

'If you all say I mustn't, I can only say very well. But, to tell the truth,' Maisie added, 'I shouldn't know how to do good in this case. You remember I had a try.'

'We remember,' said Toby. 'We both do.'

'You couldn't be a bull in a china-shop,' said Ann. 'Perhaps a delicate gazelle, but no, never a bull.'

'The bull would make more impression than a gazelle,' said Maisie, smiling. 'But I will promise. I won't try to do good.'

As they rose to go 'Bless you all,' she said, 'and always.'

Toby kissed her, as the others did, but on her upper lip.

'You still somewhat fancy Maisie, do you?' Ann said as they drove away.

'Rot,' he said, and she did not go on.

She duly wrote to Adrian, and had a brief reply. He had in fact written to his bishop, in the hope of advice or help.

'But', he added, 'I don't think he'll be very sympathetic to an incumbent who can't stop himself being assaulted by women.'

'Dear, dear,' said Ann, 'it looks as though the whole business has its funny side. He's quite fun, in a way, even through his distress. We'll have to wait and see what happens next.'

What happened next was a note to Toby, unsigned, but he and Ann had no doubt of the provenance.

'Tell your friend to keep her sticky beak out of my business.'

'What does it mean?' Ann said.

'Maisie, of course. I was afraid she'd try it again. I'm going to ring her up and see whether I can go round this evening. You'll come, won't you?'

'No, I won't,' said Ann. 'It's Mary's day off, and I've got poor Percy coming for a drink.'

'But we could eat out, and Percy could be put off.'

Ann said that the fewer people involved in the Rita affair the better. No, he must go alone.

He telephoned to Maisie and made an appointment.

When Maisie saw him she looked alarmed. 'What's the matter?'

'You are the matter,' he answered, 'and very much so. You've been calling on Rita again.'

'How did you know?'

He showed her Rita's note, and saw her flinch. Then she said, 'Come and sit down and then you can scold me all you like. You haven't brought Ann with you.'

'No. We both felt that the fewer people scolding the better.'

In silence she gave him a drink, poured one for herself. Then she sat beside him on the springless sofa, looking very pretty and very apprehensive.

'Well,' he said, 'why did you go and what happened?'

She said she had called on Rita after lunch, when she knew Len would not be present. 'I felt like a deputation. I said that she'd been hurting Adrian, and that I didn't believe she'd do that if she thought about it. She said she meant to hurt him; it was all he deserved. I asked her to think again, but she said she'd done too much thinking and I could get out. I went on persisting, just like a canvasser at the door, and said I was sure that nobody had put the whole of the matter to her yet, so far as I knew. If she loved him, she couldn't want to hurt him.

'She said she did love him and did want to hurt him and hurt that currant bun of a wife of his. Is she like a currant bun?'

'There's a little in it,' Toby said drily, 'but she's a very nice woman. Then what happened?'

'She's got another knife —'

'Dear God almighty!'

' — and she showed it to me. She said she'd use it on me or on herself if I didn't go away. She was bluffing, of course, and she's pretty mad, but by this time I really did feel like an unwanted visitor. So I went.'

Toby said, 'You know that you oughtn't to have gone there.'

'I felt that somebody must. But it was no use.'

Toby, trying to be strict, said that she had been very silly. The only person to take steps in the matter was Adrian, if he had to. Besides, Rita was obviously crazy, and nobody could be really sure that she didn't mean what she said. 'So you know what I think of you going into that lion's den.'

'I know,' said Maisie meekly, 'but I did feel something should be done.'

'You're not to go again, do you hear me?' He gripped her round the shoulders. 'Now, promise. Promise me you won't

173

embroil yourself anymore.'

She sat very still. 'I wish my mother was home. She'd know what to do.'

'I'm sure. Ask Rita to a picnic.'

'I don't think you ought to talk to me like that, and please let go of me.'

'Maisie, we're very old friends. This is only meant for your good.'

'It looks to me', she said almost bitterly, 'that everyone is trying to do everything for everyone's good. I know I've been silly, so don't rub it in.'

But he did not relax his grip. 'That's my good girl.' He could tell that she was somewhat overwrought and he gathered that her visit to Rita had been even worse than she had told him. She was not very far from tears. If Edward were there, she said, he would have been able to advise all of them. There were times when she missed him appallingly.

'Of course you miss him,' Toby said, 'but I don't think he could have worked out this situation any better than we have.

'All right, pet,' he went on. 'I'll let you go if you get me another drink. Don't turn me out. Rita's the one for that.' Her eyes filled and brimmed over. Toby, alarmed, put his arm around her waist. 'Don't be like that, darling, over such a ridiculous affair.'

'Let me go,' said Maisie, mopping her face, 'and don't call me pet names. Ann would hate it, I'm sure she would. I'd hate it, if I were Ann.'

Toby told her that Ann would not resent a few endearments, that he was only trying to comfort her, that he was shocked to see her so upset. 'Pet,' he repeated, 'I hate to see you like this.'

She said forlornly, 'Everything seems to be going wrong all round me. When Edward was alive I never cried, because he took all troubles off me. And when I see Adrian being persecuted without any redress I feel worse. Perhaps I've meddled a bit, but I only did what I thought Edward would have done.'

'He wouldn't have tried to see Rita,' he said. 'I'm quite sure of that.' He thought that Maisie was missing less a husband than a lover. The flowers, the potpourri of Haddesdon, were alive in his memory. He saw Maisie sitting in the garden threading a daisy-chain, the Maisie his mother had tried to paint. 'Listen, you'll always be someone precious to me. Even if we both live to be a hundred.'

She smiled weakly, and turned the conversation to his stepsons. They had been very well behaved throughout the holidays, and Toby actually felt they liked him. Tim was going up to Cambridge and Sam, the younger boy, to Charterhouse. Yes, all happy there. What about Clemency?

But just then the nurse came in bearing the pretty child. 'Bedtime, Mummy,' she said, and Maisie rose.

'I'll be back in ten minutes.'

But she was longer than that, and Toby felt that he should be getting back. He would not tease her anymore.

When she came back he had already risen. 'Must go, Maisie,' he said, 'or dinner will be spoiled. Take care of yourself, and no more secret meetings.' Then he kissed her, not on the mouth but on either cheek after the smacking Russian fashion. 'God bless,' he said, and left her alone.

On his way home he began to consider whether his mild flirtation with Maisie would seriously upset Ann, did she but know. He thought it would not. After all, the past did not die away just like that. And in the end, after Maisie's rejection of him in favour of Edward, he had been somewhat in love with her. These things might die, but could not totally be hushed away. Satisfying himself with these thoughts, he went home just in time to meet Percy Clover on his way out. 'Hullo, Colonel,' Toby said falsely, 'sorry to have missed you.'

21

In the spring of the year, Toby had an instinct that Ann's feelings towards himself had changed. Now she was more demonstrative, much of her airiness gone. He was gratified, and he was not. He had been annoyed by her habit of locking herself out of the way to do her exercises or to apply a face-mask, neither of which he felt was necessary, and puzzled that she should give up her job at Bush House. But she only said that she was tired of it, and that she liked to be in when he came home. Her light had been as through a bowl of alabaster, clear but remote; now the light was like red coals spilling over. In her forty-fourth year she seemed to him more attractive than ever, but he did not think he could bear the strain of always watching her fighting to subdue the years. For him she was as beautiful as ever, whereas, when they married, he had only thought of her as handsome. Sexually, she was as willing as ever, riding him sometimes as if she would ride age back.

When they received another letter from Adrian she was more sorry for him. Things were going from bad to worse. Now Rita arrived about every other Sunday and sat in the front row of the church. He would not let her walk back to the parsonage with them, for he guessed that tongues were wagging already. 'I can only hope they think she's a relation. Probably I do more harm in that respect by leaving her at the porch. It might be more natural if she did come with us.'

'Poor, dear, beautiful Adrian,' said Ann, half-laughing,

'and not exactly made for this kind of thing.' They were happier when they heard that Ruth was expecting a baby. 'Surely that will deter her,' said Toby, but Ann said that nothing would. 'Just as nothing will deter poor Percy. Oh dear, and I used to be rather flattered once. Not now, though. I can hardly bear to sit through his visits.'

And indeed she managed, by some art of her own, to cut his visits down to once a fortnight. Toby could not imagine how she had done it, but noticed that the little man was somewhat woebegone. However, he said, 'Well done. You've suffered enough for Mike's sake, I think.'

Ann smiled, but made no reply. In April, there came a bombshell, in the shape of small print from the evening paper.

'WOMAN FOUND STABBED. Mrs Rita Cuthbertson, divorced, found dead on her bed. Her friend, a West Indian, admitted the stabbing and was held by the police, whom he had at once informed of the crime.'

'So the world's safe for Adrian!' he cried, shocked into callousness. 'Try as I may, I can't feel much sorrow for Rita. She had it coming to her. Let's hope Adrian's name doesn't come into it; that would be the last straw.'

It did not. At the inquest Leonard Lovejoy gave evidence. They had been living together for three years. She had maddened him by taking his money, or cajoling it out of him, to pay mysterious visits to a friend in Lincolnshire, and he had been too much in love with her to protest. But suddenly he felt he could not bear it and denied her the money for her journey, whereupon she threatened him with a knife. They were in the bedroom at the time. He tore the knife from her and stabbed her three times; then, when he was certain she was dead, he laid her on the bed and called the police.

'I wonder how Bob will feel,' said Ann. 'I must say I'm

sorry for the unfortunate Lovejoy.'

He came up before the magistrates, and was remanded for three weeks without bail.

Bob wrote a letter. 'Dear Tobe, I expect you have read about Rita's death. Poor little devil, she must have asked for it. It's lucky that she hasn't been to see Estella for years, so I shall have no explaining to do, anyway not till she's grown up and asks about her mother. I am marrying Carol next week. You must both come and see us afterwards.'

'Nobody cares about Rita,' said Toby. 'I thought she was a bit pathetic and I hated her to die as she did. But I keep thinking of her red dress and her grubby little white boots.'

'Sentimentalist,' said Ann. 'But now I know that she actually tried to use that knife I shiver in retrospect for you, and for Maisie on her ridiculous call.'

One paper had found out the name of her former husband – Professor Robert Cuthbertson, FRS, and Ann and Toby expected that he might be badgered by the press. From the same paper they learned that Lovejoy had been a waiter at a restaurant within the sound of the division bell. They guessed that he must have made a good deal in tips.

The trial opened at the Old Bailey in June. Toby and Ann were in the public gallery, and so, to their dismay, was Adrian, not even in mufti.

'God,' Ann whispered to Toby, 'I hope he's not there to take the blame.'

But even Adrian had not contemplated that.

There was a stir of interest when Lovejoy entered the court. For he was handsome, as handsome – nearly – as Adrian. Ann murmured, 'The girl had taste.'

Lovejoy pleaded not guilty of murder.

'He'll go for manslaughter or for self-defence,' Toby said to Ann.

The empanelling of the jury took some time. Three black

men were accepted, a fourth was not. It was a young jury, it seemed to Toby.

He listened to the opening speech from the Crown, and then for the defence. As he had thought, they were going for manslaughter. Self-defence, for a man of Lovejoy's build with a small woman, was not to be considered.

Lovejoy took the box, his fine brown head held erect.

How long had he known Mrs Cuthbertson?

'About three years,' Lovejoy said.

'And you were in love with her?'

'Yes.'

'And jealous because she used your money for visits to another lover?'

'Yes.'

'Do you know who he was?'

'No. She would never tell me.'

'No idea whatsoever?'

'No.'

'She attacked you with a knife because you would not pay for more of these mysterious visits?'

'Yes.'

'She attempted to stab you?'

'It seemed like that.'

'You got the knife away from her and in self-defence struck her?'

'I don't exactly know,' said the truthful defendant. 'It seemed like that.'

A good deal of cross-questioning, but Lovejoy was immovable. His splendid head seemed to attract all the light there was to the witness-box. He wore a sharp-cut navy suit and had shaved himself very clean.

'You had been building up resentment against this woman?'

'No. But it was hard to bear. She was alone so much

when I was out.'

'Did you suppose she had a lover in London?'

'No.'

'Where, then?'

'In Lincolnshire.'

Toby saw Adrian flinch, as if someone had threatened to hit him.

'And you don't know his name?'

'Of course I don't.'

'You don't think you were unreasonably jealous when you knifed her?'

'No,' said Lovejoy, and then, on a burst of electrifying feeling, 'and nor would any man. I dare them to say they wouldn't.'

'You struck her in a burst of rage, didn't you? And you're saying that wasn't murder?'

'She was trying to knife me.'

'Oh, how feeble! You were twice her size.'

'But she was determined to knife me.'

So it went on, hour after hour. When at last there was a lunch-break, Toby and Ann joined up with Adrian, who said, 'I couldn't bear to eat.'

'But we could. And you can accompany us,' said Ann rather sternly. 'What made you come here?'

'I thought I owed Rita something.'

'You weren't afraid of the press?'

'I haven't been, up till now.'

The case went on. There was much reference to the mysterious lover. As time went by, Lovejoy seemed to lose interest and to flag. Once, when defending counsel was examining him, the judge asked him if he would like to be seated, but he said no, he could stick it out.

He did, until the judge's summing-up, when he fumbled gratefully for a chair.

The judge spoke for thirty minutes. He seemed to dismiss the charge of murder, and, on account of the defendant's physique, of self-defence. He rambled around these ideas, but said nothing of manslaughter – which is what the jury brought in after only twenty minutes. Toby guessed that they had spent the time less in conferring than in having a smoke.

The judge expressed agreement with their verdict and asked Lovejoy, before sentencing, if he had anything to say.

The man's voice was rich and musical. 'Only that I'm sorry and that I'd give anything to have her back again.'

Gratified by this expression of penitence, the judge gave him three years. 'Thank you, my lord,' said Lovejoy, and was taken down to the cells.

Toby was nervous about Adrian. He had seen him soundlessly praying and hoped he was not going to make himself conspicuous. 'Beware of any pressmen when we go out, because I wouldn't put it past any of them not to winkle you out.'

But he was wrong; Adrian passed by unscathed and got a taxi while Toby and Ann went for their car.

'He was a great fool to have come,' said Ann. 'Of course, it's that conscience of his. It was an insignificant little trial, wasn't it? I wasn't worried about a murder verdict. The jury had taken a bit of a fancy to Lovejoy, as I'm sure I should have myself. So Rita passes out of Adrian's life. I wonder whether the parish will talk when she doesn't come on alternate Sundays anymore?'

'They may,' said Toby as they wound their way through the city, 'but I don't think they will. Thank God there was only a smudged photograph of Rita which might have been anybody. And she, blessedly, left no unposted letters behind her. Though Adrian says she didn't write during her spell of district visiting. The whole affair must have been a great relief for Ruth, who just got insulted all the time. Damn you, taxi! You nearly slammed into me.' He dropped Ann off at home, then made straight for the office, having had a sketchy lunch.

The bank was bright with window boxes containing dwarf daffodils. Clive came to his room to ask the news. Toby had confided to him the whole story of Rita and Adrian. 'Manslaughter, three years,' he said.

'I suppose Rita had asked for it for ages. Her husband wouldn't have clocked her if she hadn't been a born victim *provocateuse*.' Clive did not know Bob, but had heard all about him. Toby, who did not usually deal in confidences, had found his own good listener in Clive. There was little work to be done that day, so the two men sat talking for nearly an hour. 'I wish I could have met the *dramatis personae*,' Clive said, 'so does Clarissa.' He had told the whole tale to his wife.

'I don't know why it should make one feel rather grand just to be on the perimeter of a murder, but it does. One shares the fierce light that beats upon the dock.'

'Just as David Copperfield felt rather grand when he had been bereaved, and felt that it had given him improved status among the other boys.'

'I'm rather surprised the judge didn't give him a suspended sentence,' Toby went on. 'They're fond of doing that these days. But the crime wasn't a very nice one.'

That evening Bob telephoned, and wanted to hear everything. Ann answered him. 'I feel I've something to do with it all,' he said. 'You ask Tobe if I haven't. If I hadn't sloshed her, would she have wanted a divorce? It makes you think.'

'It doesn't make me think,' said Ann. 'You are quite guiltless and it would be absurd to pretend anything else.'

Toby and Ann could not keep from discussing the case all through the early evening, though both employed opening gambits in order to have a change.

'One thing,' said Ann, 'you can never say Rita wasn't a picker of good-looking men.'

'I wasn't going to say so. You know, I'm on the jumpy side waiting for the telephone to ring.'

'Who by?'

'Adrian, I suppose. I'm still frightened that some journalist will have tracked him down. He was lucky to get away this morning, and a damned fool to have taken the risk.'

'Adrian may be all kinds of fool,' Ann replied, 'but never a damned one. His place seems to me pretty secure in Paradise. And, of course, he will take Ruth with him.'

'I'm hungry. What's for dinner?' And, indeed, he had not eaten much that day.

'Chicken.'

'A dull bird.'

'I can't think of many things you don't find dull. I shall have to ask your mother.'

But nevertheless Toby ate heartily. 'What would I really like to eat?' he said thoughtfully, as coffee arrived.

'And don't say a nice raised pie, because I couldn't make it and nor could Mary.'

'Well, a duck would be a change.'

'Beloved, you shall have duck.'

After dinner was over, Maisie telephoned to know if she might come round. Toby assented with some alacrity. The same old story would have to be told, but it would stop him and Ann mulling it over in private. 'Yes, do come,' he said.

She arrived at nine o'clock, wearing, as Toby noted, a black skirt and one of her favourite frilled blouses. She looked young and very fresh.

So they went through the whole day's adventure again.

Maisie said, 'It is dreadful to think of poor silly Rita

stabbed. I can't help feeling sorry for her.'

'That's no use to her now,' Ann replied, her tone of voice verging on the acerb. 'You might be sorry for poor Lovejoy, goaded beyond his control. He was handsome, by the way, and had a most beautiful voice. He made an excellent impression on the jury; but, of course, they couldn't let him off.'

'No,' said Maisie, looking depressed.

'My dear, it's all over now,' said Toby, 'and nothing we could say would bring her back, even if we wanted her, which I don't.'

'I told the story to Mother, and asked what she could have done, and she said keep her mouth shut and, so far as Adrian was concerned, put up with the — rather mild, she thought — persecution. She would have said he was stupid to appear at the trial, but that, apparently has done no harm. She said, "We shall see."'

'Amanda is wonderful,' said Toby, 'but with luck I think we won't see.'

He looked covertly at Maisie, sitting in the light of her own green lamp. She looked pretty and morose.

'Listen, dears,' Ann said, 'we simply must change the subject, even by an effort of will.' She included them both in her endearments. 'There's a war in Vietnam. Let's talk about that.'

But nobody had anything to say about Vietnam.

'Then let's have another drink. It may divert us from our original intentions.'

22

It so happened that Mike's mother, who was well into her seventies, had been ill and wrote asking Ann to come and see her. She lived on the far side of east Sussex, and Ann said she had better spend the night there. 'It will be the only time we've spent a night apart,' she said to Toby mournfully. 'I shall miss you horribly.'

'It's only one night, love,' he said. 'Don't look so glum and don't worry about me. I shall eat at the club. Bless you, and don't get too tired.'

As he kissed her he noticed for the first time that she had some fine wrinkles under her eyes, and guessed that this would deeply trouble her. For she was not quite his high-riding, cool Ann of earlier days; she was becoming dependent on him in some respects.

It was a fine July morning when she left, having clung to him as if they were to be parted for years. When she had gone, he found himself at a loose end. It was a Saturday and the hours stretched ahead of him. What should he do with himself? He startled Mary by asking for a duster, and set to work on the books in the drawing-room, of which there were many.

After half an hour of this, he came across a book picked up by Ann from a second-hand shop. It was called *Under the Sunset* by Bram Stoker, author of *Dracula*, intended for children and bound in dingy cream leather, with magnificent illustrations – calculated, Toby thought, to send any right-minded child into fits. He remembered that Maisie had expressed interest in it, and had said that she would like to borrow it some time. What better time, he thought, than this evening? He would take a chance on finding her in and alone and, if she was, could always ask her, as a grass-widower, to dinner. Having come to this decision, his enthusiasm for the remaining dusty books waned. Ann would not mind if he asked Maisie out, he told himself. She was sure of him and of Maisie, despite the past. All would be understood. There was nobody like Ann for understanding things. He followed her in his mind down the Sussex lanes, and he missed her. He had hardly known to what extent, since they had been so much together since their marriage. It depressed him that the jars of various unguents on her dressing-table increased. She had begun the war against age, and he had hoped she never would. Her concern was an irritation to him.

But should he take the book to Maisie? Since their telephone had been installed, his parents were accessible. He could send Mrs Roberts away from her work and straight to the kitchen if he rang her up. So he did not ring her up. Her work was more important than his stomach. At six o'clock he started for Hyde Park Gate.

And he did not find Maisie alone. She was with an elderly woman who appeared to be selling her some new charity.

However, when Toby came, she immediately left.

'How ever did you know that I needed rescuing?' Maisie said. 'She was driving me mad. Oh, is that the book we talked about? How kind of you. But where's Ann?'

'She's buried in the wilds of Sussex with her former spouse's mother, who has been ill. And I'm going to ask you to dinner, to help heal a temporarily broken heart.'

'Now, listen, Toby,' said Maisie, 'and I have to ask you because I was uncertain of you last time we met. Is this going to make Ann angry?'

'Good God, no,' Toby answered, 'she's a civilised woman. Why should she be angry?'

'Because', said Maisie, looking suddenly sturdy despite her delicate physique, 'she knows about you and me in the distant past. She told me so.'

Toby did not know how to take this and his freckles stood out all over his face. 'Suppose she does? That's over now — or is it, pet?'

'If you are going to talk like this, I shall be asking you to go away.'

'I'm only offering you a rather good dinner, and some conversation. Now tell me about Amanda.'

Apparently Amanda's picnics were in full swing, and he felt vaguely misused that he had never been invited to any one of them. 'I hope she still has the string quartet,' he said.

Maisie laughed. 'No, they began to bore her. They never got on terms with the other guests, and when they weren't playing they whispered amongst themselves.'

He thought how well she was looking, in a closely beaded black dress, with a string of pearls. She would not need to change. He accepted the drink she gave him and sat back on the flawed sofa. He believed he might go through it at any moment.

'Do you ever think of Cambridge, pet?'

'Don't — what you said — yes, I think of it a lot and how I disgraced Mother by coming down with only a two-two.'

'What can that matter now?'

'It rankles. You got a First, which was expected of you. Naturally, no one expected that of me. Perhaps a two-one, but not a two-two. No, I was entirely disgraced.'

'And how much difference has it made to your life? You married Edward.'

'Certainly I did. He expected nothing of me, but I gave

188

him something, I know.'

'He was madly in love with you. One day, on our way from Haddesdon to Cambridge, he warned me off the course.'

'I don't like that horsy metaphor,' she said, 'but I loved him back. You have to believe that.'

'I'll believe whatever you tell me to,' said Toby.

'He was a wonderful man. More than any of you knew.' She took out her handkerchief and dried her eyes, which had begun to fill.

'He was the wise old man of the tribe.' Toby was determined not to be embarrassed, but he did realise that Maisie was a long, long way away. He had used the term before.

'Let's eat early,' he said. 'Would you mind? Do you like L'Abri?'

'I've never been there.'

'Ann likes it. French cooking, but without any messy sauces or an excess of garlic.'

'Garlic is disgusting,' said Maisie, with the air of one who has discovered a universal truth.

'I am inclined to agree with you. I like it only in moderation but, finding I can't get it in moderation, I ban it from the kitchen.'

'Toby, you sound like the lord and master.'

'I try to sound like that. Ann is so forceful that I have to put up a show. All the small things I deal with. The grandiose ones I don't.'

She laughed. 'Dear Toby, you are still much the same.'

'You called me "dear Toby", pet.'

'Don't be silly. It is only a social custom.'

'Hooray. And, having decided that, shall we go? We must have a taxi as Ann has taken the car.'

L'Abri was a small restaurant in a basement, not too dimly lit, with checked tablecloths and red candles. There was an admirable smell of cooking. Also there were 'no smoking' notices, at which Maisie demurred. 'I know I'm smoking too much lately, but it's inevitable. I find this wowser activity uncomfortable.'

'What's wowser?'

'Australian for spoil-sport. The anti-smoking lobby remind me of the Puritans, who stopped bear-baiting not out of pity for the bear, but because it gave pleasure to the spectators.'

Toby thought how much she had matured. She was no longer the little, admired girl of Cambridge and Haddesdon, but unmistakably a woman. A small one, but with backbone. He felt dimly that perhaps he didn't like this. The one thing by which he could clearly identify the old Maisie was her appetite. Just as she had been delighted with eggs on chips in the cafés, so she enjoyed the expensive food here. They had a bottle of wine between them and as she drank it she seemed to spring to new life. 'Coq au vin', she said, 'would be wonderful.'

A vase containing a single rose was in the middle of the table. Stretching out her hand to touch it, its rounded shadow fell on her forearm. Toby put his fingers to it and said, 'Pet.'

She said quietly, 'Don't. We're not boy and girl now.'

'But I can't forget when we were.'

'You must, or I shall have to leave this nice food and go home.'

'If I say I'm sorry?'

'And mean it.'

'I'm sorry to have upset you, and I do mean that.'

She said she was not upset, but that she wanted him to know where they stood. Then she changed the subject to Mrs Roberts. Was she still working hard? Was she really enjoying her honour? Maisie thought that she might have had a bigger one, but supposed she had begun too late.

And Toby listened, admiring her as she spoke. The light from the candles was mellow, and it became her. His heart stirred. Supposing it had always been Maisie? No, that was mad thinking. It was Ann he really loved, of course. Ann the tall and graceful, with whom he shared so much. He realised that he had done wrong that evening in taking Maisie out.

'Listen,' he said, 'I'm not going to tell Ann. As you say yourself, it is all girl-and-boy stuff, and not meant to worry her. So don't you tell her, either.'

'Oh dear,' she said, still not raising her voice, 'you are making me do something deceitful. I think you should tell her that we had dinner together, and don't say how badly you've been behaving. I can't bear to look at her and lie.'

'I will do whatever you want.'

'You're making me a sharer of a secret. Well, I won't share it. I shall just say you brought me a book and then took me out to dinner. No more than that.'

'As you like. I don't imagine that she'll mind.'

Maisie said nothing more on the subject, but instead changed it to talk of her daughter, and how much she had meant to Edward. Then she said, 'It's getting late.'

'Well, drink up your coffee and then you can go.'

He took her to her door. 'I don't imagine I may come up for a nightcap?'

'No, you may not.'

The light of a street-lamp was full upon her. He kissed her before she could resist. 'Dear, darling Maisie.'

'That's enough. You've got a good marriage and a beautiful wife. Be content with that.' She took out her key and let herself in, closing the door upon him abruptly.

All the way home, his thoughts were in a turmoil. He had a good marriage, of course, and didn't mean to spoil it, but the sight of Maisie disturbed him as it had done long ago. He began to think that there was something to be said for polygamy. The thought made him smile, and he was in no ill humour when he arrived home. Indeed, the bedroom without Ann reminded him of how much he depended upon her. He was ashamed of his early uxoriousness, but more ashamed because he knew that he had not quite liked that recently she had reversed the rôles. No, he was not going to try to make Maisie an accomplice. He remembered all too well how he had deserted her for Claire, and how Claire had rejected him. That had only left him with bruised pride, but Edward's announcement that he was going to marry Maisie had been a bitter shock. He had really loved her then, and too late.

Ann came home next day at noon, her arms full of flowers from Mrs Thorold's garden. She put them down, and then came to him, kissing him as though she had been away for a month.

'And how is the old lady?' he enquired.

'Doing very well, as a matter of fact. She's got a friendly nurse-companion living in, and I should say she was chipper.' She sat down and, to Toby's surprise, lit a cigarette.

'Fallen from grace, darling?'

'Yes. It was being away from you, I think. But my ration is likely to be one a day. Now tell me about you. I hope you didn't mope.'

He lit a cigarette himself. 'No, though I was inclined to. I took that grisly book, *Under the Sunset*, to Maisie and, as she was at a loose end, asked her out to dinner. I was remembering your advice about caring for widows.'

'Specious,' said Ann. 'Aren't you thinking a bit too much of Maisie?'

'That's rubbish, love. I only think about you.'

'Nevertheless, I have seen signs. I've even told you so. I'll go and put those flowers in water.' She left him abruptly. While she was out of the room, he worked his brains as to how he should answer this. It was, of course, untrue. Nothing was more dead than an old affair, and he had merely flirted a little with Maisie, teasing her. She would not take him seriously.

Ann came back with the filled vases. 'Has Mary left us anything to eat?'

Toby said he hadn't enquired.

He spoke shortly, and she looked at him in surprise. 'Darling, what's the matter?'

'The matter is what you said about Maisie. There isn't a word of truth in it.'

'Because, if there were, I might be jealous for the first time in a long life.' The midday sun fell harshly upon her, revealing the fine lines below her eyes and beside her mouth.

'Of course you wouldn't. You've been educated out of all that.'

'I might find my education lacking. Toby, I want your honest word that you aren't falling in love with Maisie again.'

'And you have my honest word. Come and kiss me. I love you, as you well know.'

'Somehow you don't seem to show it so much. But I do take your word for it.'

So the small storm blew over, leaving Toby guilty and, though he fought against it, a little withdrawn.

He said to himself, as he went through the Sunday papers, that he was certainly not in love with anyone but Ann. The trouble was that she wanted signs of it as he had once wanted signs from her. At last he said, 'We're going upstairs after lunch, my pet. I had a dreary night without you.'

He took her rather roughly that day, and it seemed to please her. She was at least sexually secure, as she had seemed to be in all other ways. He looked at her nakedness. No signs of ageing there, not so far as he could see. She was so light-skinned that she might have been made of icing sugar. The skin of her neck was still firm. Playing with her gently at last, he ran a finger down from her nose to her breast. 'Remembering you, my girl. We've been too long apart.'

'I shan't go away again, not without you. And don't feel to see whether I've a double chin yet.'

'I can reassure you that there's not a sign of one.'

'Touch wood. Oh, I do so want to keep nice and trim for you.'

'You are both nice and trim. There's nothing whatsoever to worry about.'

'Come downstairs now. I haven't looked at the colour supplements.' However, she did not dress again, but put on the dressing-gown he admired. 'And if Percy looks in', she remarked, 'it will be just too bad.'

23

Mrs Roberts was very content. She was making money now by the sale of reproductions, though she had never allowed her impression of Maisie in a meadow to be reproduced. Since her living expenses were small, she prudently put her money in a deposit account, and asked her husband whether she should buy some shares. 'Don't ask me,' he said. 'Ask Toby.'

Toby, who was there for tea, said he thought he could help, that he knew a good stockbroker.

'Shouldn't I feel grand with my stocks and shares?' said his mother. 'I can hardly imagine myself.'

'You want to make money work for you, and not just sit in a swollen deposit account earning peanuts.'

'Have you any shares?' she asked him.

'Quite a few and all doing well.'

'Then you can help me yourself.'

'You'd better have a broker, Mummy. I'm a rank amateur and mine does all my work for me.'

'I see. I'd like it if it was you, though.'

After tea, she took Toby up to the bedroom to inspect her latest work. What he saw made him gasp with surprise. It was an unpretentious portrait of himself in profile, easily recognisable. All was there, the upturned nose, the freckles, the reddish hair. It could have been done by an amateur, if it had not had Mrs Roberts's skill with colour.

'You know who that is?' she said triumphantly. 'It's my first real portrait, and I dare say I shan't do any more.'

'It's me to the life, Mummy. Congratulations.'

'You're not going to have it, though. I'm hanging this downstairs to remind me of you when you don't come here for weeks.'

'I do come as often as I can, bless you.' Toby kissed her cheek: they were not a demonstrative family and this pleased her. 'You must show it to Ann when she comes next.'

'I hope she'll come soon,' said his mother rather stiffly. She had never really taken Ann to her heart, though she liked her.

'We shall come before long.'

'I wonder what Maisie would think of my picture?' said Mrs Roberts, showing as much pure naughtiness as so austere a woman could convey.

'She'd like it. I saw her the other week. She sent you her love.' It was a relief for Toby to talk of Maisie, even to his mother, who would understand nothing. 'We had dinner together when Ann was in Sussex with her mother-in-law.'

He stretched himself out on the bed — just like old times.

'Doesn't Ann mind?'

'Mind if I take Maisie out for once? Not the least bit in the world.'

'More fool she,' said Mrs Roberts.

'Now, Mummy, that's not kind, neither to Ann nor to Maisie.'

His mother disregarded this. 'And how was Maisie?'

'Much the same. She's very much over things.'

'Over Edward, you mean?'

'More or less. But Edward seems omnipresent.'

'I don't understand that big word, but I take it you mean that it's as if he was always there.'

Toby said that was what he meant.

'Silly girl, to marry a man all that older.'

196

Toby said that Maisie had loved him. And that, further-more, Edward's death had been premature.

'Well,' said Mrs Roberts, not originally, 'no use crying after spilt milk.'

They went downstairs amicably enough. Toby was never annoyed by his mother, whatever she said or did. But he was wary of her, of her insight, her sense of something awry.

'You must paint Ann some time,' he said.

She did not reply.

Mr Roberts asked Toby how he had liked his picture, and was warmed by his praise. 'Your mum's a marvel,' he said, 'no pretending she's not. It's as like you as if you were two peas. I tell her she must do more portraits, but she fights shy of them. She always was on the shy side.'

The rest of the evening passed uneventfully, until Mrs Roberts said suddenly to her husband, 'Toby's been taking Maisie out.'

'Well,' said her husband comfortably, 'young people are like that these days. Permissive society as they call it, and all that.'

'Too much permissiveness', said Dora Roberts, 'always leads to trouble.'

'Mummy, you're not suggesting that there's anything between Maisie and me? You couldn't be farther from the truth.'

'Things grow, big ones from little ones,' said Mrs Roberts, like a sybil.

'There's nothing to grow from, Mummy. Please be sen-sible. Maisie and I are still friends. And she seemed to be lonely.'

'Maybe.'

'Ann and I have been married for four years and we're happy.'

This seemed to satisfy Mrs Roberts, who hinted no more. But Toby did not much enjoy himself.

He began to watch Ann covertly. The long row of bottles on her dressing-table, looking like the New York skyline, irritated him. He wished she would get rid of the lot of them. He went one evening a week to his club, but believed she was inwardly saying, Is that really where he goes? He even invented telephone calls that she could make to him there, to reassure her. He also thought that the presence of the boys broke any tension, though Tim was about to go by himself to Morocco, and Sam was making a Greek cruise with a party from his form, led by one of the masters. Ann was cool and pleasant with them in a way that Tim obviously appreciated, though Sam was still at the age to want demonstrative affection. This she gave him, though she teased him about it. She was trying to wean him from her.

With Toby, in private, it was she who called for the affection. As the weeks went by, the thought of Maisie grew more faint, and it was an absurdity to think he could ever have contemplated an affair. He felt that he and Ann were a properly settled couple, and their house well ordered. 'We are comfortable, aren't we?' he asked her.

'Very comfortable,' she said, looking slightly surprised.

The fortnightly calls of Percy Clover did not annoy him as they had once done, though the old man's amorousness got worse, not better. Toby thought him a little mad, and wondered whether he had ever sent anonymous letters to anyone else. He remembered how Percy had wept at their wedding, and hoped everyone else had put this down to a general wedding reaction.

One evening when Clover called Ann was out. He had an air of determination, and when he had been given a drink said to Toby, 'You're good to that damned fine girl, aren't you?'

'Of course.'

'Because, if you weren't, you would have me to reckon with.'

'Out of pure interest, how?'

'Never mind. I said, you'd have me to reckon with.'

'Ann and I get on excellently, thank you. Let's change the subject.'

'Cool feller, aren't you?'

'I don't know and I don't care. Do stop it, Percy, because Ann would be furious if she knew we discussed her.'

'Hah. Ann being furious would be something new. Are you changing her?'

'Percy, if you go on like this I'll have to ask you to leave before she comes home.'

Clover's eyes, mapped by red lines that might have been rivers, clouded then brightened. 'Oh, you are expecting her in?'

'Yes, I am. Have another drink.'

'Not under your roof,' Clover said, his voice slurring, and Toby realised that he had drunk too much before he came.

'Well, under Ann's when she gets back.'

Clover quietened down. He said, 'Damned fine girl,' but still refused a drink.

Toby heard Ann's key in the lock, and remembered when the sound of it had excited him. He still found it a pleasurable sound.

'Hullo, dears,' she said as she came in. 'Why, Percy! How are you?' He lurched a little when he got up. She kissed him.

'I must be going on my way. Meeting a friend at the club.'

He still would not have another drink, and Toby was

glad of it. But he sat staring at Ann almost in silence, for another ten minutes. Then he did take his leave. 'Remember,' he said to Toby *sotto voce*.

'Remember what?' Ann said when he had gone.

'He gave me a lecture on what he would do to me if I ill-treated you. Really, darling, he is rather mad.'

'But not enough to be shut up. What did you say to him, darling?'

'I denied the aspersion. I don't exactly beat you, do I?'

'Not so that I've noticed. You must take care not to be alone with Percy very often, because when he gets a bee in his bonnet it never stops buzzing.'

'I didn't ask to be alone with him tonight.'

'No, you didn't, and I was rather late. I'm sorry, but I got caught up by some BBC people. They might offer me some television work, if I wanted it. They think I'm photogenic.'

'I've never seen a photograph as nice as you are. By the way, my mother's done a portrait of me, in profile. You can't miss who it is, and for an amateur it's remarkable.'

'Surely you can't call Mrs R. an amateur?'

'Well, she's had no training and one needs it for portrait painting.'

'She really is wonderful,' said Ann.

Percy, whom nature made to be a comedian, had left a disagreeable taste in Toby's mouth. He asked Ann whether she thought they should stop him calling.

'No, dear,' she replied, 'we can't. He has so very little in life. He's a widower of twenty years, and it means a lot to him to come here.'

'And make love to you under my nose. It makes me feel like a pimp.'

'Oh, it's all so harmless, all words. Poor old thing, let's not throw him out.'

'I could have thrown him out literally tonight.'

'That would have been unfair. He's such a little shrimp.'

'Yes. I could have caught him and shelled him.'

She laughed. 'Bully,' she said. 'That's quite a new role for you. You can't possibly be jealous of Percy.'

'I'm not, but I don't like him prying into my private affairs.'

She said that it was obvious that Clover had been rather drunk, and said that to the drunk many things are forgiven. Toby said he would forgive him this time but not the next. He was indeed disturbed; it was rather as though the old man had hit on his secret thoughts.

He thought that, just as Rita had been Adrian's tormentor, Clover was likely to be his. Rita. He had scarcely thought of her since her death, yet she had been for so long the focus of their interest. Death left a blank that would not be filled. Maisie had been at her wedding, so dainty and so kind. The secret planner stirred in him; inch by inch. He did not recognise it.

Nothing came of the BBC offer and Ann was rather disappointed. She would have liked to be in front of the cameras for once. 'Would you mind awfully if I took up my old job again?' she asked him. 'There's nothing to do all day except miss you.'

'Of course I wouldn't mind, if that's what gives you pleasure. I can always work a bit later so that I come home more or less the same time that you do.'

'Then I'll get in touch with Bush House and see if they've still got room for me.'

'I bet they have,' said Toby, encouraging her. It would leave him freer. Freer? For what? He did not know. He only knew an expansion of the breast, of the lungs. 'Darling, that's a fine idea. The more I think about it, the better it is. I know you've been rather dull alone all day here. Let's be a working couple again.'

Ann frowned for a second, then her face cleared. She was still a beautiful woman, and she liked him to feel it.

24

Two letters. The first from Claire, from Venice.

'Hullo, Duckies. How are you both? We are having a good holiday in this wonderful place, but Alec says it is hard on the legs. Now for my news. Anneliese is expecting a baby in November! If it's a girl, the parents will be murderous. I try to get it into their heads that it is the *man* who determines the sex – I have my odds and sods of knowledge. But they won't believe a blind word of it. Hairy is immensely happy but longing to get away from Germany, which he should be before the baby is born. What do you think of it all? How are you, Ann? Do you ever see Maisie? I think she's been wonderfully calm since Edward's death. Lots of love from both of us.'

The second from Adrian, mostly on a similar theme. 'Ruth and I are expecting our child round about Christmas. Naturally we are delighted. Ruth seems wonderfully well, and it is hard for me to stop her exerting herself too much. Everyone in the parish has found out, of course, and seems really delighted, too. On a more sombre theme, I find it hard to get Rita out of my mind. I never pick the mail off the mat without a shudder, just as though she was still writing to me from beyond the grave. Poor girl, I always feel I could have done much more for her.' ('Damned fool,' Ann put in.) 'I could, perhaps, have given her more attention.' ('He *is* a damned fool,' Ann reiterated. 'She would have been much worse.') 'I pray for her constantly and hope she understands.

'You must come for a week-end again soon – that is, if you can stand it. Billy is now turning into quite a good little curate and takes a lot of work off me. As you can imagine, we are over the moon about the baby. I did think I'd never get married, let alone become a father, but it is surprising how things have turned out. Love from Ruth and me, Adrian.'

'What a lovely flood of infants,' Ann said. 'It almost makes me jealous. Do you wish it were me? You've never said anything about it. But I'm afraid I'm past it now.'

He caressed the nape of her neck, which seemed proudly arched. 'You're quite enough for me,' he said, 'and I never expected it. Besides, the boys would be unlikely to welcome a newcomer. They're too old.'

'Everyone's too old,' she replied rather sadly. 'And you're probably partially right about the boys. Tim is mature enough not to loathe a new brother or sister, but I'm by no means sure of Sam. Still, I shall go on not taking precautions.'

He had always believed that she was taking them. Now he realised that she had always lived in hope. 'That way or this way,' he said, 'it'll be all right by me.'

But the secret planner crawled a millimetre, then withdrew.

In September, Maisie telephoned to Ann to say she was in touch with Bob Cuthbertson, and they were both going to Greece with his new wife Carol.

'She's a buxom girl,' Maisie said, 'and very, very good for him. We're not taking Estella this time, because she's too young and Mrs Flax adores her anyway. We leave on the fifteenth.'

'Let me get at the phone,' said Toby. 'Maisie? You're going to Greece with Bob and his wife? When?'

'On the fifteenth. I told Ann. I'm looking forward to it all no end. I think it's kind of Carol not to mind sharing Bob with me, though she must have realised that I have no designs upon him. No designs on anyone, come to that.'

'Time will pass,' said Toby.

She answered, 'Nobody who had been married to Edward would ever want anything else,' and Toby quailed a little. The secret planner seemed to stir beneath its carapace. He said, 'Shall we see you to say good-bye?'

'Oh, Toby, I'm not going to the moon!'

'It sounds like it. Let me consult Ann – Ann, Maisie for dinner next week?'

'Certainly.'

'Maisie, can you come to dinner next Tuesday? We have quite a lot of news about Hairy and Adrian, and I shan't appease your curiosity by talking about it now.'

When she had accepted the invitation, she rang off.

'So at least you'll see her,' said Ann, reducing him to muteness.

Maisie duly arrived, in a long-sleeved, long-skirted, violet dress. Toby and Ann both admired it.

'I'm glad you like it. I'm giving it a first airing today in your honour. Oh!' She had noticed the cat on the patchwork quilt for the first time. 'Isn't that lovely!'

'I think so,' Ann replied. 'But Mrs R. has done a wonderful portrait of Toby, the easy way, in full profile. But she doesn't want to give or sell, bless her.'

Maisie sat down in a big armchair, tucking her feet beneath her. 'I'd love to see it. Do you think I might call, Toby?'

'You know damn well you may call. Mother would love it. And you could smoke a cigarette with Father.'

'I smoked one last time I was there,' said Ann. 'I have now succumbed to the extent of one a day. I'll have today's after dinner.'

'Now tell me all the news you wouldn't tell over the phone.'

'Both Hairy and Ruth are having babies. Lord Llangain is already frothing about the sex of Hairy's, and Adrian is taking immense comfort from laying the ghost of Rita.'

'That's very good news. But poor Rita will be such a hard ghost for him to lay.'

'Do you suppose there was a ghost for Bob?'

'I think not. I think he's disliked her almost since they married. After all, she was like a foot across his path,' Maisie said. 'I believe he hardly thinks of her. After her housekeeping, Carol seems to make everything look like Claridge's. She's a wonderful cosy girl, a real homemaker. And, furthermore, a wonderful cook and nursemaid. He could not have done better.' Maisie spoke with a new authority that had not been hers when Toby was having a love-affair with her. She had certainly greatly matured in Edward's company.

Half-way through dinner the telephone rang and Toby answered it. It was Amanda. She had called at Maisie's flat and had been told by the doorman that she was dining with Mrs Roberts. 'I expect she meant Ann, didn't she?' Toby replied that she had, and asked her round for coffee and a drink.

'I'll come if I may,' said Amanda, 'because I may not get another chance to say good-bye before she goes to Greece.' He said they would expect her in a few moments.

Maisie, however, seemed a little put out. 'Mother's not one for saying good-bye till the very last minute. She must be up to something.'

Within fifteen minutes, Amanda's big car was outside. She stepped into the hall, looking regal in a caftan, her gipsy bun of hair even more streaked with grey. She was a big woman but soft-moving.

'And how are all you dears?' she exclaimed, with a look that somewhat excluded Toby.

'Well, Mother,' said Maisie, 'though why you should have been in such a state about me I don't know.'

'The greatest medal children can give to their parents is an acknowledgement of concern,' said Amanda, rather astringently. She added, 'Still in half-mourning? Surely that's not necessary?'

Maisie said, 'No mourning. It's just a nice dress.'

Amanda questioned her. Why was she going to Greece in such an uncomfortable way? It would have been much better to take a cruise.

'Because a cruise would cost more than Bob can manage, and because I like it better this way.'

Amanda spread herself out on her thick hams upon the sofa. She was still handsome but her eccentricity had become more apparent. Some years ago she would not have questioned her daughter in this fashion.

'We could just about manage a picnic at Haddesdon, if you and Ann were free to come,' she said to Toby.

At once he had a violent desire to go. 'I'm sure we should be,' he said.

'Only a small group, and indoors if the weather's unkind. You two, and Claire and Alec, and Ruth and Adrian. And a new poet whom I've got my eyes on. And Philip, who will play to us.'

Ann received this last with enthusiasm. 'Would he really?'

'He will, for me.'

'He's glorious,' said Maisie, 'he really is,' and Toby remembered a green day of sun and shadow, when Philip had played 'L'Île joyeuse'.

'Children,' said Amanda, 'you're all looking chuff, as Edward used to say. Let me be chuff, too, and make it a real party.'

She crossed her legs. They were a little swollen beneath the straps of the gold sandals.

'But I haven't much time,' said Maisie, 'what with packing and all that.'

'I can organise it within a week.'

'And no string quartet,' said Maisie with a touch of impertinence.

'I could never understand you taking against them. They were really very good.'

'As instrumentalists,' Maisie added, 'but not as guests.'

'So I am put down by my own daughter. Do you hear that, Ann?'

'It wasn't a putting-down, I am sure.'

'Yes, you're sure. You have a sure look about you, which is very comforting, I must say. Shall we ask the Llangains?'

'And get in some vodka for Moira,' Toby answered. 'It ought to be fun. I haven't forgotten your marvellous parties, Amanda.'

'And I haven't forgotten your attendance.'

But this was a little hard to endure, as her bottom lip snapped shut, altering the whole of her face. He knew that she had not forgiven him, but that she had felt free to ask him (safe, naturally) back to her home.

'We'd love to come to Haddesdon,' he said, 'but I shouldn't ask Adrian and Ruth.'

'Why should I not?'

'Because he's a handsome bore, he means,' said Maisie, 'and a little goes a long way.'

'I've never met a more handsome man, and I doubt whether you have,' said Ann firmly.

'That is admitted and agreed,' said Maisie, 'but it would be nice if he had a party piece. He won't even play paper games.'

'Nobody need play any games if they don't wish. You can't say I've ever compelled people.'

'But, Mummy, they all have to in the end.'

'Anyway, I shall ask Adrian for his mother's sake. Adrian and – what's her name? – Ruth.'

'They're going to have a baby,' Ann said.

Amanda beamed. 'If that isn't wonderful news! I hope it will be the image of Adrian.'

'It may be the image of Ruth,' said Toby, 'so we must be prepared.'

'Why, isn't she pretty?'

'She is not,' said Ann, 'but she is a great dear.'

'Well, if Adrian had married a beauty it might have been too overwhelming.' Amanda looked comforted. 'So I can make the party today week, can't I? That will give you days before you go.'

'I can manage today week,' said Maisie.

'Oh, this is just like old times!' Amanda cried. 'And shall I ask the children? They make such a nice background.'

'Small children make not such a nice foreground, darling,' Maisie retorted, 'and, anyway, I wouldn't bring Clemency. She's always car-sick.'

'Then that's the one thing that keeps her from perfection,' said her grandmother. 'All right, I won't ask the children, but I don't promise not to ask Adrian.' She added to Toby, 'Do you think your mother might come?'

'I could ask her. *But.*' (And, when he did so, Mrs Roberts replied that she had done quite enough gadding about.)

And so they came to Haddesdon.

It was at the end of the first week in September and, though sunny, was too cool for any thought of a picnic. They might, however, have their first drinks outside before taking off their coats.

They stood under the princely cedar, looking across

grass and flower-beds, brilliant with chrysanthemums, to the little stream which Amanda herself had made there.

Philip, the pianist, was not his usual taciturn self. He had recently shared the Tchaikovsky Prize in Moscow with a Russian violinist and could not hide his satisfaction. He promised to play anything they liked after lunch. Maisie came out from the house to welcome them, as in the old days. Bob and Carol arrived, and Amanda swept them both into the group. 'I've been hearing so much about you, Professor,' she said.

'This is a very nice place,' Bob said admiringly, and Carol echoed him. She was a tall, rosy girl with a lot of light hair and a snub nose.

Claire and Alec came across to the Cuthbertsons and introduced themselves. 'Hullo, Bob and Carol,' she said, 'good to meet you at last. Cambridge is so near that you must come here often – and to my place, only a stone's throw away. How's Estella? I've heard so much of her. By the way, I'm Claire and this is my husband Alec.'

'Estella's a posy,' said Carol with enthusiasm.

The next arrival was Adrian but without Ruth. 'She was feeling a bit tired,' he said. 'I'm sorry.' He knew everyone, including the pianist. But he shivered a little. Ann was more than admiring of the house and gardens which, she said, had magic. She was wearing a fur-trimmed suit of lavender tweed, and looked, Toby thought, exceedingly nice.

'You', said Amanda sternly to Adrian, 'are as thin as a lath. I can see the wind blowing through you. Into the house, children, it really is a bit chilly.'

But Toby hung behind, making for the stream. 'Won't be five minutes.' Ann stared after him, but followed the others into the house. He was thinking of the days long ago, when big grey Edward had suggested *bouts rimés*, and

Maisie had been a girl in a queer tam-o-shanter such as no one else wore.

He was wondering now how he could possibly get her to himself.

As it happened, he got his chance at once. She was coming through the hall with a tray of drinks, which he took from her, and in doing so kissed her cheek. 'I didn't greet you properly before,' he said.

'And you're greeting me improperly now,' she said, looking flustered and angry.

'You must know that I've never got over you.'

'Don't stand here talking such nonsense. Let's join the others.'

'I suppose we must but, Maisie, I only want a quiet half-hour with you.'

'You can't have that. You're with Ann, and she would be angry.'

'Oh no, no—'

Without a word she went into the drawing-room and he followed her with the drinks. Ann had taken off her jacket and was admiring the pictures. 'Look, Toby,' she said easily, 'that's a Bonington.'

'You like it?' said Amanda. 'I bought it during the war when prices were at rock-bottom. And did you see your mother-in-law's paintings in the hall?'

Ann said she had, and lovely they were. She particularly admired the self-portrait of Mrs Roberts in the kitchen, leaning over the stove.

'Yes, I was clever to buy that,' said Amanda. 'It was one of the few still unsold at her first show.'

Claire had gone to talk to Adrian, Adrian to Alec. Ann went to talk to Bob and Carol, who never left each other's side.

Toby felt an inner turbulence which was like a threat.

He knew he had done wrong, but told himself that it was very natural. He did not think he would enjoy Amanda's sumptuous lunch as much as usual. The pianist came to talk to him, giving him a glowing account of Moscow. 'When they do anything big they make it big,' he said. 'I've never eaten so much caviare.'

'I expect you'll have another chance today. It's usually on the menu.'

Amanda was in her element, bearing down upon first one and then another. She was still a good-looking woman, and her energies did not flag. She was never happier than when she was entertaining and, if she did so more opulently than other people, well, that was her life-style.

Toby, less comfortable than ever, remembered the day in Greek Street when she had told him that she knew about him and Maisie. He fancied that, naturally beneficent, she had not swept away the memory of this, any more than he had himself. It had taken her more than five years to invite him to Haddesdon again, and this only because Ann was with him.

All the same, he found his appetite returning as they moved into the oval dining-room where china and glass glittered even more than at the Baumanns'. Caviare, yes, there was, and whitebait presumably in memory of Edward who had loved it so.

Ann did not seem to be at all disturbed, but ate her *bœuf à la mode* with enthusiasm. Perhaps, he thought, he had done no harm. He had only made Maisie angry, but he was glad to have had any effect upon her at all. When the pianist began to play for them, he asked for 'L'Île joyeuse', hoping to stir her memories still further. No games were played that day, which, Toby thought, would be something of a relief to Bob and Carol, but when the music was ended they just sat round talking.

'It's rare for me to have a scientist at one of my parties,' said Amanda, 'and I know you're a very distinguished one. In the Royal Society, and so young.'

'Oh, I don't know about that,' Bob said.

'He always talks down about himself,' said Carol, smiling warmly at him. 'You don't need to accept him at his face value.'

'I expect you have to entertain a lot at Cambridge,' Amanda went on.

'A fair amount, but I usually do it in Hall. Now Carol's allowed in it's all right.'

Amanda, who had heard all about Rita, was silently marvelling at him: Toby knew. Her eyes always seemed more protruding when her interest was sharply aroused. But, not surprisingly, nothing was said about Rita that day.

When it was time to go, Maisie kissed everybody, including Toby. To have ignored him would have caused talk. She was staying at Haddesdon for the night. Claire insisted, once they were in the drive, that the party should continue for a little. The Bull would be open in ten minutes, and they would all go and play shove ha'penny. 'If it's all right for you to play, Adrian.' But he said he would not, since he was staying the night with Bob and Carol, and would have to be up very early in the morning to get to Lincolnshire. So the idea of a further party dwindled away, and Toby and Ann, with a final good-night, got into their car.

It was a beautiful evening, with a harvest moon, and still the long strips of sunset behind the trees. 'Well, did you like it?' he asked Ann.

But she did not reply to this. Instead she said, 'What have you been doing?'

25

He saw that she was furiously angry. She did not look at him, because she was driving and kept her eyes upon the road, but there was a red spot high on the cheek that he could see.

'Darling, what on earth do you mean?'

'Don't call me darling, not now. I'm talking about Maisie. You never had your eyes off her the whole of the time, and you were alone in the hall together.'

'This is absolute nonsense, but if you're persisting in it for God's sake let us get off the road, or drop into a pub.'

'There's no need for that. I'm tired and I want to get home quickly. Yes, Maisie. Do you suppose I'm a fool? And the others must have seen.'

'They didn't see anything, because there wasn't anything to see. So stop it.'

'Do you suppose I'm jealous? Well, I am. I'm human, though I doubt if you thought so.'

The September night was coming down around them.

'Pet,' said Toby – rather soapily, he feared – 'I thought you were having such a good time.'

'That is what I wanted them all to think.'

'There is nothing at all between Maisie and me.'

'Oh, there may not be on her side. But there is on yours.' Her voice was high, and Toby was sorry he had ever sentimentally thought of her as an 'ice-maiden'. There was nothing icy about Ann now, and he knew it.

'Listen, my boy,' she said, 'I am not blind, deaf or dumb.

This old thing with Maisie is coming to life again and I don't like it. I don't suppose it's gone far, but I mean to stop it before it does.'

Toby said, 'You make me seem like a Casanova. I can imagine how wild my mother would be.'

'Your mother loves Maisie, next to you, best of anybody in the world. Mind you, I don't think she'd urge you to desert me.'

'I'm not deserting you. And I think you should stop all this.'

'I am weak enough to plead with you. Is this true, and if so, what does Maisie know about it?'

'Maisie would never have me, not even if I were free as a bird. She simply isn't like that.'

'So far as that goes, I believe you. But I am hurt and, yes, angry. I felt so put on one side. I shall always hate Haddesdon.'

'Hate Haddesdon? You must be mad.'

'Mad I am, in the slang sense.'

Neither of them spoke till a few more miles had been covered. The harvest moon, coloured like a blood-orange, still shone out of the dark sky. There were stars. The headlights raked the hedges as they drove, and an animal was caught in them.

'You aren't going on being silly, are you?' Toby said steadily. 'Because even if you are, or even if you're not, I shall suggest a pub, and drive the rest of the way.'

She did not demur. They parked the car in the courtyard of a cubic, white public house and went in. It was surprisingly comfortable inside, with horse-brasses and leather-covered benches. Toby asked her what she would drink.

'Half a pint of beer,' she said. 'That will be enough for me.'

'You like beer, don't you, darling?'

'I told you not to call me that again.'

To other customers, they must obviously have been quarrelling, and this gave Toby a lift of spirits, as though he had at last brought Ann down to a more human level.

When he came back with the beer, he found her sitting very upright on the bench, her legs crossed. It was only in part her air of distinction that made people look in her direction.

'Thank you,' she said stiffly, as to a stranger. She swallowed half the beer in a gulp.

'We'll have to be thinking of getting back soon,' Toby said. Then he realised that she was all too human; she had her hand across her mouth and her back was stiffer than ever.

'Want to be sick,' said Ann.

'Darling! I think the Ladies is behind that curtain.'

'Can't wait.' She got up, hand still before her lips. She hurried from the pub and Toby, his beer untouched, followed her.

She was standing in the forecourt, bent over from the waist and was very sick indeed, most of it on the stones, but some on the fur revers of her jacket. When she had stopped retching, she tried to clean herself with her handkerchief. Toby gave her a bigger one. He could not bear to see her humiliated like this. 'I must have drunk too much at Haddesdon.'

But he knew she had not. 'Come on, let's be going.' He took the two handkerchiefs from her and threw them behind a shrub. 'I expect', she said, speaking with difficulty, 'that they often find repulsive things here from time to time.' He helped her to the car, where she insisted on sitting in the back. She might, she said, sleep for a little while. She did, in fact, sleep at once and for the best part of the way home. A faint smell of vomit came from the rear of the car, for her cleaning had been imperfect.

When they got home she took off her jacket. 'Cleaners,' she said, and went straight upstairs. 'You'd better go in the spare room,' she called down to him.

'I'll do nothing of the sort. How do you feel?'

'Pretty horrible. I'll be better after a shower.'

He gave her twenty minutes, then turned off the lights and went upstairs. She was sitting in the bed, fresh-smelling, her hair still damp from the water.

He bent down to kiss her and she did not repel him. This time her mouth smelled of toothpaste and mouth-wash.

'I'm so sorry,' she said.

'Don't be. We all do those things sooner or later.'

'I didn't mean being sick. I meant saying all those things to you about Maisie. I must have been mad.'

'Mad you were,' said Toby with some severity, 'but you're all right now, and it's all right.'

'We can always have Maisie here if you want her.'

'That's begging the question, darling. Let's not talk about it anymore.'

'Something just came over me,' she said with a rather childish air. 'I won't do it again.'

'Not if it makes you sick outside pubs.'

'It was all very silly of me. Still, I shall never go back to Haddesdon again.'

'I'd be sorry for that, even if it was only for Amanda's sake.'

'I think that I might smoke my second cigarette.'

Toby lit one for her, and took another for himself. 'You are going it,' he teased her, feeling that in her lowered state she would be unable to fend him off. Furthermore, she did not want to fend him off. She had been scared that day and had lost all control of herself.

Later, he lay down in bed beside her, but did not try to

touch her beyond a slight caress. She said, out of the darkness, 'I shall never be like that again. I give you my word.'

'I believe you.'

'I am pretty vain. I expect you have guessed that.'

'No more than you should be.'

'So it was wretched for me, this evening.'

'Forget it. I shall. Anyway, I never took you very seriously. And, if you want to know what Maisie and I were doing in the passage, I was taking the tray from her and looking at my mother's pictures. I told her about the cat on the patchwork quilt.'

'I suppose you forgot that she saw that in our house.'

'Yes, I did. And now shall we drop the subject? It's always tiring driving from Suffolk. When we go to the Llangains, which Claire and Alec want, I think we'll go by train and take a cab from Sudbury.'

'I don't think I want to go anywhere again,' said Ann, sleepy and subdued. 'I don't know how I shall look you in the face tomorrow.'

'I don't know what else you're going to look me in. Now go to sleep again. I'll go back to my own bed.'

He, however, did not sleep for a long time. He told himself that he had really hated to see Ann disgraced. He loved her a lot, though not as intensely as when they had first married. He would try not to love anybody else. He had exaggerated his feeling for Maisie and was sorry. It had all been tomfoolery.

Later, he heard her get out of bed and, without turning on the lamp, make for the bathroom under which a bright line of light appeared. She was away for some time till he called, 'Are you all right?'

'I'm just coming,' she called back. 'I forgot my throat cream, that's all.'

He was tired of her lotions and her creams, but he did not

tell her so. Almost at once she was back and between the sheets.

Tomorrow he must try to get Ann back on her comfortable pedestal. That she should be on one was part of her lifestyle, and inherent in her looks. Obviously it would be no easy matter, since she would certainly brood over being sick in the pub car-park, but he must try. Yet next day she came down to breakfast looking cool and composed. 'By the way, how old is Maisie?' she said towards the end of the meal.

'My age. I don't think she looks as much.'

'She doesn't,' Ann agreed, and picked up the paper again.

So that was at the core of her anxiety – Maisie's youth. It seemed to be a worry foredoomed for her and to grow worse with age. What would it be like when Toby was fifty, and she sixty? He would never be able to look at a woman. No, with her plight of the past day, a whole world had changed for them both. He must try never to let her down. And there was no reason why he should let her down, if only he kept his head.

She left early in order to take her suit to the cleaners. He only hoped she would not refuse to wear it ever again, because it much became her. But he could only think of the splash of vomit on the fur.

All in all, she had made Toby miserable, a state rare in him, and the absence of which made her grateful. Theirs had been such a serene household, the tone mostly set by herself but to which Toby could easily make a contribution. They must return to this, as if yesterday's ugly scene had never existed. He looked across the room at Maisie's green lamp. He guessed that Ann would be glad to see the back of it, but knew it would be like a confession of guilt if he got rid of it without asking her. It had shone on his love-makings, to Maisie, to Claire, to herself. He marvelled that she had felt no jealousy of Claire, but thought the latter's brisk and comradely airs did not encourage amorous speculation. As for himself, he had got over Claire completely, and now enjoyed her company as if they had never been lovers. Besides, she had no feeling for him. Had Maisie?

He believed she had, though held firmly down. When the pianist, at his request, had played 'L'Île joyeuse' he had seen her colour rise and had noticed the way she had gripped her hands tightly in her lap. Somehow, he could never see Maisie vomiting in a car-park. But, then, would he ever have thought he should so see Ann? He hated life's disturbances, especially those of an improbable kind. He was glad they had promised to go with the Baumanns that night to see *Tosca*, though at most times opera bored him, and it would doubtless do so again. But it would remove the necessity of making conversation. They had better avoid much intimacy for the next few days, after which the day-before-the-day-before-yesterday would seem genuinely far away.

It was a beautiful autumn day, the mist standing thinly between what seemed to be Japanese trees. He passed a barrow full of giant chrysanthemums, and the peppery scent of them took him uncomfortably back to Haddesdon. Amanda had grown such giants in her greenhouse, like curled white and yellow heads. When he got to the bank he found the window-boxes filled, too, with chrysanthemums of a smaller breed. The worst of life, thought Toby, is that it makes it so difficult for one to forget anything.

26

Ann's work, however, did not prove so demanding. She was often in before him. One evening he found her playing a Beatles record, and leafing over a new book in her lap, by Ian Fleming.

'You know, Toby, James Bond and I are never going to be on the same wavelength.'

'Don't pine about it. Thousands of people are.'

She turned off the record-player and came to kiss him. 'Busy day, darling?'

'I think there may be news for me soon.'

'Don't say that we've got to go and live in Frankfurt!'

'Nothing like that. But I shan't tell you what it is till I'm more sure.' In fact, he believed that he was working up to a junior partnership. Then he would really feel himself a merchant banker. Mrs Roberts would be pleased, and her visions of himself behind a grille would be dissipated.

In the first week of November, Claire telephoned in great glee. 'It's happened, darlings! Hairy has got a son and the parents are crazy mad about it. Anneliese will be really popular now, which she wasn't before. He has the remark-able name of Rhisiart Hans, and because he was a bit early he was rather small. But he's heading for five and a half pounds now. Anneliese seems to have given birth with the sang-froid of a peasant woman in the fields. Think of it – I'm an aunt!'

'Congratulations to you and to Hairy,' Toby said. 'I think it's wonderful. I'll tell it all to Ann.'

When Ann was told, she said at once, 'I'd better ring Maisie. She'll love to know.' But Toby rejected this quixotry.

He said casually, 'I shouldn't do that, darling. She'll have heard. I bet Claire's telling half London.'

The following January Winston Churchill died, mourned by the nation that had acclaimed him in war but dismissed him in peace. 'Not surprisingly,' said Alec, when they were dining there one night, 'they didn't turn *him* down; they turned out the Conservatives. And with their pre-war record it's not surprising. Still, he was a great old man. He judged the mood of the country when he offered us nothing but blood, sweat and tears. The British are very masochistic.'

'No politics this evening,' Claire ordered. She was looking very handsome, her flaxen hair tied with a Mozart ribbon. 'We're going to discuss the new Hairy.'

'Oh, come, darling, he's been discussed from his head to his toes. And there is only one Hairy.'

'The parents approved of Rhisiart, by the way, but not of Hans. They thought it an unnecessary concession to Anneliese. "Why not Adolf?" Mummy said, quite nastily for her. People are never satisfied.'

After dinner they played bridge, at which Toby was very bad and Alec very good. Both Claire and Ann were competent.

Toby thought they must seem a pleasant middle-class quartet.

But they had not been home for half an hour when Mr Roberts telephoned. He was agitated.

'Son, your mum's had an accident. She's in hospital being X-rayed. She fell off a step-ladder when she was hanging some curtains and seems to have ricked her back.'

'Good God! Where have they taken her?'

'Bart's. She didn't want to go, but the doctor said there was no time to waste.'

'Shall I get along there?'

'Not tonight. But she'll want to see you tomorrow. Poor little woman!' said Mr Roberts, sounding very upset indeed.

Toby, even as he was telling Ann all this, thought of his mother's intense passion for being in her own home, and of how badly she would take to a hospital. She would feel caged there, trapped for ever.

'Is it hurting her much?' Ann asked.

'Not very, Dad says, when she lies quite still. Can you see her keeping still? I can't. Not voluntarily.'

He was as upset as his father. He went to see Mrs Roberts next morning, and found her lying flat in a trim bed in a large ward. No private sector for her, though she could have afforded it. Toby leaned over to kiss her. 'How are you?' he said.

'Not in much pain, if I lie here like a dummy. I never thought I'd come to this. How Stan will manage I don't know.'

'Ann could come in and cook an evening meal for him.'

'Not in my kitchen, she won't.'

'Mummy, for Pete's sake be reasonable! You may be here for quite a little while, and we all know Dad's helpless around the house.'

The nurse came up with the flowers Toby had bought, already in a vase.

'Are those for me?' Mrs Roberts asked. 'Very, very nice. I could paint those roses.' Her little body barely made a hump in the bed. 'I wonder when I shall paint again?' She looked as if she might cry.

'Have you had your X-ray yet?'

'Yes, but the pictures aren't out yet, or if they are I

223

haven't been told. Maisie's coming to see me this afternoon. Your father rang her last night after he'd rung you. If Maisie wants to lend a hand at home, I might let her.'

Toby's heart had lurched. 'Don't you think Ann will feel a bit out of things? She told me she'd do anything in the world for you if she could.'

'Maisie knows where things go,' said Mrs Roberts obscurely.

Then two doctors and a nurse came in and the curtains were drawn about the bed. Toby lingered outside the ward, feeling miserable. He was not alone long, since a nurse came and called him back. One of the doctors spoke to him. 'Well, there's no fracture, thank Heavens. She just seems to be rather badly bruised. I'm afraid it's bed for her for the time being. We'll keep in touch.'

When the doctor had gone, Toby returned to his mother.

'I've broken nothing,' she said. 'That's a lot to be grateful for.'

'Can you sit up?'

'I can, but I'm not comfortable. You just leave me be.'

But she had a look, not so much of pain, but of terror. Through her window she could see rooftops and pigeons. Free birds; nobody locked them up.

'Is there anything I can bring you from home?' he said. 'I'm free all this morning.'

She considered. 'Another nightdress. You know where to find one? In the airing-cupboard. And I'd like my dressing-gown and slippers.'

'Then I'll just go home and get them all. I'll be back with you in an hour.'

'I hate to be a trouble,' she said. 'I just hate it.'

'Don't just lie there and pine, then. You've done nothing serious and you'll be out of bed before you know it.' He kissed her three times and went away. In the corridor he met the nurse who had brought the flowers. 'She'll really be all right soon?'

'Well, I don't know, but I should think so. She doesn't like hospitals, though. Some people love them. Takes all sorts, doesn't it?'

When he returned with her clothes, which he had found clean and dainty, she was fast asleep. She looked curiously young with her hair down. It was reddish and a little sparse and did not reach below her shoulder-blades, but it made a tidy little bun when it was up. He considered that he had never seen her so before.

'Better leave her,' the nurse whispered. 'She didn't have much of a night. By the by, is she some sort of celebrity? The flowers haven't stopped coming all the morning.'

Toby told her about his mother's painting. The nurse was admiring. 'Fancy that! I thought she looked clever.'

In the clean polished corridor, he ran into Maisie, her arms full of flowers. Both checked momentarily, then fell into conversation.

'Oh, poor darling! Shall I be able to see her?'

'She's sleeping at the moment, but she'll wake up soon. There seems nothing seriously wrong.'

Maisie smiled her lovely curved smile. 'Oh, I'm so glad! What can I do to be of use?'

'Just talk to her, I think. She's behaving like the Prisoner of Chillon.'

'I know, fettered to the wall. I'll do my best.'

And Maisie passed on. Toby watched her go. He wondered how on earth he was to get out of the problem of two women wanting to come in by the day, decided that they must somehow share it between them. He could not have Ann hurt. In a manner he dared not confess even to himself he was excited to have the chance of seeing a good deal of Maisie. But he said nothing to Ann about the project for helping his father in his mother's absence.

Next morning, when he went in to see her again, he found her sitting up against a pile of pillows, a look of strain on her small face. Flowers had multiplied; there was not room for all of them at her bedside, so they were put on a table at her foot, for the general delight of the ward.

'Is it hurting?' he said.

'A bit. But I suppose I must get used to it. Can't lie on my back all my life.'

'Mummy, about looking after Dad. You can't just have Maisie without hurting Ann. Ann's jealous of her, and for no good reason.'

'Oh ho?' said Mrs Roberts.

'For no reason at all. But I wanted to tell you that the best thing would be for Ann and Maisie to share the work. It would make them both very happy and take a lot off your mind.'

'No,' said Mrs Roberts, 'and I should just like to know what you've been doing.'

'Mummy, you must. It will hurt Ann dreadfully if I go back and tell her you don't want her. Please be reasonable, for my sake. Please.'

Mrs Roberts did not reply at once. She moved restlessly, and winced. A Chinese nurse came in with a cup of tea for her.

'I don't want it.'

'Now, be a good lady. It will buck you up.'

Mrs Roberts shrugged it away.

'Did you know there was a bit about me in the *Standard* yesterday? That's where all these flowers come from. People have got to be thanked. Ann could always do that for me.'

'She will, if I take down a note of the senders. But she must come in and help. You like her quite a lot, don't you?

226

And so does Dad. I have never insisted on anything before, have I, Mummy? But I must insist on this.'

'He insists,' said Mrs Roberts mockingly. 'Oh, very well, have your own way. Make your own arrangements. I shan't be long in here, anyway, and then I'll get back to work.'

Toby thought she was looking desperately tired and very thin. He thanked her for the concession, and told her that Ann would be in to see her that evening.

'Yes,' she murmured, 'but I do wish I knew what you'd got up to.'

'Mummy, you used not to hedge me round with suspicions. What's the matter with you?'

'I remember how you were with that Claire.'

'It didn't matter as much as I thought at the time. But that's years ago. Let's drop the subject now. Shall I bring you something to read?'

'Well, I get all the papers here. But I wouldn't mind reading *Anna Karenina* again; I liked that, though it was pretty miserable. Drop it in some time, if you will. I can't read much, it's too uncomfortable sitting up. I long for the afternoon when they let me have a sleep. Not that I get much with blood-pressure tests, and thermometers, and so forth.'

It was a cold and windy day outside and the rain streamed down the windows. There was not a pigeon in sight. A dreary view for a prisoner.

The doctor stopped by the bed. 'How are we today, Mrs Roberts? Feeling better?'

'That's what you think.'

'Oh, come, come! Still much pain? We'll give you a couple of Distalgesic tablets; that will ease you a good bit.' To Toby he said, 'We're going to get your mother up in a chair for a bit tomorrow. Can't have her getting stiff.'

She groaned. 'Can't you leave me in peace?' She was not one of those who were overawed by hospitals and doctors.

Simply, she did not like them.

'Now, now, you'd really be sorry if we did, wouldn't you? We're trying to get you well again. I know it's hard at first.' He took her reluctant hand, felt the pulse, then squeezed it. He passed on.

Strange, wedding flowers arrived from Alec and Claire. Stephanotis. The smell was pungent.

'She would,' said Mrs Roberts darkly.

In the evening Ann went to her, and came home looking puzzled.

'I think she'll be all right,' she said, 'but she hates it so. Listen. She wants Maisie and me to take turns in looking after your father. In fact, she's already given me her key. Isn't it an odd idea?'

'It would be more strain on you if you had to do it alone.'

'I suppose so. But there we are. I'm going in tomorrow morning to feed and water Blackie, and change his tray.' (He was not an outdoor cat.) 'Then I shall dust around a bit and take your father a steak and kidney pie for his supper. Mary will make it, and hers will be far better than mine. Maisie will go in the day after.'

'Don't you think my father could cope with Blackie? He can't be entirely helpless.'

'That's what I thought, but Mrs R. said no. I shall have to bring Blackie tins of cat food. I'll take a fortnight's leave from Bush House, by the way.'

He asked her if that would be difficult. No, she said, so long as she made it up another time; she almost wished now that she hadn't gone back.

Maisie rang her up to make sure of the arrangements between them. No bother about a key for her, she said; she would look in at the shop and borrow Mr Roberts's. She was brisk on the telephone, and wasted no time.

Toby drove Ann to SE1 next morning, himself taking

time off. As they entered the little house they were greeted with a loud, offended mewing. Blackie was sitting on the cushion made from Ann's patchwork quilt, erect and proud. Obviously Mr Roberts had fed him only a few scraps from his own breakfast (which he was capable of cooking) and the pan smelled. 'Work to do here,' said Ann. She put on one of Mrs Roberts's aprons, opened a tin and lavishly fed the cat.

'I say,' said Toby, 'if you give him all that much he'll only be sick.'

She gave the cat a warm stroking. 'Oh, no, he won't. He doesn't want to cause me extra trouble. You run along, Toby, and let me look around. I'm going to give everything a thorough dusting.' Then she took out the pie and put it on the kitchen table with a note: 'Give this an hour at No. 7 just to cook the pastry through.'

'No, I'll wait for you,' Toby said. 'You can't have much more to do today.'

'Well, I'll dust and tidy and polish a bit. Where are the tools of my trade?'

Toby told her and she took out broom, dustpan and brush. 'I want everything to be as she left it. I can imagine her fretting there in bed. Do you hate hospitals, too? Once they take you in they strip you of your *mana*. Though I imagine they'd be hard put to it to do that to Mrs R.'

She started to work, and Toby made a cup of tea. She drank it slowly, Blackie, haughty and gorged, on her lap. His purrs were satisfactorily loud. 'Do you know,' she said wonderingly, 'I feel quite happy and right doing this. Perhaps it was what I was meant to do. Don't you think so?'

'I'm not so sure,' he said, 'but you look very pretty in that apron.'

'Thank you. I'll wash it out before I go so that it will be all ready for Maisie. It's plastic, so it won't need ironing.'

This imitation of humble domesticity pleased him, too, though he hardly knew why. Up in the bedroom was the step-ladder exactly as it had fallen, and the curtain was hanging from three hooks. 'Now, that I can do myself,' said Toby, and did it. They tidied up this room, too, taking care not to disturb a half-finished painting on a chair.

'I'll get *Anna Karenina* while I'm about it. Do you see it anywhere about?'

At last they found it, with a row of recipe books, on the kitchen shelf.

'Now,' she said, 'at last we're finished. But I must leave Mr R. a note about feeding Blackie. He's perfectly capable of following instructions. Meanwhile, Maisie can cope with his pan. Poor Puss, are you a martyr to human neglect? I know you're missing your mother.'

As they were about to leave the house, Toby took hold of her and kissed her. She gave a laugh of joy. It had been a very odd morning for them both. 'Now, I think I'll look in at Bart's tonight, and reassure Mrs R. that all is shipshape and that you helped me. I know she'll be fretting about that hanging curtain. Nothing to do but lie there and fret. I shouldn't fret if it were me, but, then, I can never take household affairs very seriously.' They went out into the mournful grey day, somehow exhilarated.

27

When he called at the hospital next day, he found his mother sitting in a chair with his father beside her. It was about two o'clock, and Toby guessed that the shop had a 'closed' sign up.

'If my back didn't hurt so much, I'd feel thoroughly spoiled,' said Mrs Roberts, trying to smile. 'Look what I've got from Mrs Ferrars,' she said, and displayed a book of French Impressionist painters, the plates large and finely produced. 'I can look at that when I can't read anything,' she said. 'It was ever so kind of her.'

'You deserve spoiling,' said Mr Roberts, 'that you do.'

'Just turn and look what's on the wall.' Both men did so, and found that where a seascape had been hanging was a reproduction of her schoolchildren coming home for lunch. They exclaimed. 'You can't guess how funny it was. There's a nice woman who calls once a week, and gives everybody a chance to choose. She had a big – portfolio, is it? – with her, and among the pictures I found mine. She seemed to know about me, because she said, "Oh, we must have that." So there it is.'

'It looks fine,' said Toby. 'Now, tell us how you are, apart from the back.'

'They're going to do another X-ray this afternoon, bother them. I hate riding in those hard wheel-chairs, and then having to wait. I don't know how I shall stand it.'

This was heard by a nurse, who stopped and said, 'We might get you a stretcher, Mrs Roberts. Not to worry.'

'Everyone tells me that.'

'Can you walk at all, Dora?'

'I can walk to the toilet. It hurts less when I stand up. Never mind about me. How are you getting on, Stan?'

He said that he was getting on fine, that the girls had been doing great work and that Blackie missed her.

She told him he must stroke the cat and have him on his lap when he came home from work. Was her husband being fed all right?

'Like a fighting cock,' he said. 'Ann brings things her Mary makes, and very good they are, but Maisie cooks herself.'

'I hope they're both keeping my kitchen tidy.'

'As a new pin. Everything's as you'd like to see it.'

She seemed satisfied. Toby thought it odd that she did not mention going home, but seemed to have settled down. He thought she must know how hard the work of the house would seem to her, until the pain had subsided.

He commented gingerly on this and she replied, 'Oh, I'm all right here for the moment.'

Mr Roberts said, 'But it's lonely without you, Dora. Get well soon.'

'It's nice to be missed. Are you taking your tablets?' She had herself started him on a course of Vitamin C.

'Every day, cross my heart and hope to die.'

'You don't have to die. You'd better both get going now, because the stretcher may be coming at any moment, and I don't want you to see me looking like the Lady of Shalott.' Toby laughed; he liked his mother's rare literary references.

They both got up to go, and both kissed her, Mrs Roberts lifting her thin small face as though she could not really be bothered. 'The other patients are quite nice,' she said, 'so I can't be lonely myself.'

232

When they were out in the street, Mr Roberts said, 'I don't like that back of hers. They ought to do something about it beside pills.'

'She seems to be getting plenty of attention. I liked the way they hung her own picture. I expect the nurses told everyone she'd painted it.'

His father said, 'Have you got your car? Could you give me a lift? I hate to leave the shop for too long. You hear such things about burgling.'

Toby said that, barring unusual pressure of traffic, he could get him home in ten minutes. The secret planner, who never lets its owner know what it is thinking, stirred in him.

It was Maisie's day to work in the house. 'Drop me off at the shop,' said Mr Roberts, 'and then you can cut away.'

Toby found Maisie in a white nylon overall, zealously mopping the kitchen floor. 'Hullo, Cinderella,' he said and took the mop from her.

'What are you doing? I've no time to play. The oven's got to be cleaned before I do any more cooking.'

He kissed her, and to his delight she responded, though only to draw away a second later.

'No, Toby. None of that.'

'You know I haven't stopped caring for you.'

'If you do care for me, you'll let me get back to my work.'

'And you care for me, just a little. Now, don't you?' He lifted her suddenly and sat her on the kitchen table. She was so little and so light.

'Jump me down,' she ordered him. 'You know you've got no right to speak to me as you do. It isn't fair to Ann. We shall go on being friends, Toby, but nothing more, nothing ever.'

'You can't stop me from loving you a little.'

233

'But I can stop you saying so.' She jumped down by herself and took up the mop. Toby promptly took it away again.

'You'll drive me out of here,' she said steadily.

'Remember that night at Haddesdon? And when we first went to Paris? There were black crabs on the wallpaper.'

She seemed on the verge of tears. She said, 'I remember that I loved Edward.'

'I shall never forget when he told me you were going to marry him. I was quite broken up.'

'Nothing will ever break you. You're not made that way.'

He watched her as she abandoned the kitchen floor and began to lay the table. 'You think I'm being disloyal to Ann,' he said, 'but I'm not really. It will always be Ann and me, I suppose. But I want you, too.'

'That's detestable. I'm angry with you, Toby, and I want you to go away.'

'I can't help the way I feel.'

'Oh, yes, you can, if you try. Now will you go?'

'I suppose so. But let me kiss you once more.'

She wavered. 'Then only once.'

When he had kissed her — and this time she did not respond — he did not at once let her go. Neither of them heard the key in the lock.

'Playing house?' said Ann.

'I only looked in when I'd taken Dad back to the shop.'

Ann sat down. The cat leaped at once upon her lap and began to make dough.

'Come to that,' said Toby boldly, 'what are you doing here?'

'Mrs R. asked me to look for her second pair of glasses. Which is what I shall do, and then you can drive me home.' She looked hard at Maisie, who was red in the face. 'I don't ask you what you and Toby have been doing,' she said, 'only to say that I can guess and that it hurts. I have become a jealous woman, Maisie, so you'd better keep out of my way for a time.'

She rose, and looked in the kitchen drawer for the glasses, which were not there. She then went into the parlour, and in a moment or two came back to them. 'Come on, Toby.'

Maisie said nothing, and looked the picture of guilt.

'All right,' he said, and to Maisie, 'Good-bye.'

In the car with Ann he said, 'You're barking up the wrong tree.'

'And which is the right tree? Surely not Claire?'

'I meant that there's nothing in what you say. Surely you can trust me?'

'And why should I?'

'Because I tell you to. I only went there through chance, and I'd even forgotten it was Maisie's day. We were just playing around.'

'I resent you playing around. I may be too old for you—'

'Don't say that.'

'I shall say what I please. But if you're going to amuse yourself elsewhere I shall divorce you.'

'Darling!' said Toby, genuinely shocked. He thought of the problems of a divorce, how it would upset the boys, and of the dividing of property. He thought of the disapproval of the Llangains and the Baumanns. It all sickened him.

So he assured her that he loved her, that Maisie was quite innocent of offence, and so was he. Then he said, 'You don't mean that.'

'No, I don't. I shouldn't make it that easy for you.'

'You're making an enormous mountain out of a molehill.'

He looked at her. Anger made her look older and plainer. 'I don't think I am.'

235

They had reached the house. She got out and went inside, and Toby, when he had put the car away, followed her.

She was standing, still in her outdoor clothes, in the middle of the sitting-room. Her fists were clenched.

'Don't make yourself miserable over nothing,' Toby said. 'I was only teasing Maisie a bit, that was all. She was annoyed, if that's any consolation to you.'

'So you weren't entirely blameless.'

'If you think teasing Maisie is significant, then perhaps I'm not. And I love you. And if you don't unbend you'll get stuck like it.'

All at once her rigidity left her. He put his arms round her and she cried on his shoulder. Tears were so rare with Ann that he was alarmed. 'Quiet, pet. All over now, and nothing to cry about. Do you believe me?'

'I must believe you, or I couldn't bear it. Oh dear, and I am not a crying woman.'

'You've been a very silly one. I hate to see you in tears, though they rather become you.'

She smiled weakly, slipped off her coat and sat at his side. 'Now kiss me,' he said, 'and don't let's have any more scenes like this. They don't suit us.'

Indeed, he had thought they were both a perfectly balanced, rather cool, couple. That image had now been destroyed.

They were not pleased to be called on by Percy Clover, who seemed to have forgotten any offence he had ever given.

'Hullo, Percy,' Ann said, 'we haven't seen you for some time.'

'Hullo, my girl. Why, what's the matter? I sense thunder in the air.' His nose twitched. 'Oh, yes I do. Don't put me off.'

236

'Percy,' said Ann, without much inflection, 'if there's been any thunder, it's our thunder. It's over now, though. Have a drink.'

He said to Toby, in a jocular tone, 'Mind you treat this girl right, or, I've told you, you'll have me to reckon with.'

'Do mind your own business,' said Ann, 'or I shall have to ask you to go away.'

'Sorry, sorry, I barge in, I know.' He accepted the drink and drained it at once. 'There, I'm a good boy now.'

'Then stay good,' she said. She went upstairs to erase the ravages of her tears. Toby looked at the Colonel. 'You really mustn't butt in, you know. Ann and I were having a commonplace domestic scrap, if that will satisfy you.'

'I suppose it must. But I've kept an eye on her ever since she was a young thing. She's just a girl to me now. She and Mike never fought.'

'Change the subject. Ann's coming down.'

She came, face freshly powdered, as much like the Princess Lieven as ever, Toby thought, and he marvelled at her control over herself. She began to tell Percy about her mother-in-law; he, at least, had not heard the news, nor did it seem much to concern him. Still, her story served to pass the time until he said that he must go. 'See you soon,' he said, and kissed her. He patted Toby's shoulder. 'Expect you think I'm an old limpet,' he said rather surprisingly. That was exactly what Toby did think.

Clover went off, straight-backed, jaunty, and when he had gone Ann began spontaneously to laugh. 'Oh dear,' she said, 'it is really dreadful to be caught out, and especially by Percy.'

'I wish you could get rid of the man for good and all, though.'

'I've tried, I've tried, I've truly tried. But it's like the cat who always comes back. He's getting very old now, and I

237

rather hate to spoil one of his few pleasures, which is — I have to say it — seeing me.' She rested her head on his shoulder and he put an arm round her.

'I can see that's a pleasure,' he said, 'but I wish he didn't also come to lecture me. I'm too old for that sort of thing.'

'I do love you,' she said. 'That's why I behave so badly.'

'Since your behaviour is perfect most of the time, I think I can allow you a small lapse.' He knew that, by her outburst of tears, she had delivered herself into his hands. If anyone felt guilty now, she did.

She clung to him that night as if it were the first time they had slept together. In the dim light of the lamp she looked at him wide-eyed. He thought that, as they would inevitably stay together, he must put all idea of Maisie out of his head. In any case, it had all been a fantasy. She had indeed been fond of him, but not enough to be a party to wreckage. And at the thought of wreckage Toby shuddered. He must put the whole of the Cambridge dream, Haddesdon dream, Paris dream, behind him, and for ever. Ann had gone to sleep with her head on his chest, which was very uncomfortable. After a while he gently removed her, and returned to his own bed.

28

They were at breakfast next morning when the doctor telephoned to Toby from Bart's. His mother was not so well. She had had a very slight stroke and, though he expected she would recover almost entirely, would like to see her son.

'Shall I go with you, too?' said Ann. 'But, of course, it's my day in SE1.'

'I'd better go alone. I'll ring Dad.'

When he arrived at the hospital Mrs Roberts was back in bed, looking frightened. Her mouth was twisted, and he had difficulty in making out what she was saying. 'My right hand,' he managed to hear, 'it won't work. I shall never paint again.'

'Of course you will,' he told her, trying to sound confident. 'I swear that you will.'

Mr Roberts arrived, looking even more scared than his wife. The doctor came, and spoke to them both. 'Listen, this is very slight. Her mouth will be all right in no time and she'll be able to speak properly. Perhaps her hand will be weak for a while. Of course, this was entirely an unexpected development. It happened in her sleep.'

'Are you talking about me?' Mrs Roberts said drowsily.

'Yes, giving you lots of hope when you've got over all this.'

'Shall I be able to paint?'

'I don't see why not,' said the doctor. 'Cheer up.'

He called the nurse. 'And we won't make her get up today, as she may be shaky, but tomorrow she'll be back in her chair.' He said to Toby, 'Ring up here as often as you like, if you're anxious. But I'm sure there's no need to be.'

'Fool,' mumbled Mrs Roberts when he had gone. 'I know a bit about myself.' She looked at them both, her small, once bright eyes dulled. 'But don't you two go worrying.'

'What?'

'Worrying,' she said with difficulty. 'Just see your dad's looked after.' She added, 'I can't talk anymore.'

'Is there anything you'd like brought in, Dora?' asked her husband.

'No. What should I want?' And she turned her back to the wall so that they would not see that she was crying.

Both of them came back on the evening of that day, and so did Ann. Mrs Roberts was now sitting up against the pillows, wearing her best Viyella nightgown. A nurse had put her hair into the little bun, and it seemed to them that the slight distortion of her mouth was disappearing. Her speech was still affected, though when they took her hand in theirs it seemed to respond by a slight pressure.

She managed to say 'Thank you,' to Ann – or, rather, mouthed it – and to Toby and her husband, 'All right. Better now.'

But, since communication was difficult and a strain on her, Toby offered to read her the newspaper. She nodded, and slipped down in the pillows. After about a quarter of an hour, she indicated that he should stop. She seemed very tired. With eyes half-closed she murmured something to Toby, which sounded like 'Don't let them turn me.'

'Turn you?' Toby asked, thinking this was some hospital routine. 'No, we won't let them.'

She shook her head. Ann leaned over her. 'What was that, Mrs R., dear?'

The reply was whispered. Ann looked puzzled, then said, as Toby had, 'No, of course we won't let them.'

Mrs Roberts looked satisfied. Her eyes closed. After a few moments Toby said, 'She's asleep. We'd better go.'

Ann stopped to kiss her, and so did Toby and her husband. They made their way out of the bright bustle of the ward, and met the doctor half-way down the passage. He stopped to talk to them. 'I'm sure she's better, though this has been a shock to her. She worries about her hand. I gather that she paints.'

'She's quite a well-known painter,' said Ann. 'It would be dreadful to her if she really lost the use of her right hand.'

'Is she? That's interesting. I don't keep up much with these things.'

'She's sleeping now,' said Mr Roberts, obviously as a warning not to awaken her. 'She said something about "don't turn me".'

The doctor frowned. 'I expect she meant, don't turn me and wake me up.'

'It wasn't that,' Ann said, 'but I don't know what it could have been.'

'Well, leave her to us. We'll do nothing she doesn't like.'

They drove Mr Roberts back to the shop. On the way he said, 'I don't like the look of her.'

'She had a fair colour,' said Toby, 'more than yesterday.'

As his father got out of the car, he saw Maisie just up the street, with a shopping-basket. She went into the house.

It was not until they were at home that Ann said, 'I think I knew what Mrs R. meant. She said, "Don't let them burn me."'

'And what did that mean?'

'I have an idea, but I'm afraid of upsetting you. She may have been thinking about death. Has she ever expressed a fear of cremation?'

He was appalled and shocked. 'I don't know. But she

isn't going to die, and she's going to get the strength in that hand back again. I know it. And she couldn't have said what you think.'

Ann said, 'I think it was. I wondered first if it meant anything they'd done to her in hospital which she associated with burning. Then I realised that that was absurd. I do love your mother, Toby, though she's luke-warm about me.'

'I'll go back again tomorrow,' Toby said. 'God, but I hate hospitals. The smell of disinfectant, the bustle of it all. I've never been in one myself.'

They were not long in suspense. On the following morning the doctor telephoned and broke the news. Mrs Roberts had had another stroke, a massive one – and was dead.

In the black days that followed, Toby was stunned with grief. He had never thought, when his mother went, that he could ever feel anything like this. His father looked lost and bewildered. It was Ann who took charge of all the funeral arrangements. It was to be private, family flowers only. A memorial service to be held later.

It was she who had told of the death to Maisie. It seemed to have healed the breach between them immediately.

'Don't cry,' said Ann. 'She'd have hated that.' When she hung up she said, 'It's quite extraordinary how we always seem to know what the dead want. Toby, we must start to make plans about permanent help for your father. I'd ask him to stay here, but now the shop and the house are all his life. We must get a good woman in who will stay all day. We'd better advertise.'

As it happened, the advertisement was answered in an astonishing fashion. Mrs Cassell, their next-door neighbour with whom Dora had never been intimate, called upon Mr Roberts that night. She was at a loose end (he told Toby later) after her husband died and had nothing to do with herself all day. She was a good-looking, cheerful woman, with clear blue eyes. She would come in to wash up the breakfast things, clean, shop, prepare his lunch-time sandwiches, go back home for a couple of hours, then come back to get his supper at six o'clock and wash it up. Did he think she would do?

Mr Roberts said he was sure she would, and his face cleared with relief. It was something to have someone whom he knew, however slightly.

On the following day was the funeral, in the small cemetery near St Joseph's Church, in which Mrs Roberts had never set foot. Mr Roberts, Ann and Toby followed in a black Daimler. They had agreed not to wear mourning, which they did know Mrs Roberts had hated, but Ann was in grey. The day was fine, and as they went through the streets Toby stared dully at the girls in jeans, the men with long hair, both as a rule wearing a cross or beads. Ann and Toby had bought red roses, and for Mr Roberts a bunch of lilies of the valley and parma violets.

Toby held back tears. His imagination was morbid.

He could see the little body in its Viyella nightdress lying beneath the earth, and slowly rotting. To worms, to a skeleton, and then to dust.

He could not get warm.

That evening, Ann telephoned Maisie and asked her to come round. Toby saw her with pleasure, the first he had felt all that day, but without any troubling of the heart. She was in black, not funereal black, but black nevertheless. She had brought them a bunch of tiger-lilies. 'I know it said only family flowers, but I've got these for you.'

Ann kissed her. 'That was kind.'

'I was thinking about you both today.'

'We bore up pretty well,' Toby said, 'but my poor dad looked so lost. By the way, we've got an excellent woman to

243

be with him, so your chores can cease. And thank you a hundred times.'

They were having a simple slab put on the grave, nothing upstanding. They wondered what to put on it.

The three of them discussed the matter, as if in some macabre parlour-game, but it diverted them from other thoughts. Suppose, Toby had thought, Amanda had suggested as a game the composing of epitaphs?

It was Maisie who had the final idea, though she put it to them diffidently.

Dora Roberts

PAINTER

1903–1965

'I think that's a good idea. I'm sure Mrs R. would have approved of that,' said Ann. 'What do you think, Toby?'

'I think it's a good idea, too. Thank you, Maisie.'

Then they discussed plans for a memorial service, to be held a month later, at some central place. 'I think there will be a crowd,' Maisie said. 'I hope so.'

'I don't know how I'm going to go through with that,' Toby said. 'I feel I've had enough.'

'I can make the arrangements,' said Ann efficiently. 'You don't know her favourite hymns?'

'She hadn't any. She never went to church.'

Maisie made a sound half-way between a giggle and a sound of distress. He thought of her at Haddesdon, with a small crowd at his mother's feet. That had been a magnificent day, the great cedar multi-green in the light. But it was not of Maisie, for once, that he was thinking. All that was over, and she knew it. He wondered what her own feelings were for him, and thought that if she had any she would always keep them under control. Edward's ghost was much

244

with her.

The women talked as though there had never been a rift between them, Maisie without shyness, Ann confident.

Toby believed that Ann had lost every vestige of suspicion. He watched her busily making notes, her dark hair glittering beneath Maisie's green lamp.

'It's very important', she said, 'that the service shouldn't be mournful.'

'What about St Martin-in-the-Fields?' Maisie asked.

'Very nice, if they'll let us. I'm not up in these things really, but I'm going to be.'

'I wish I were with my father tonight,' Toby said, 'but he specially asked to be left alone. He's made too much of an effort today to make more. And he's attached to the house and shop.'

This was meant as an explanation should Maisie query his presence. But obviously she did not.

'There was that song, wasn't there?' Maisie said. ' "They that found out musical tunes And recited verses in writing"?'

'It might be a good idea,' said Toby, somewhat refreshed. 'There's nothing in the Bible about artists, is there?'

'We might have a lesson from St Luke,' Ann suggested. 'He was supposed to have painted.'

So they went on, in the bright room, the walls white and the pictures looking down. Toby now found the source of his refreshment. It was because his life with Ann had settled him, and he no longer had hankerings after Maisie. It was odd that his mother's death should have brought this about. His morbid thoughts of her had left him, too, and he could only see her in the bedroom, painting away between the two chairs. And he saw her at her first private view in Cambridge, sitting sedately on a chair fetched for her by Edward, looking well in her blue dress and coat which

Maisie had bought for her. Suddenly he felt very tired.

'I'm going up to bed,' he said. 'Don't bother about me.'

Maisie jumped up. He kissed her cheek. 'Good-bye, Maisie dear, and thank you for all you've done.'

'It was nothing,' she said. 'Nothing.'

Nothing. No quickening of the pulse.

Ann came up to bed within half an hour. 'I'm rather tired, too. I thought I'd find you asleep.'

'Too many thoughts, pet.' He might have been speaking to Maisie, but was not.

'I'll give you a Seconal,' she said.

He thanked her. 'It's been a long day.'

'Poor Maisie is as upset as anyone. I thought we could take her out of herself. She deserves it.'

'And her chores are over, and so are yours. Mrs Cassell comes in tomorrow. Thank God, Dad's able to afford her. Did I tell you about the will? All her money to Dad, all her paintings to me. But there won't be many unsold.'

He drifted into a dreamless sleep.

Christmas was hard on him that year, because he could not feel festive. Ann was, however, 'making a Christmas for the boys', with a lighted tree, and holly disposed about the walls. 'They're too young', she said, 'to have the Christmas I should like, which is none. I might appreciate it more if it came every five years, and didn't burden us every year. Expense and hard work, that's what it is. And I hate cooking a turkey.' Mary was off to her own home for the long holiday.

The boys duly came back, both of them taller. 'I'm so sorry about your mother,' said Tim, on a kind of gasp, as if he had been practising this all the way home. 'I'm sorry, too,' said Sam, 'awfully.' He was now in long trousers.

Toby told them they were both kind, and that his mother would have liked them both. As it was, they had never met

246

her.

Christmas Eve came. The boys were sent early to bed. Ann piling presents around the tree. Then the turkey, which she had managed to undercook so that it had to be sent back to the oven. Then the Christmas cake which was too rich fare after the luncheon pudding but which both the boys wolfed. Then, quietly and blessedly, a spell of television while Tim and Sam played with one of their presents, a game of L'Attaque.

29

The New Year brought bad news from Adrian. Ruth had miscarried – 'through riding that bicycle once too often,' he wrote, adding that the doctor had recommended it for her rather than standing in bus-queues. Adrian was down-hearted, though the doctor assured him that there would be other children. 'But I'd hoped for one of my own *now*, and I don't feel stoical in the sight of God.'

'Poor dear,' Ann said, 'it's very sad. And I wanted to see whether that wonderful face would appear on another generation.'

The memorial service was indeed held in St Martin's. Toby had dreaded a poor attendance, though his mother had rated a third of a column in *The Times*. But the big church was three-quarters full, despite the lashing rain outside. Everyone he knew seemed to be there. Maisie, of course, smiling at him beneath the brim of her wide blue hat. The Llangains. Claire and Alec. Two dealers, and the owner of the Cambridge gallery, Mr Driffield. Amanda, of course, not even in suggested mourning, but upright and gipsified, was wearing a soaring hat of yellow felt. Who else? Everybody. He could not keep count. He sat with his father at the front of the church, noticing that, despite Mrs Roberts's prohibition, he was wearing a black armlet and tie. Well, if it made him comfortable it could not annoy her. The voluntary: 'Jesu, Joy of Man's Desiring.' The church struck cold, though they had the central heating on. Hymn: 'Immortal, invisible.' Prayers, Collect. A reading from St

Luke, whom, the vicar reminded them, was said to have painted the Virgin Mary. Anthem: 'Let us now praise famous men', apparently according to Maisie's suggestion, but which he thought unfortunate. His mother would have shrunk to describe herself as famous, and she was not a man. Address by the novelist, Peter Coxon, one of Amanda's finds and an admirer of Mrs Roberts. Today he had discarded his bow-tie, and wore a long one striped with blue and silver. He had put off his small affectations, and spoke audibly, briefly, and to the point. As the service drew to its close, Toby realised that he and his father would have to greet people at the door. His father would not like that, not at all. Voluntary (outgoing): the third movement of the Fourth Brandenburg Concerto.

Then out into the porch, sheltered from the rough wind and rain, and the greetings.

'It was beautiful,' said Claire to Toby, 'simply beautiful. She'd have adored it.'

Since Mrs Roberts had not been to church since she was twenty, Toby wondered how Claire knew. 'Fine,' said Alec. 'Beautiful,' said Moira Llangain, who had previously fortified herself for the event, 'simply beautiful. God bless you.'

Maisie said nothing, but gripped his hand for a moment and then was lost in the streets black with umbrellas. He would see her again, but never the same again. Lovely Maisie.

Toby vaguely shook a hundred hands and saw his father doing the same.

'She'd have liked all this, eh?' said Mr Roberts. Toby observed that it would have made her shy. At last, the thanks to the vicar and the organist. All over. He felt warm to his father, who had carried it off well. Since his wife's death, Mr Roberts had seemed far more secure. He must have leaned on her a great deal, and now Toby wondered whether he was leaning on Mrs Cassell. Toby invited him to lunch, but he said, 'Not today, son. I've got to get back to the shop.'

There were several journalists present, with whom Toby found it quite easy to cope. At last he was able to say to Ann, 'Home.' But there was a couple still waiting for them: Peter Coxon, with his delicate snake-like head and oval eyes, and Amanda, with her yellow hat flaring against the greyness of the square, where the fountains were blown sideways and the pigeons had gone to roost out of the wind and the rain.

Toby congratulated Peter on his address and thanked him warmly. 'I knew he would do it beautifully,' said Amanda, 'and I was right. It was a wonderful service.'

'Ann planned it really. She and Maisie.'

'How pleased your dear mother would have been!' Amanda nearly mimicked herself. Toby doubted it. He thought his mother would have been far from pleased at 'such a fuss'.

'Now, then, Mr Roberts, Toby, Ann, you must all come and have lunch with me. After all, we have just given thanks for your mother's life, so there's no need to be sad. I've got a car coming in a minute.'

Mr Roberts said no, and thanked her. He said again that he had to look after the shop. Toby and Ann said they were very sorry, but that they had to go home.

'What a pity! Have you got your car, or shall I run you back in mine? It wouldn't take ten minutes.'

For this they thanked her. They were otherwise going to look for a taxi in the rain and slush. The car came round, chauffeur-driven.

'Now I shall go abroad for a month,' Amanda said. 'I put it off because I didn't want to miss Mrs Roberts's memorial service. The wind and the rain get through to my bones here.'

Toby wondered how they would get through, for Amanda, still comely, was putting on weight. Peter, who was silent, fiddled with his tie. Ann asked him if he were writing. Yes, he said, he had another novel half-way finished.

'And the critics will love you as usual,' Amanda said.

Peter said he always fancied novelists in an enclosure for sacred cows. Some had only just got in, and there was a man with a stick outside always ready to drive them out. The most established had bells round their necks, and the most sacred of all had their bells growing into the grass.

'I'm in the enclosure,' he said, 'at last. But only just inside the gate. The man with a stick may be waiting for me. It needs only one hatchet job.'

They laughed at this conception. But Amanda said, 'Nonsense, Peter. I have known novelists survive many a hatchet job. Well, here we are. I'm so glad to have had you to myself even if only for a few minutes.' Toby never saw her again, for she died in Marrakesh later that year.

He and Ann were relieved to be alone indoors. 'Do *you* think she'd have liked it?' he asked her.

'Mrs R.? Isn't it hard to tell? She'd probably have wondered what the bother and the singing were all about.'

'She'd have liked Peter's address, though. Very short, very apposite.' He was feeling close to Ann – more so, perhaps, than any time since their marriage. Her display of weakness had strengthened his feeling for her, and he no longer resented even the time she spent at her dressing-table. It was true that he had noticed the slight puckering under her chin and had found her pulling out a grey hair. Before, he had been cowed by his own comparative youth, hating her to assume a maternal rôle. Well, that was all over; it had to be. He was especially tender with her these days. They saw Maisie often, but no shadow was there.

Claire and Alec came to visit them, and so did Hairy and Anneliese, bringing the baby in a carry-cot and stowing it away under the piano that was never played. 'I don't think I want anything more out of this life,' Hairy said. He knelt, and held the baby's finger. He was in civilian clothes, which made him look less trim.

'He's such a good little boy,' Claire said. 'He hardly ever yells.'

'And what should he yell for?' said Anneliese, smiling. 'He has the best of everything. Plenty of food, plenty of love. And he gets fed on demand.'

'Our two were quiet babies,' said Alec. 'But I hear from her mother that Claire was not. Nor is she now.'

'Come off it, Alec. You're making an ass of yourself, not me.'

Claire knelt down by the baby, and Hairy got up, stretching himself. 'I have given much satisfaction to my parents, and it's probably few sons who can say that.'

'That's true,' Claire said. 'I'm glad I've got Alec, or I'd be left right out in the cold. Hullo, little Heir. We won't call you Hairy. You'll always be Rhisiart to us.'

'I'm glad of that,' said Anneliese, in her none too fluent English. Toby thought what a pretty girl she was, with her ballet-dancer's hair-style, and her balletic grace. Hairy had done well for himself.

It was a Sunday morning and they had all gathered before going back to their respective luncheons. The baby started to cry.

'Ruining your reputation, my lad,' said Hairy.

'He thinks it is his dinner-time, and so it had better be,' said Anneliese. 'May I take him somewhere to feed him?'

Ann said she would take her up to her bedroom. The

baby was taken, dripping wet, out of the cot, while Anneliese took up a clean napkin she had brought with her. 'He will not be ten minutes,' she said, undoing the top button of her dress as she went.

'Yes, I'll have another Scotch,' said Hairy. 'I feel like celebrating every day. Of course, I'd have been as pleased —'

'Liar,' said Claire.

' — if it had been a girl, but the parents wouldn't have been so joyful. Really, they behave as if we were a royal house.'

'Agreed,' said Claire. 'As I told Toby once, they are terrible snobs, but he wouldn't believe me.'

'Having had such luck through Lord Llangain,' Toby retorted, 'I only care to think the best of him. So do you, really.'

'Of course,' she said, 'but I don't like to let it show.'

In ten minutes precisely, Anneliese came back with her sated son, who promptly went to sleep again. She wrapped the soiled towel in paper and tucked it in at his feet. 'Better go now,' she said, taking up the cot. Toby leaned over it; the usual baby smell, milky, slightly faecal. He felt a twinge of envy; this was never to be his. He had, in fact, half-hoped that despite her age Ann would conceive, but the months went by and she never did.

When they had all gone, he sat down with Ann to lunch. It was perfectly satisfactory, his life, or he would make it so. A well-laid table, a well-cooked meal and a handsome woman to preside over it. What more could a man want? If there were dissatisfactions stirring somewhere in his soul, he was scarcely aware of them, or else thought they were a manifestation of indigestion. Toby always preferred the material to the metaphysical. Now he was going to care for Ann all his days, with no more yearning for the Maisies of this world. As if there were one more Maisie in this world!

He felt pure and unscathed, and he enjoyed his roast beef.

In February came the good news for which he had waited. He was offered a junior partnership, with a commensurate salary. He came home to Ann in fine fettle. 'This is something like it!'

'Oh, dear Mrs R.! How thrilled she would have been.'

'I doubt it.'

'You know you always said she thought of you spitting on your finger to count dirty pound-notes.'

'That idea would have been hard for her to dispel.'

'Really, darling, I am so proud of you. I always knew you'd make it.'

But was there anything else to make? He had gone up one step, perhaps two, on the stairs of his life. And the restlessness which was like indigestion moved in him.

Claire telephoned to congratulate him; she had, of course, heard the news from her father.

'Wonderful, ducky!' she exclaimed. 'Now you're a great man. Alec sends his congratulations, too. Did you know this was coming to you?'

'I had a faint idea, but it was only faint. And a faint hope.'

'Daddy's awfully pleased with you. He says you're really on top of the job. Mummy is having an extra vodka in celebration. Is Ann happy? I'm sure she is. Give her our love.'

It occurred to him that Claire was the only one who had not suffered in the least from the past. He remembered, all those years ago, when she had sat up in bed with him and drunk wine. And how she had rejected him. Painful for him, for at least a while, but not for her. She simply went her way, taking all things as they came. He had never known such a clear-minded woman, but now he was glad that she had not accepted him. Fairly high-spirited himself, he believed her own leaping spirits would have been too much for him. But she could have given him children. Still, the lack of them was Toby's own fault. He had married Ann in the knowledge that it was unlikely.

They went out, well wrapped up, to walk in the Royal Hospital Gardens. Hardy Chelsea Pensioners sat around smoking their pipes and children played tag across the grass, with their mothers or nurses keeping a weather eye on them. The trees were bare, apart from a few evergreens. They paused for a while over the map and the memorial tablet. This had been Ranelagh, scene of eighteenth-century revels.

'I wish I'd known it then,' Ann said. 'I always feel I was designed for the eighteenth-century.'

'And so you were. I can imagine you here, taking part in the dancing.' He took her hand and held it for a moment. 'With beaux all round you.'

'Poor Percy,' she said, 'I expect he'd have been the only beau.'

'Poor Percy nothing. That was your mistake.'

'To encourage him? But I hadn't the heart to get rid of him.'

They walked on. She spied a clump of snowdrops in one of the beds and said, 'Spring, believe it or not, is coming.'

But the winter's evening was fast closing down, and the few birds had gone to bed. 'My hero,' she said sardonically, but Toby knew that in part she meant it. His spirits flagged a little. How was he going to keep up the business of being a hero?

'I suppose I'd better tell my dad the news, though God only knows what he'll make of it.'

'You underrate your father.'

'"Must see to the shop". How many times have I heard that? But he doesn't seem unhappy.'

They walked home under the lights of Royal Hospital

255

Road. It was a longish walk, and they were chilled when they got in.

30

Dinner at Baumann's. A celebration. Toby tied his tie in a glass placed at precisely the right height. All things were right in Ann's house. She was wearing another white dress and the double string of pearls that he had bought her for her birthday. Cultured, of course, but expensive enough. The zircon flashed on her hand as she raised it to comb her hair. He felt proud of her, as he always did when he took her out. She could still make heads turn, and this put him into good conceit with himself.

He kissed the nape of her neck. 'Nice,' she said.

At Baumann's, the same brown drawing-room and the picture-lights. Clarissa greeted both Ann and Toby with a kiss. 'I must add my congratulations!' she said. Toby could think of nothing modest to say, so he simply thanked her. 'This is a very small party, just the people you know. To celebrate your promotion.'

Plump, smiling, she said, 'You're the first. We wanted you to be.'

The next arrivals were Claire and Alec, then the Llangains. Hairy without Anneliese — she could not leave the baby, who had a slight cough.

'Have you called the doctor?' said Llangain, his hair seeming to stand on end with anxiety.

'It's nothing to fuss about,' Hairy told him. 'Of course we will if it gets any worse.'

'Then mind you do,' said Moira, who had been drinking before she came. 'You can't be too careful.'

'I think you can leave it to Anneliese,' Claire put in. 'And, Mummy, you're not to fuss.'

'Beautiful child,' said Alec. 'Bigger than ours at that early stage.' He added, 'I love children.' It was true. He was a devoted father.

The next person to arrive was Maisie.

Toby started. Why was she here? He imagined that Claire, who knew nothing of recent troubles, had asked Clive Baumann to invite her. He and Clarissa greeted her eagerly. 'We've heard such a lot about you from Claire,' Clarissa said.

She was wearing dark blue and her hair was cut quite short, though not short enough to prevent it curling on her forehead, glistening as though she had just been under a shower. Why had she accepted this invitation? Toby asked himself.

She came forward gaily to offer him her congratulations, kissed him and Ann, Claire and Alec, the Llangains. She had a new, light, almost a dancing, step.

In the dawn, Toby had awakened from a nightmare. He was passing between the privets to his old home, *in deadly dread of his mother*. Before he could put his key in the lock she opened the door to greet him. She was wearing an apron and the small blue hat Maisie had helped her to buy for her first exhibition. She beckoned him, smiling but saying nothing, upstairs to the bedroom. There were two pictures by the wall, each covered by a towel. She asked him if he would like to see two portraits. Then she uncovered the one. Maisie, she said. The canvas was blank but for the outline of a curling smile. Now for you. I hope you'll like it. She twitched away the second towel. No smile here. The canvas was quite blank. That's you, she said. And she began to laugh, as she had never done in her lifetime, silently, uncontrollably. Shall I give it you for a present?

He had awakened, sweating. Why should the mother to whom he had been devoted appear to him in the guise of a tormentor? To dream such a thing seemed an insult to her. For a long while he feared to sleep again.

And now here he was, with Maisie smiling, knowing nothing of the dream canvas. She was talking to him. One of Edward's plays was to be revived by the National Theatre. He would have been so delighted. Toby asked her which one, and she replied, *The Hostess*. It was one of his very best, Ann suggested, and Claire and Alec concurred. Maisie said she was very happy about it.

'What's this?' asked Clarissa. 'Something else to celebrate?'

Toby's momentary black mood passed as the dream receded.

They sat down to dinner in the bright room, with the candles and chandeliers. This time there was no flower in a glass beside each place, but a small orchid with accompanying pin. 'How lovely!' said Ann, fastening hers to her dress. The other women followed suit, and the men put the flowers in their buttonholes.

'There's nothing much else this year,' said Clarissa. 'The shops are almost empty except for forced flowers which look wrong in February.'

They all drank to Toby with the first glass of wine, to Edward's memory with the second. Maisie's face clouded for a moment, but her smile soon returned. 'Not a third thing to celebrate?' asked Baumann. 'Things are said to run in threes.'

They disclaimed any third thing, but Toby thought that, if they only knew, his reconciliation with Ann would have been worth a glass. Claire was on one side of him, Moira Llangain on the other, and Maisie was opposite. 'Shall we tell them, Alec?' Claire shouted down the table.

'If you like.'

'We're expecting another, and we don't care what sex it is.'

'Then there was a third!' Baumann exclaimed, and glasses were refilled. 'This time, Alec and Claire.'

'Thank you,' Claire said, 'but it only seems toastworthy the first time. Maisie, how's Clemency?'

'Very well and very lively. It's all I can do to keep up with her. Thank Heavens there's that old-fashioned thing, a nanny.'

'I don't know what I'd do without ours,' said Claire. 'I'm longing to get them to day-school.'

Clarissa said, 'Clive and I never had any children, but I'm sure I'd have longed for a day-school if we had. I'm so physically lazy that I'd make a poor mother.'

'You lazy!' Moira protested, with the crumpled look about her mouth which accompanied drinking. 'You're always sitting on committees, and that *I* could not bear.'

'But that's a sedentary occupation,' Clarissa retorted, 'and it makes my figure spread.'

'May we drink to the memory of Mrs Roberts?' said Maisie, and Ann echoed her.

'In champagne,' said Claire, 'that's what you said she liked, Toby.'

'I didn't say she liked it, I said she had twice managed to drink half a glass. It was really against her principles, though she would never admit it. She said she couldn't bear the smell of alcohol.'

Alec sipped at his glass. 'She'd like the smell of this. Anyone would. What is it, Pommery?'

'Taittinger,' Baumann replied. 'I'm glad you like it. To the happy memory of Mrs Roberts, then!'

Toby thanked them. He said, 'Her remaining pictures are selling like hot cakes. Now, that would have pleased her.' The dream of the night was almost entirely dissipated. He felt on top of the world, free of Maisie (so far as he knew) and with the prospect of new worlds to conquer.

'Do you remember in Proust', said Alec, who was full of surprises in his quiet way, 'how the hostess – I forget her name – introduced Mme de Villemur, I think it was, to Detaille, because she said (though he hadn't) that he wanted to paint her neck? That isn't quite right, but nearly. She said it to get rid of a boring guest, of course, and leave her free to circulate. I'd want to paint Ann's.'

'You're not the first person to say that,' said Toby.

Ann looked down at her pearls, to seem shy.

The pheasant was followed by an ice-cream with a chestnut purée. Toby thought it was a long time since, an undergraduate at Cambridge, he had wondered what pheasant was like. Well, he had known since, at Haddesdon, Glemsford and elsewhere; even his mother, in the days of her prosperity, had cooked the bird with all accessories, only to be met with the comment from her husband that it smelled. It is a bit high, she had replied, but that's the way it ought to be. So eat it up, and don't be fussy. He had said Phew, but with a wry face had eaten it.

After dinner they returned to the drawing-room, not separating. The men drank port, the women brandy, with the exception of Moira who asked for another small drop of vodka. After a while Hairy thought he had better go home and see how things were.

'I shall go with you,' said Moira. She attempted to get up from the low sofa, but flopped back again.

'No, don't, Mother. You'll only bother Anneliese.'

She made another struggle to arise, and was pulled up by her son, as in some game of Nuts in May. She staggered backwards first, then regained her balance. 'I am the child's grandmother,' she announced magisterially, 'and of course I shall go.'

'Oh, chuck it, Mother,' Hairy said rudely. 'I'm not going to let you. I'll tell you what, though. When I get back I'll find out how things are and telephone you. You'll be here for the next half-hour, won't you?' he added to his father.

'If Clive will have us,' said Llangain. 'No, you go along, and we'll wait for news.'

The spell of the party had broken, with everyone listening for the telephone. Talk was no longer general. Maisie chatted soothingly to Moira, Ann to Clarissa, Alec to Clive. Some of the talk turned on Vietnam, and became slightly quarrelsome. At last the bell rang. The manservant came in. 'Mr Falls for Lady Llangain, madam.'

Moira went to answer it, weaving slightly as she went. She came back again jubilant. 'Ivor says it's quite all right. Rhisiart isn't coughing now and is sleeping soundly.'

Everyone expressed pleasure. 'And now,' Moira said, 'if I might have a tiny drop more vodka. I'm so relieved.' Toby noticed that this time she took a hard chair, and no risks. The spell re-exerted itself; it might have been a birthday party.

Maisie said to Ann, 'It's hard on Hairy having the usual infant worries, but if ever I saw a healthy child that is one. I remember when Clemency had bronchitis and it nearly drove Edward mad.'

'Didn't it drive you mad?' Toby asked curiously.

'I was anxious, of course, but I realised that with antibiotics she was going to get better. Which she did, after just one injection.'

The air of general relief was disproportionate to its subject. Llangain was saying to Alec that the war in Vietnam wouldn't last out the year, and Alec was saying mildly but firmly that he disagreed. 'It ought never to have been started. That's one thing for which we have to thank Kennedy.'

'But you'd let the Reds run South-East Asia?'

'It's the Vietnamese's country. They should have been left alone.'

'Ah, you're a dove, as they say,' said Llangain and let it alone.

'He's my own dove,' said Claire, 'and it's high time we went home.'

The Baumanns seemed to want to stop them. 'But it's early yet! You must all have another drink.'

'Not for me,' said Moira, stately, as if rebuking them. 'Your hospitality has been all too lavis – lavish.'

'Nor for me,' said Maisie. 'I must be going myself. It's been lovely, Mrs Baumann,' she said to Clarissa.

'Did you bring the car, Maisie?' said Ann. 'Because Toby and I could give you a lift.'

'Thank you very much, but I did bring it. Taxis are such a risk these days.'

'And so eshpensive,' said Moira. Her husband looked at her and, before she could struggle up for herself, lifted her gently from her chair and steadied her. Toby had never seen her really drunk before and, indeed, Claire had asserted that she never was. But it was something Llangain seemed to take in his stride.

'Are you staying the night in London?' Clarissa asked.

He said that they were. In fact, they had kept a house there for some years, at which Toby used to sleep with Claire. It occurred to him for the second time that he had slept with three women in that room, and the drink stirred him to a flash of Juanesque pride. 'And you come along,' he said to Ann.

'And don't look so beautiful next time,' said Clarissa, 'or I shall be eaten up with jealousy.'

'And that goes for you, too,' she added to Maisie, who flushed.

All said their good-byes. Moira was fairly steady now, and ignored her husband's arm. Toby looked at Maisie with an air which, though he did not realise it, was slightly proprietorial. Fortunately Ann was looking the other way.

Out of the house, out of the scents of flowers, drink and cooking, the night was cold and bright. Stars were even visible above the russet veil made by the London lights shining through pollution, and he thought he could make out the Great Bear.

'You'd better drive,' he said to Ann. 'You've had less to drink than I have. You'd pass a breath test.'

He was not in the least drunk but he cried out when she swerved to save a black shadow racking across their path, going into a skid and pulling as featly out of it. 'A poor pussy,' she said equably. 'I couldn't have killed him.'

'You nearly killed me, darling.'

'I'd like a pussy of our own, wouldn't you? An Abyssinian, I think. Shall I call at Harrods' pet-shop or watch the ads in *The Times*?'

'Whichever you please. But you'd better consult Mary and see what she says. She may be an ailurophobe.'

'A what?'

'A cat-hater. There are plenty about.'

'And I always say there must be something wrong with them.'

'There is. A phobia. But I'd rather like a cat myself, to purr at me when I come in of an evening.'

'Don't I do that?'

'Yes, but you're rather big for me to pick you up and scratch you behind your ears.'

'Let's mull over the evening when we get in. That's the nicest part of it all.'

He agreed.

She said, 'I hate to see Maisie going home again to a

house with only the child in it. I hope she'll marry again.'

'I hope so, too,' said Toby; but he was not quite sincere.

At home, they talked for more than an hour before Ann said that she was dropping with sleep. She would not have her usual shower, but would take off her make-up — she used little — and go straight to bed. Toby said he would follow.

In bed himself, he felt his sleepiness slipping away. He lay on his back in the dark, watching the reflected head-lamps sweeping the ceiling. Neither he nor Ann liked a totally dark room. His thoughts raced furiously. He felt almost scared to go to sleep lest he should encounter that vengeful mother in his dreams. Poor Mrs Roberts, to whom he had been so close and in whom, of very few people, he had confided. He had never been so badly shaken by a dream in his life. But from that his thoughts began to stray all over his past life. Early childhood near Epping Forest, the unexplained move to the house in SE1, his school days at a grammar school, scholarship to Cambridge. Discovery that his mother's paintings were worth attention, not merely an amusement for herself. His friends Bob and Adrian — Bob with tragedy behind him and a bright future before him, Adrian rubbing along somehow in his strag-gling parish. Maisie and Claire. His own attempt to become a historian, from which he had been saved by Llangain. Ann, and marriage. A fan of light swept the ceiling. He had been faithful to her in deed, if not altogether in thought or word. He would be faithful entirely now. His partnership, and a new office. A secretary of his own, a very plain girl with protruding teeth, which was a good thing. He would not be led into temptation.

'Going to buy a kitten,' said Ann, out of her sleep.

He wondered why his mother had shown him that hor-rible blank canvas. Had her ghost thought of him as a blank, with nothing written on his future? He went to the lavatory, and when he came back and was again settled in bed his thoughts became lighter. They would be truly domestic with a cat. He wondered whether Mrs Cassell was feeding Blackie properly, and, come to that, his father properly. It was not altogether inconceivable that he might some day marry her, so as not to be quite lonely. Yet he was an independent man, who had refused to accept a home with him and Ann. I'm not used to your kind of life, he had said. I'm happy where I am. And, of course, he had to mind the shop.

Considering his father, Toby marvelled at his own social rise. It was true that, when he was first at Cambridge, he had tried to seem grander than he was, until his pretensions were blown by his mother's unexpected publicity. It had been an eye-opener to him how much Maisie and Claire had liked the house in SE1 and had revelled in Mrs Roberts's groaning board. He had soon been drawn into their lives, and had eventually made a social place for himself. Between Hairy and himself there seemed now very little difference. Mike had left Ann with a good deal of money, so he really did not seem any poorer. A young man of his time, he thought, drawing new pictures from the swarming images of the night. They were blurred pictures, as though done in sepia with a dazzle around the edges. Soon he began to experience hypnogogic images, hard to catch and harder to retain. Monkeys, green and red. A girl whom he did not know. His mother's little face, grave, unsmiling.

He slept.

31

They went next Sunday to see his mother's grave, where the stone was now in position. Dora Roberts, Painter. Ann had brought daffodils and a triple vase of green tin, spiked at the bottom. She arranged the flowers, and set them in the grass at the head of the slab. It was a March day, grey and cold with rain in the wind. Ann shivered in her spring coat.

Someone came to greet them. Peter Coxon. He had brought narcissi and jonquils. 'I hope you didn't mind,' he said inadequately. Toby assured him that they didn't. 'I liked Mrs Roberts,' said Peter, 'though she thought I was smarmy. But I admired her no end.'

'We shan't forget your address,' Ann said.

'Are you very cold?' Peter asked. 'I am. There's a sort of tea-shop just up the road. Will you come and have a cup with me?'

They were pleased to. They all went into the dubious café, with soiled tablecloths and windows perfunctorily wiped. Toby asked him how the book was going.

Peter replied that he was nearing the end. 'But no "Peter's parable" about it this time. No kitsch. Just straightforward. It will disappoint some of my readers, I'm afraid.'

He had, with the years, become more masculine in appearance, though his hands and feet were very small. He looked worried. His great vogue had had its day and sales were dropping off. He had been much inflated, but all that had gone.

'It was kind of you to come today,' said Ann, taking a drink of much-stewed tea. 'Mrs R. would have been so pleased.' She echoed a thought of Toby's. 'Though how can we know that she'd be pleased?'

'She might', said Toby, 'be hoping we shouldn't stand about in the wet, and she'd have told me to put on a warmer coat. She was something of a bully in a very quiet way, was my mother.'

The tea, though horrible, had warmed them up. Soon, Peter took his leave and Toby and Ann went to the house to see how Mr Roberts was faring.

They were greeted by Mrs Cassell, who told him that Mr Roberts was asleep, though he'd wake up at six for certain sure.

'I thought you went home in the afternoons,' said Ann.

'I do, as a rule, but I had to do a bit of cleaning. Ah, here's Master Blackie,' she said as the cat came into the room. 'I call him that because he's that proud of himself.'

And certainly Blackie was spruce and well fed. He jumped on to Ann's lap.

Mrs Cassell asked if she could get them anything, but was told that they had had tea.

'Well, Mr Roberts will be down in a flash, and then I'll get his supper.'

'How is he?' Toby asked.

'Oh, fine, really. I think he gets a bit lonely at times. Sometimes he asks me to stay and have a cigarette with him.'

That was one of the things he had liked about Maisie, that she would smoke with him. Toby cast off the image of Maisie in her Frieda Lawrence tam-o'-shanter, blowing smoke into the air.

Mrs Cassell looked at them with clear Scandinavian

eyes. 'Will you stay and take a bite of supper with him? He'd like that, and there's plenty go round.'

'It's lovely of you to ask,' said Ann, 'but we have got a date.'

Toby was pondering the new smell of the house. The smell of age was still with it, and the smell of turpentine had gone; but all was fresh and clean, with lavender polish and plenty of soap.

Mr Roberts came downstairs in his shirt-sleeves. 'Why, son, what brings you two here?'

'Hullo, Dad. We've been to the cemetery, as a matter of fact. The stone looks very good.'

'I've been wondering whether we shouldn't have put something like "Beloved wife of Stanley". It almost looks as though she wasn't cared for.'

'It shows how proud everyone was of her,' said Ann. 'I'm sure it's right.'

He still looked rather troubled. He yawned deeply. 'Had a good sleep, anyway. You staying for supper?'

'As I told Mrs Cassell, we can't; we've got visitors coming.' This was not true.

'What have you got for me, Katie?' he asked. Toby and Ann were startled by the Christian name.

'Rabbit-pie. You know you like that.'

'If it's got enough onion in it.'

Toby noticed that the table was laid for two.

'Now, Stan, don't start making up your mind already. You'll see what onion it's got.'

'She's a good sort, Katie; she's a blessing to me. Knows just what I like. By the by, Toby, I've found another of your mother's pictures in the cupboard on the stairs. I've put it back in the bedroom. It seems she didn't like it much. You go up and see.'

Toby's heart beat rapidly as he obeyed his father. Yes,

there was a picture on the makeshift easel, but it was not blank. It was a half-finished flower-piece, strong and arresting, but with the usual poor drawing of the vase. Then he noticed the bed. Ann's quilt was back upon it and Blackie was in the middle. Evidently Mrs Cassell did not approve of it bundled up on a chair for the cat's benefit.

'I don't think she liked the way the vase was drawn, Dad,' said Toby, returning, 'but I shall tell Telford about it just the same.' Telford was her dealer. 'There aren't many paintings left now, but her reproductions are doing big business.'

'You must excuse my shirt-sleeves,' said Mr Roberts to Ann, 'but even if it's cold outside it's hot in here.' That was true. Mrs Roberts had installed central heating.

The rabbit-pie was borne in, brown and odorous, and Toby regretted for a moment his refusal to stay for it. But Ann, he knew, hated rabbit and hare, and refused to eat either. He watched his father make a start on the pie, starched napkin under his chin. Mrs Cassell, eating opposite to him, wore hers more genteelly over her knees.

'Katie makes mashed potatoes as good as your mother did. Don't you, Katie?'

'I'm sure I don't know. I'm just careful not to let them get lumpy, and I always add a drop of cream.'

It was a pleasant enough domestic scene. Toby was only bothered by his father's dubious acceptance of the gravestone.

'Do you know who we saw this afternoon?' he said.

'Of course I don't, son.'

'Peter Coxon, the young man who gave mother's memorial address. He'd brought flowers, too.'

'That was kind of him,' said Mr Roberts. 'He did all right at the service, but he looked like a sissy to me.'

'He's a good chap,' said Toby, not defending Peter in

that particular way.

'Yes, please, Katie, I'll have a bit more. I get hungry these days, don't know why.'

'Perhaps it's Mrs Cassell's cooking,' said Ann.

'You know you always were hungry,' Toby said.

'Do you remember when your mother cooked that pheasant? Stank, it did. And she told me that was the right way to eat it. I like to stick to the things I know.'

Ann asked about the shop.

'Well, trade's usually the same. Never particularly brisk but never slow. I've cleared the paperbacks out of the window and given them a good dusting.'

'I wonder Mother didn't do that, when she saw the state they were in.'

'Because I didn't like her to be in the shop, that's why.'

Mrs Cassell brought in pears stewed with a cinnamon stick, which had been a particular favourite of Mrs Roberts. His father ate till he was replete, then said to Ann, 'You won't have a smoke with me, will you?'

'Of course I will, if you give me a cigarette.'

'There,' said Mr Roberts with satisfaction, 'she's coming on, this girl. Shall we go into the parlour? It's aired, isn't it, Katie?'

'Let's stay here,' Ann said. 'I like it in the kitchen. And, besides, we must be going in ten minutes.'

Mr Roberts did not protest. The cloud had passed from his face, and he looked content. It comforted Toby to see him so, and he believed that his father might indeed make a second marriage. Suddenly he felt that he and Ann were intruders, that they were not really wanted in that full life.

They stood up to go. 'Well, it's been fine seeing you both,' Mr Roberts said, 'hasn't it, Katie?'

He kissed Ann good-bye, waved Toby on his way. They

stepped out into the March twilight, back to a marriage of their own.